PLANTS VS. ZOMBIES

IMPFESTATION

Written by PAUL TOBIN

Art by CAT FARRIS

Colors by HEATHER BRECKEL

Letters by STEVE DUTRO

Cover by CAT FARRIS

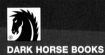

DARK HORSE BOOKS

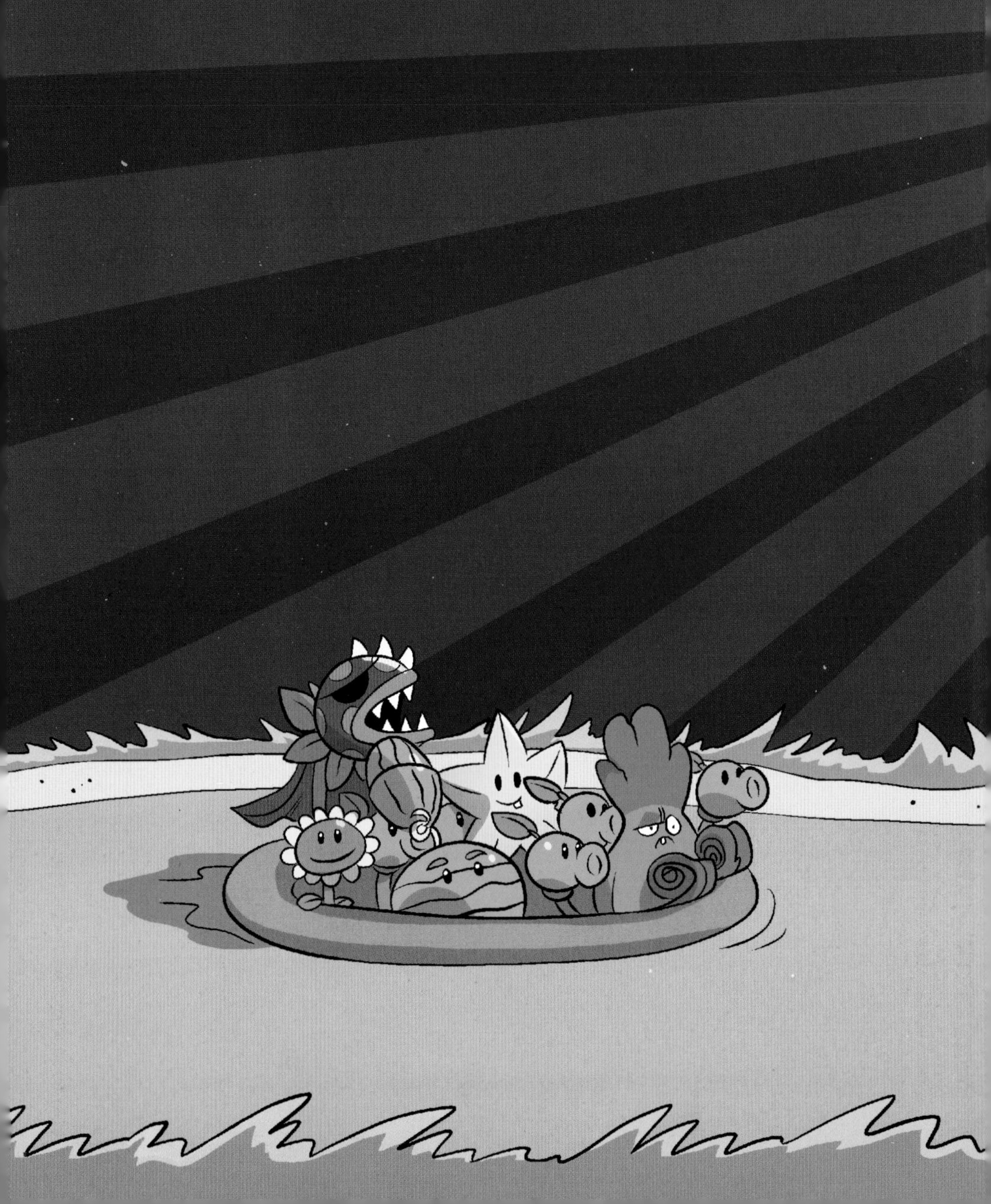

PLANTS VS. ZOMBIES

IMPFESTATION

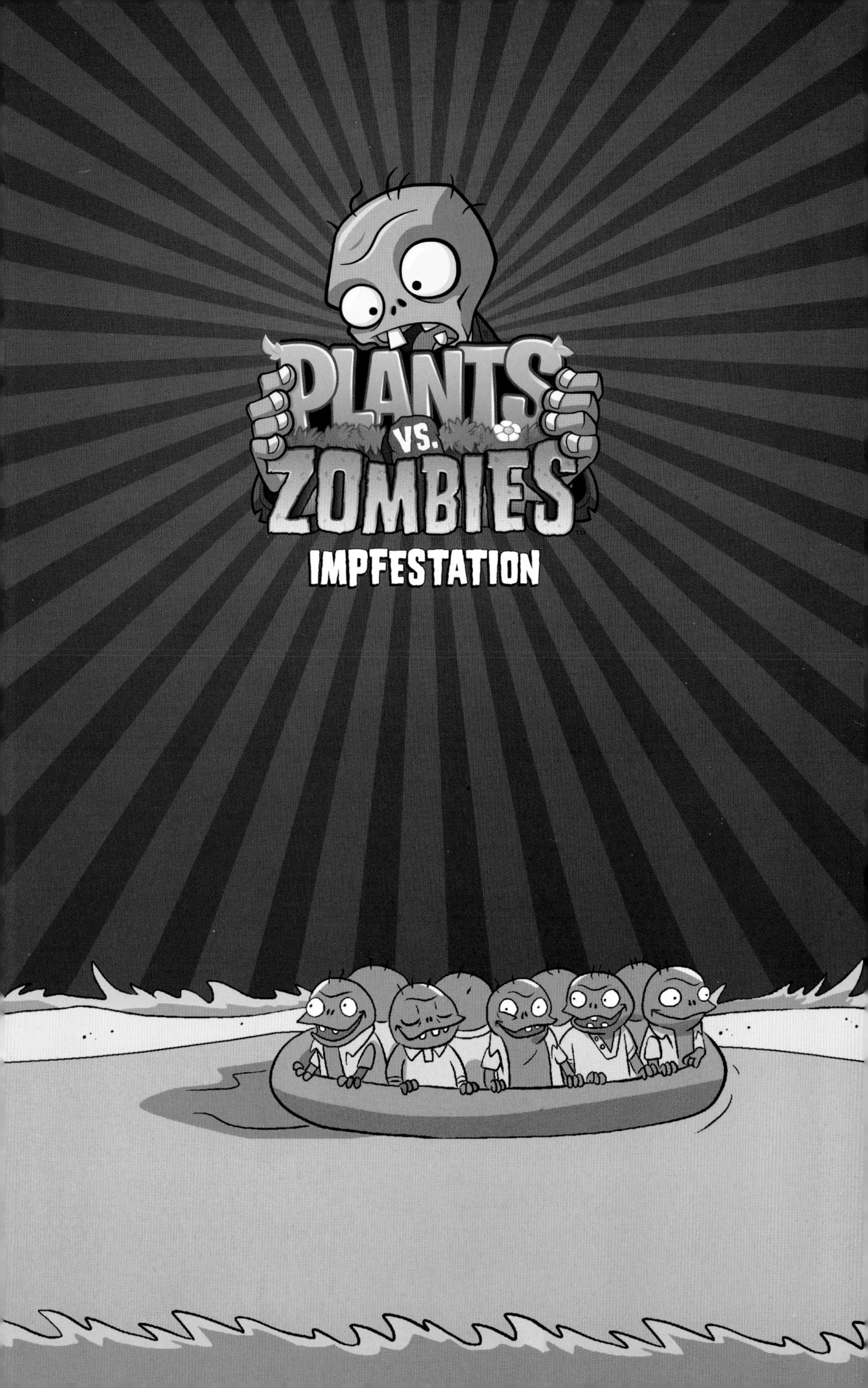

President and Publisher **MIKE RICHARDSON**
Senior Editor **PHILIP R. SIMON**
Associate Editor **JUDY KHUU**
Assistant Editor **ROSE WEITZ**
Designer **KATHLEEN BARNETT**
Digital Art Technician **ALLYSON HALLER**

Special thanks to Joshua Franks, Ryan Jones, Jessica Leung, Christopher Olsen,
Kristen Star, Matt Townsend, and everyone at PopCap Games and EA Games.

First Edition: June 2023
Ebook ISBN 978-1-50672-855-1
Hardcover ISBN 978-1-50672-847-6

10 9 8 7 6 5 4 3 2 1
Printed in China

MIX
Paper from
responsible sources
FSC® C109093

DarkHorse.com
PopCap.com

▷ No plants were harmed in the making of this graphic novel. However, the zombie named Frogpants was
definitely injured (watch out for that!) and is on the mend, and many zombie imps are now missing.

Library of Congress Cataloging-in-Publication Data

Names: Tobin, Paul, 1965- author. | Farris, Cat, artist. | Breckel,
    Heather, colorist. | Dutro, Steve, letterer.
Title: Impfestation / writer, Paul Tobin ; artist, Cat Farris ; colors,
    Heather Breckel ; letters, Steve Dutro.
Description: Milwaukie, OR : Dark Horse Books, 2023. | Series: Plants vs.
    zombies ; 21
Identifiers: LCCN 2022054736 (print) | LCCN 2022054737 (ebook) | ISBN
    9781506728476 (hardcover) | ISBN 9781506728551 (ebook)
Subjects: CYAC: Graphic novels. | Zombies--Fiction. | Plants--Fiction. |
    Humorous stories. | LCGFT: Humorous comics. | Graphic novels.
Classification: LCC PZ7.7.T62 Im 2023 (print) | LCC PZ7.7.T62 (ebook) |
    DDC 741.5/973--dc23/eng/20230124
LC record available at https://lccn.loc.gov/2022054736
LC ebook record available at https://lccn.loc.gov/2022054737

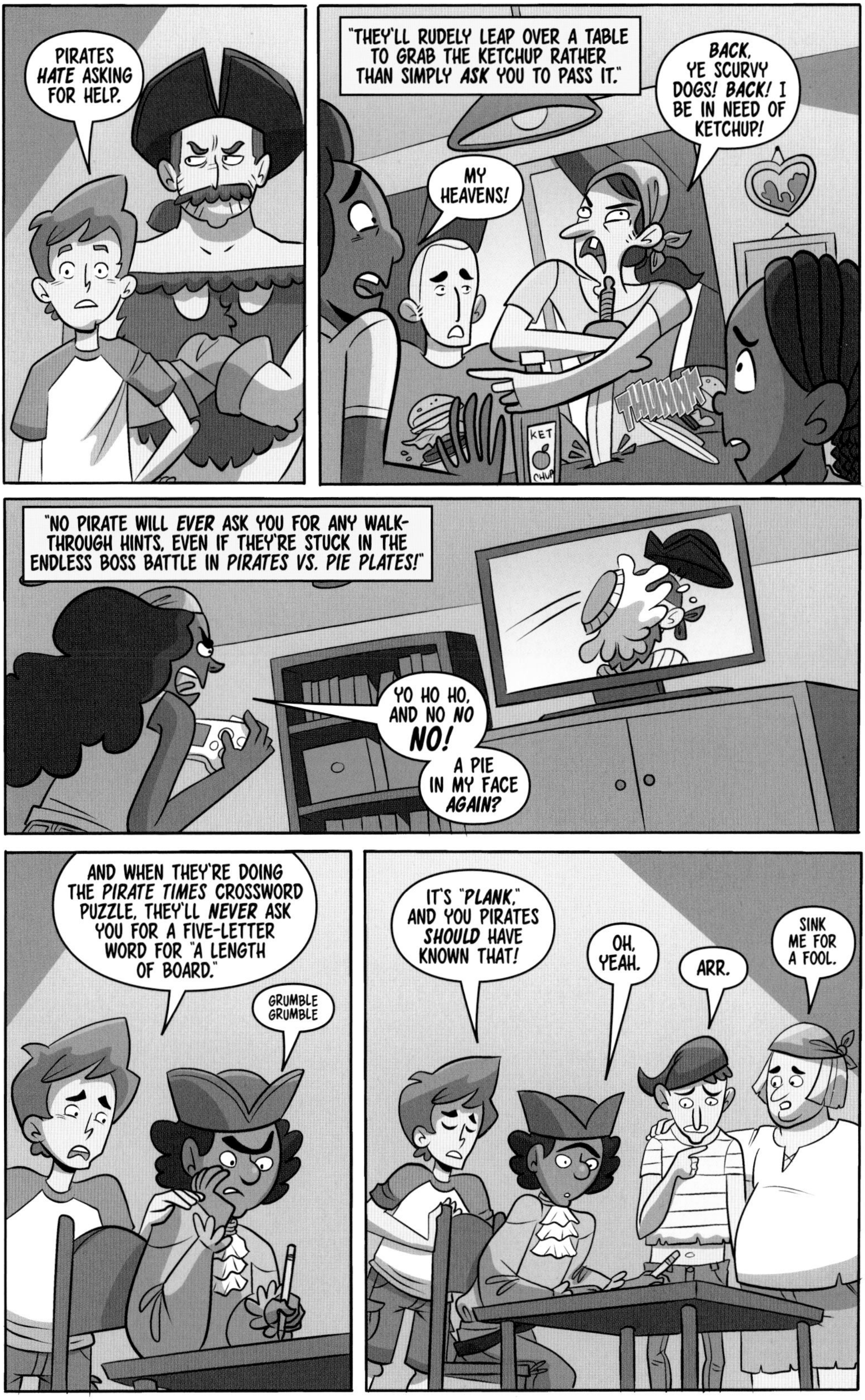
PIRATES HATE ASKING FOR HELP.
"THEY'LL RUDELY LEAP OVER A TABLE TO GRAB THE KETCHUP RATHER THAN SIMPLY ASK YOU TO PASS IT."
BACK, YE SCURVY DOGS! BACK! I BE IN NEED OF KETCHUP!
MY HEAVENS!
THUNNK
KET CHUP
"NO PIRATE WILL EVER ASK YOU FOR ANY WALK-THROUGH HINTS, EVEN IF THEY'RE STUCK IN THE ENDLESS BOSS BATTLE IN PIRATES VS. PIE PLATES!"
YO HO HO, AND NO NO NO!
A PIE IN MY FACE AGAIN?
AND WHEN THEY'RE DOING THE PIRATE TIMES CROSSWORD PUZZLE, THEY'LL NEVER ASK YOU FOR A FIVE-LETTER WORD FOR "A LENGTH OF BOARD."
GRUMBLE GRUMBLE
IT'S "PLANK," AND YOU PIRATES SHOULD HAVE KNOWN THAT!
OH, YEAH.
ARR.
SINK ME FOR A FOOL.

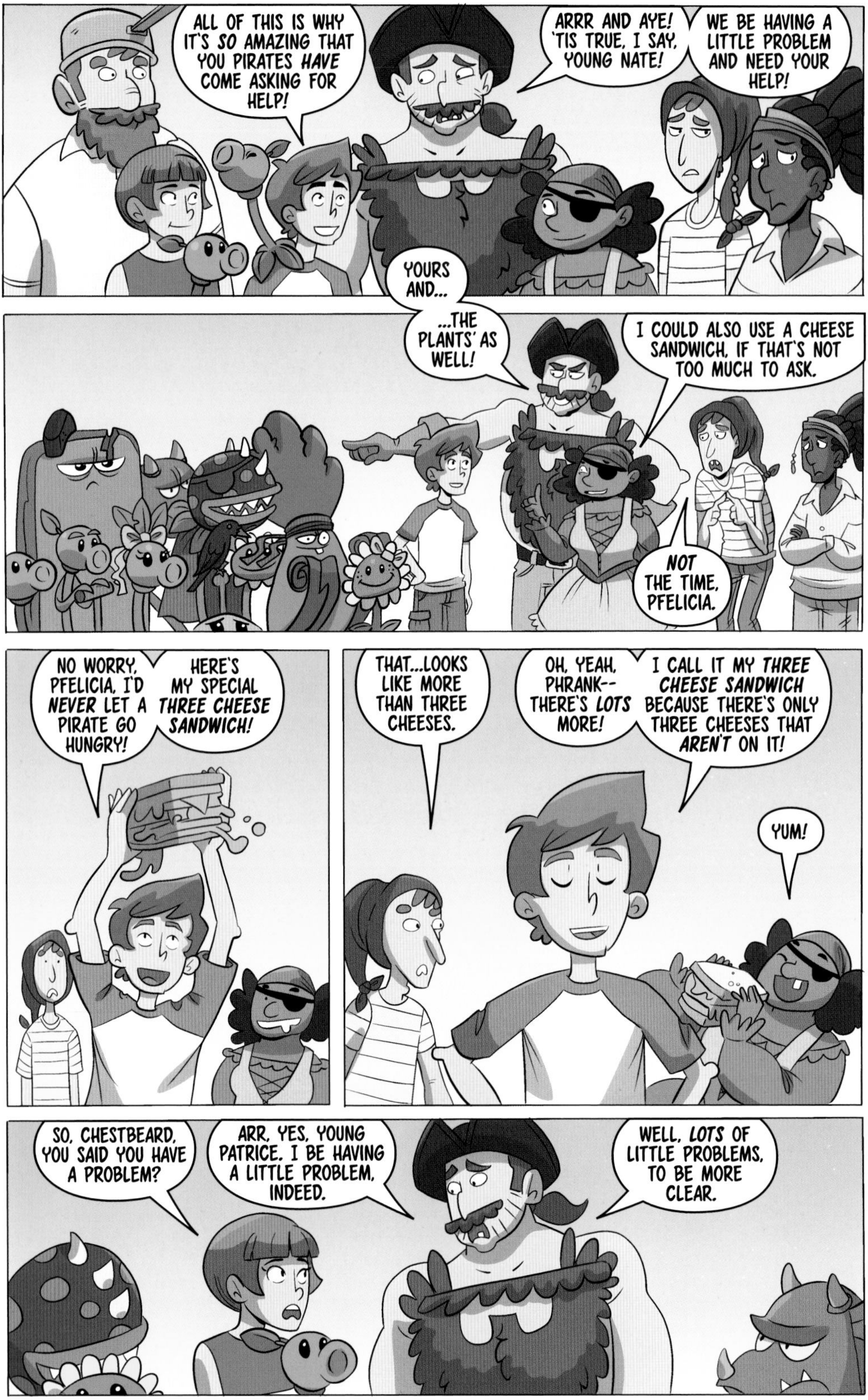
ALL OF THIS IS WHY IT'S *SO* AMAZING THAT YOU PIRATES *HAVE* COME ASKING FOR HELP!
ARRR AND AYE! 'TIS TRUE, I SAY, YOUNG NATE!
WE BE HAVING A LITTLE PROBLEM AND NEED YOUR HELP!
YOURS AND...
...THE PLANTS' AS WELL!
I COULD ALSO USE A CHEESE SANDWICH, IF THAT'S NOT TOO MUCH TO ASK.
NOT THE TIME, PFELICIA.
NO WORRY, PFELICIA, I'D *NEVER* LET A PIRATE GO HUNGRY!
HERE'S MY SPECIAL *THREE CHEESE SANDWICH!*
THAT...LOOKS LIKE MORE THAN THREE CHEESES.
OH, YEAH, PHRANK-- THERE'S *LOTS* MORE!
I CALL IT MY *THREE CHEESE SANDWICH* BECAUSE THERE'S ONLY THREE CHEESES THAT *AREN'T* ON IT!
YUM!
SO, CHESTBEARD, YOU SAID YOU HAVE A PROBLEM?
ARR, YES, YOUNG PATRICE. I BE HAVING A LITTLE PROBLEM, INDEED.
WELL, *LOTS* OF LITTLE PROBLEMS, TO BE MORE CLEAR.

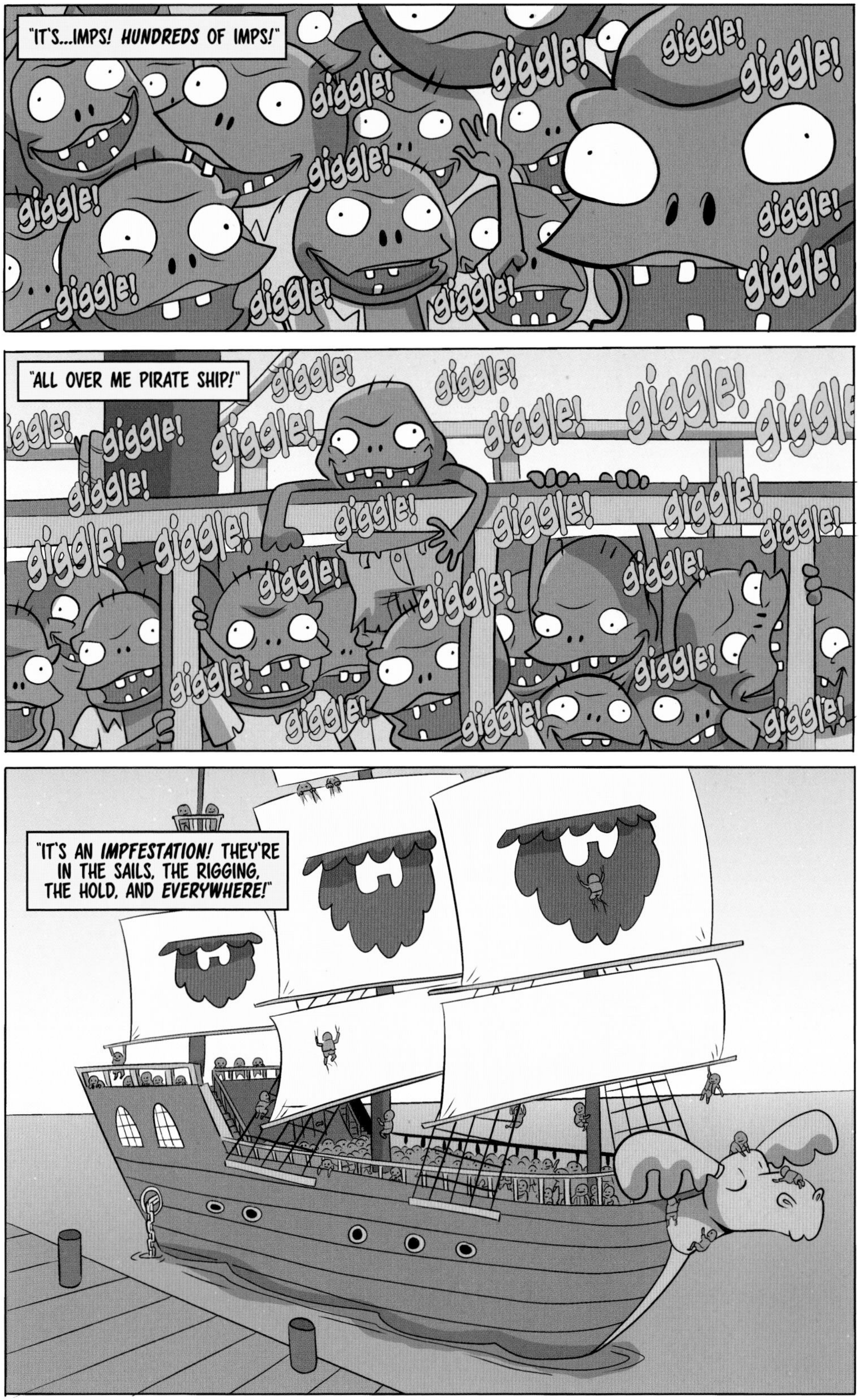
"IT'S...IMPS! HUNDREDS OF IMPS!"
giggle!
giggle!
giggle!
giggle!
giggle!
giggle!
giggle!
giggle!
"ALL OVER ME PIRATE SHIP!"
giggle!
giggle!
giggle!
giggle!
giggle!
giggle!
"IT'S AN IMPFESTATION! THEY'RE IN THE SAILS, THE RIGGING, THE HOLD, AND EVERYWHERE!"

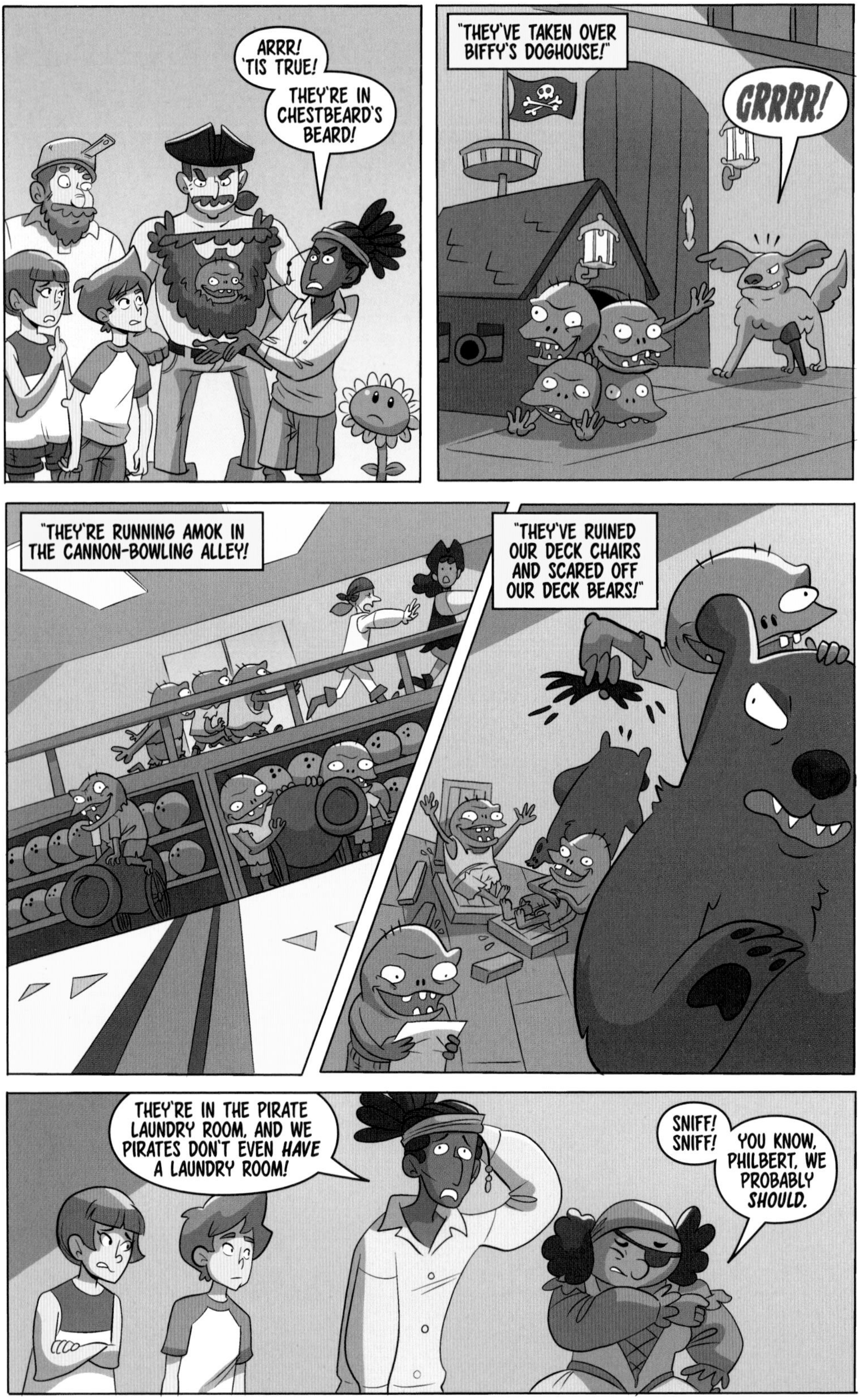
ARRR! 'TIS TRUE!
THEY'RE IN CHESTBEARD'S BEARD!
"THEY'VE TAKEN OVER BIFFY'S DOGHOUSE!"
GRRRR!
"THEY'RE RUNNING AMOK IN THE CANNON-BOWLING ALLEY!
"THEY'VE RUINED OUR DECK CHAIRS AND SCARED OFF OUR DECK BEARS!"
THEY'RE IN THE PIRATE LAUNDRY ROOM, AND WE PIRATES DON'T EVEN *HAVE* A LAUNDRY ROOM!
SNIFF! SNIFF!
YOU KNOW, PHILBERT, WE PROBABLY *SHOULD*.

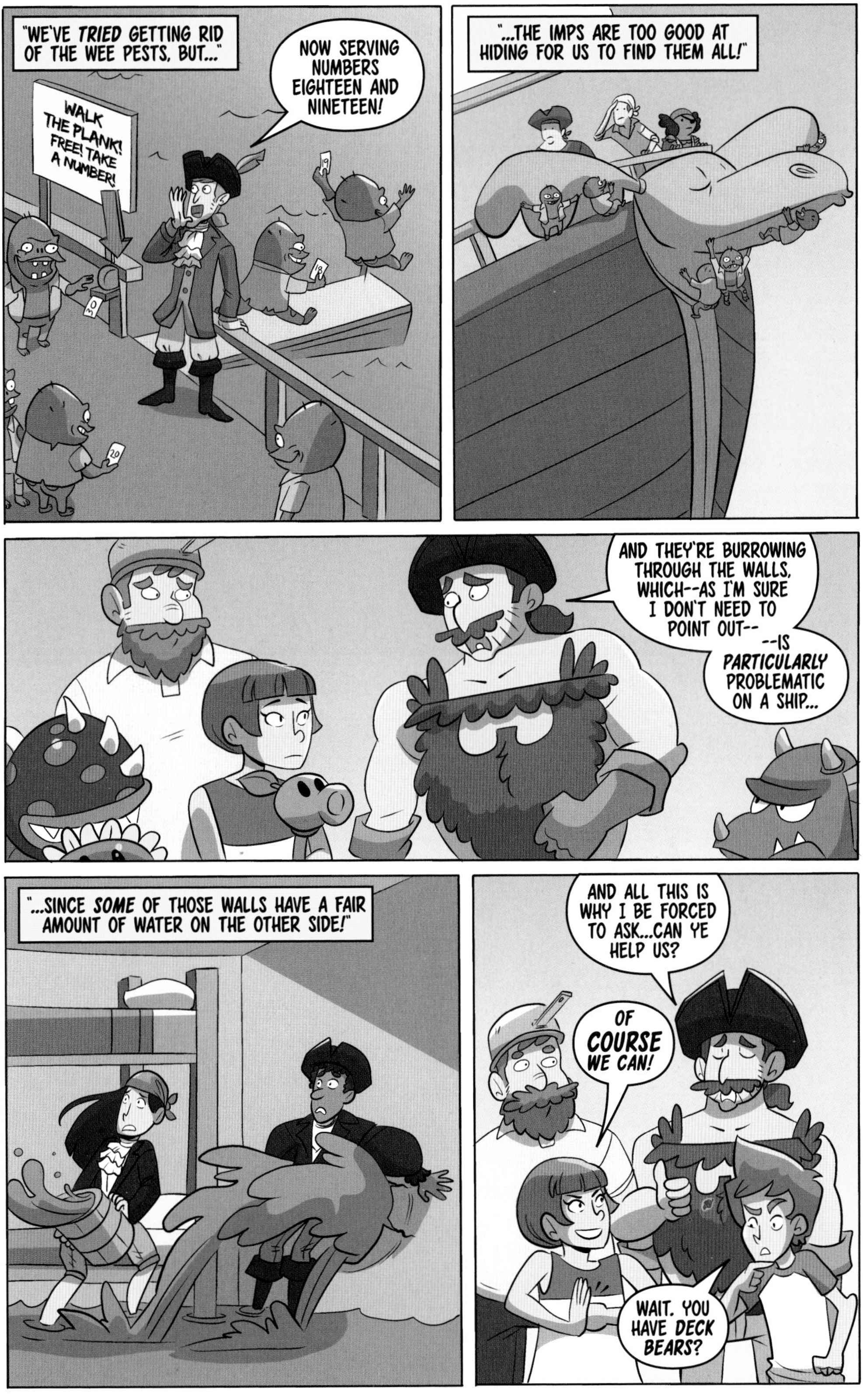
"WE'VE *TRIED* GETTING RID OF THE WEE PESTS, BUT..."
NOW SERVING NUMBERS EIGHTEEN AND NINETEEN!
WALK THE PLANK! FREE! TAKE A NUMBER!
"...THE IMPS ARE TOO GOOD AT HIDING FOR US TO FIND THEM ALL!"
AND THEY'RE BURROWING THROUGH THE WALLS, WHICH--AS I'M SURE I DON'T NEED TO POINT OUT--
--IS *PARTICULARLY* PROBLEMATIC ON A SHIP...
"...SINCE *SOME* OF THOSE WALLS HAVE A FAIR AMOUNT OF WATER ON THE OTHER SIDE!"
AND ALL THIS IS WHY I BE FORCED TO ASK...CAN YE HELP US?
OF **COURSE** WE CAN!
WAIT. YOU HAVE *DECK BEARS*?

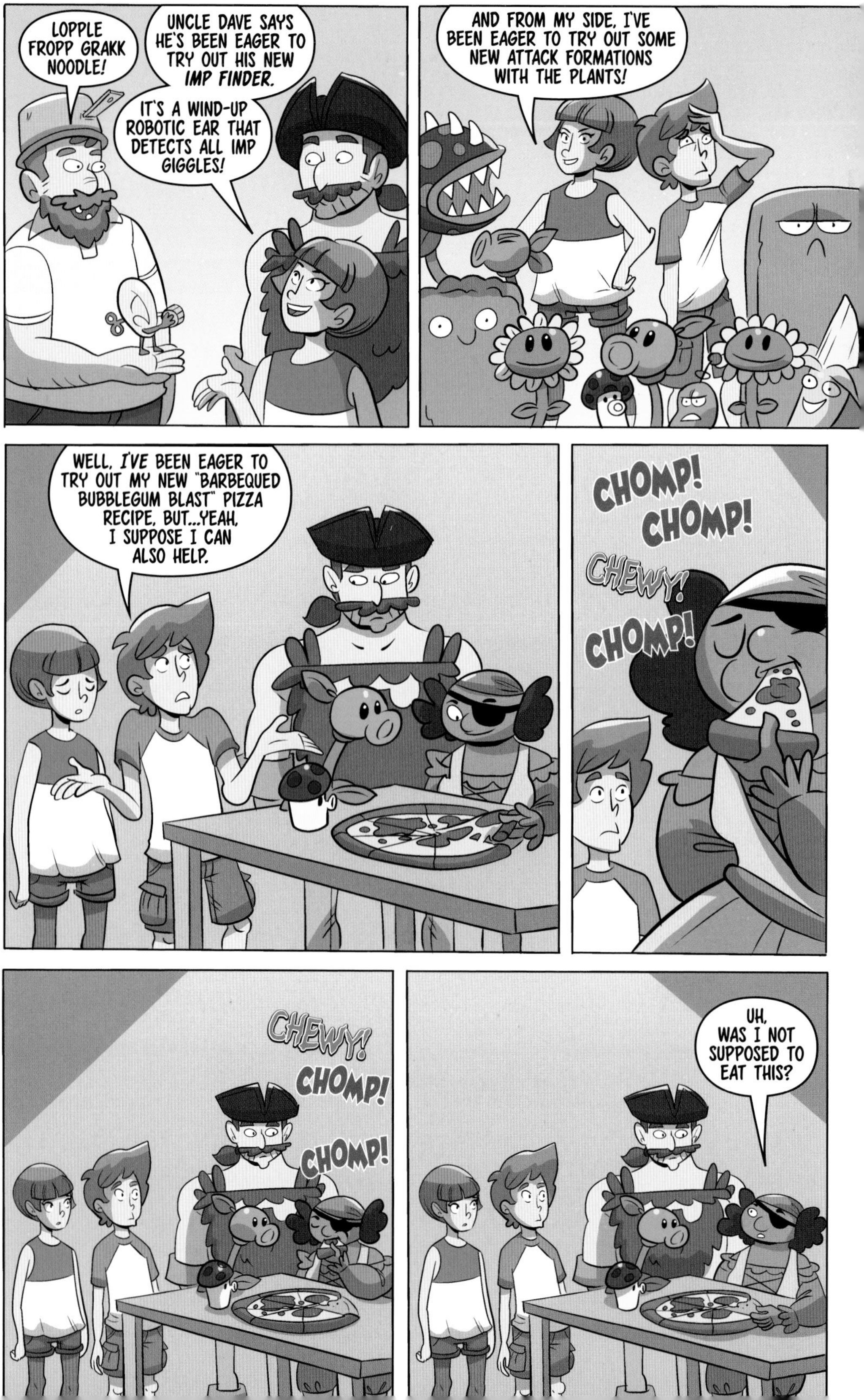
LOPPLE FROPP GRAKK NOODLE!
UNCLE DAVE SAYS HE'S BEEN EAGER TO TRY OUT HIS NEW IMP FINDER.
IT'S A WIND-UP ROBOTIC EAR THAT DETECTS ALL IMP GIGGLES!
AND FROM MY SIDE, I'VE BEEN EAGER TO TRY OUT SOME NEW ATTACK FORMATIONS WITH THE PLANTS!
WELL, I'VE BEEN EAGER TO TRY OUT MY NEW "BARBEQUED BUBBLEGUM BLAST" PIZZA RECIPE, BUT...YEAH, I SUPPOSE I CAN ALSO HELP.
CHOMP!
CHOMP!
CHEWY!
CHOMP!
CHEWY!
CHOMP!
CHOMP!
UH, WAS I NOT SUPPOSED TO EAT THIS?

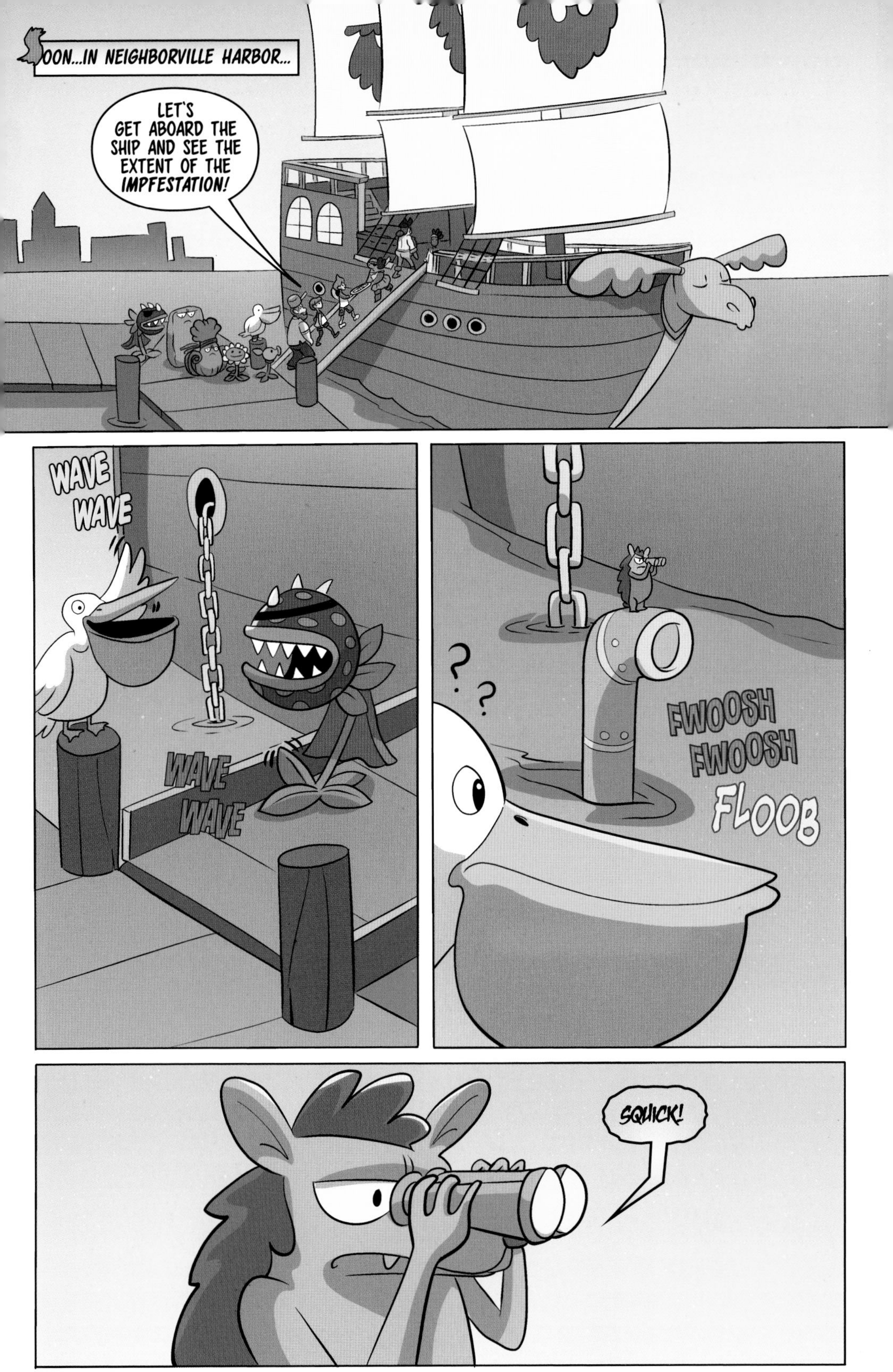
SOON...IN NEIGHBORVILLE HARBOR...
LET'S GET ABOARD THE SHIP AND SEE THE EXTENT OF THE IMPFESTATION!
WAVE WAVE
WAVE WAVE
? ?
FWOOSH FWOOSH
FLOOB
SQUICK!

MEANWHILE...

BANG BANG BANG BANG

OOF! THIS IS A PROBLEM. LOOK! IMPS IN THE PIRATE HAIR SALON!

SHRED giggle! TOSS

giggle!

ARR! NOT ME COPY OF PRESIDENT PIRATE #1!

giggle!

IMPS IN THE BLOODY HAND MEMORIAL COMIC BOOK LIBRARY!

giggle!

RRIP

PRESIDENT PIRATE!

MUNCH RRIP giggle!

IMPS IN THE SITTING ROOM!

giggle! giggle! giggle! giggle! giggle! giggle! giggle!

giggle! giggle! giggle! giggle! giggle! giggle! giggle!

IMPS IN THE KNITTING ROOM!

KNIT KNIT KNIT

Imps in the Spitting Room!

THWOOOP!

PHLURRP!

giggle! giggle! giggle! giggle!

*EDITORS' NOTE: THESE SPITTING PIRATES ARE USING SPITTOONS.

DON'T WORRY, BIFFY. THAT'S JUST CRAZY DAVE'S IMP FINDER.

BARK! BARK! GRRR! BARK!

WOBBLE THAP THAP WOBBLE

"IT EMITS A LITTLE 'CLICK' FOR EACH DIFFERENT IMP IT HEARS GIGGLING, AND GIVES A NUMERICAL TOTAL!"

WOBBLE THAP THAP WOBBLE

CLICK CLICK CLICK CLICK CLICK giggle! CLICK CLICK CLICK CLICK CLICK CLICK CLICK CLICK

spin spin whirr

!?

WHOA! IT SAYS THERE ARE... FIFTY-FIVE IMPS ON BOARD!

WAIT, NO! THERE'S...126 IMPS! HOLD ON! MAYBE 600? OR... 2,000?

IT'S... STRANGE! THERE SEEMS TO BE A NEVER-ENDING SUPPLY OF THE LITTLEST AND GIGGLIEST ZOMBIES!

WHERE ARE ALL THESE IMPS COMING FROM?

CLICK CLICK CLICK CLICK CLICK CLICK CLICK CLICK

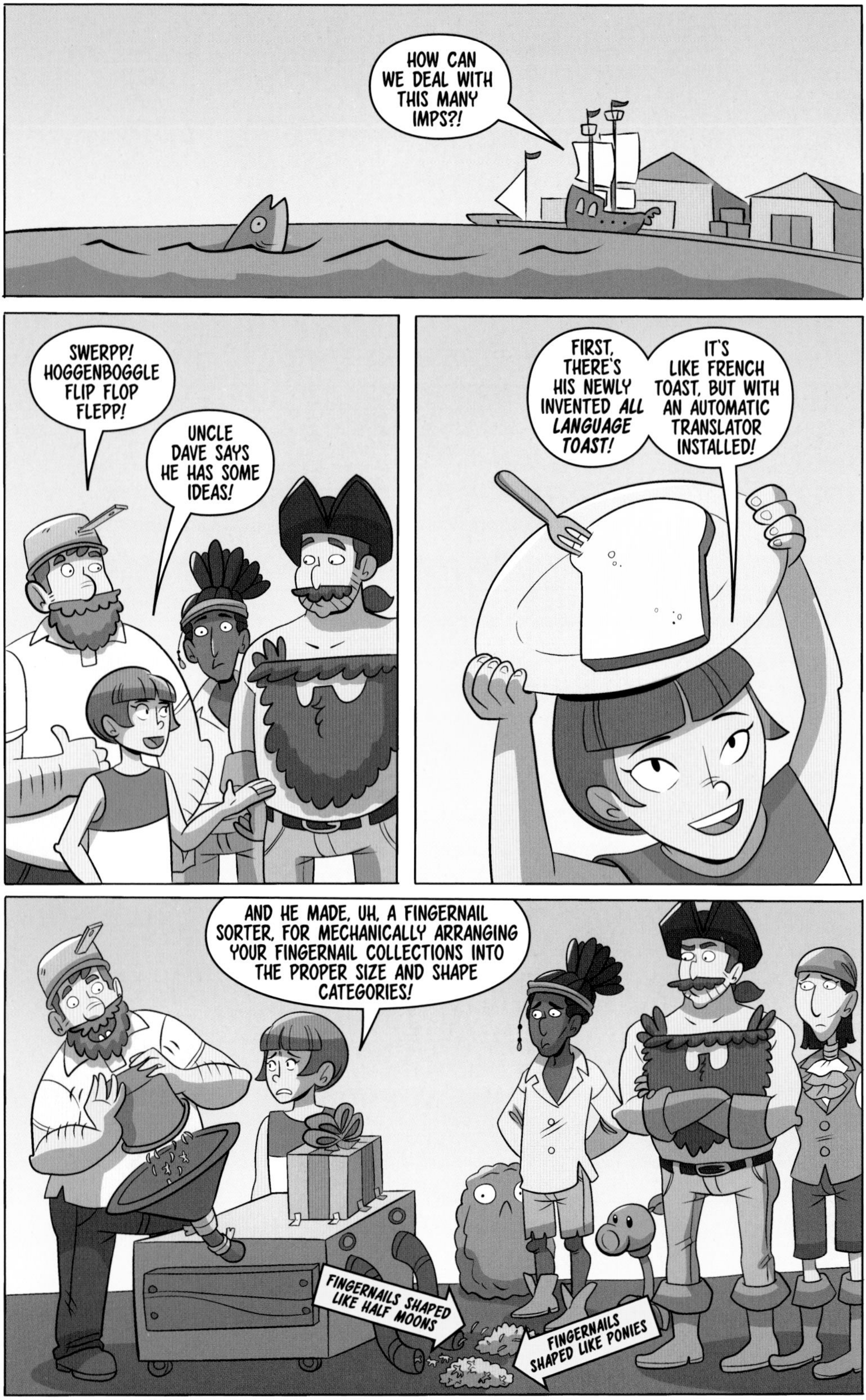
HOW CAN WE DEAL WITH THIS MANY IMPS?!
SWERPP! HOGGENBOGGLE FLIP FLOP FLEPP!
UNCLE DAVE SAYS HE HAS SOME IDEAS!
FIRST, THERE'S HIS NEWLY INVENTED ALL LANGUAGE TOAST!
IT'S LIKE FRENCH TOAST, BUT WITH AN AUTOMATIC TRANSLATOR INSTALLED!
AND HE MADE, UH, A FINGERNAIL SORTER, FOR MECHANICALLY ARRANGING YOUR FINGERNAIL COLLECTIONS INTO THE PROPER SIZE AND SHAPE CATEGORIES!
FINGERNAILS SHAPED LIKE HALF MOONS
FINGERNAILS SHAPED LIKE PONIES

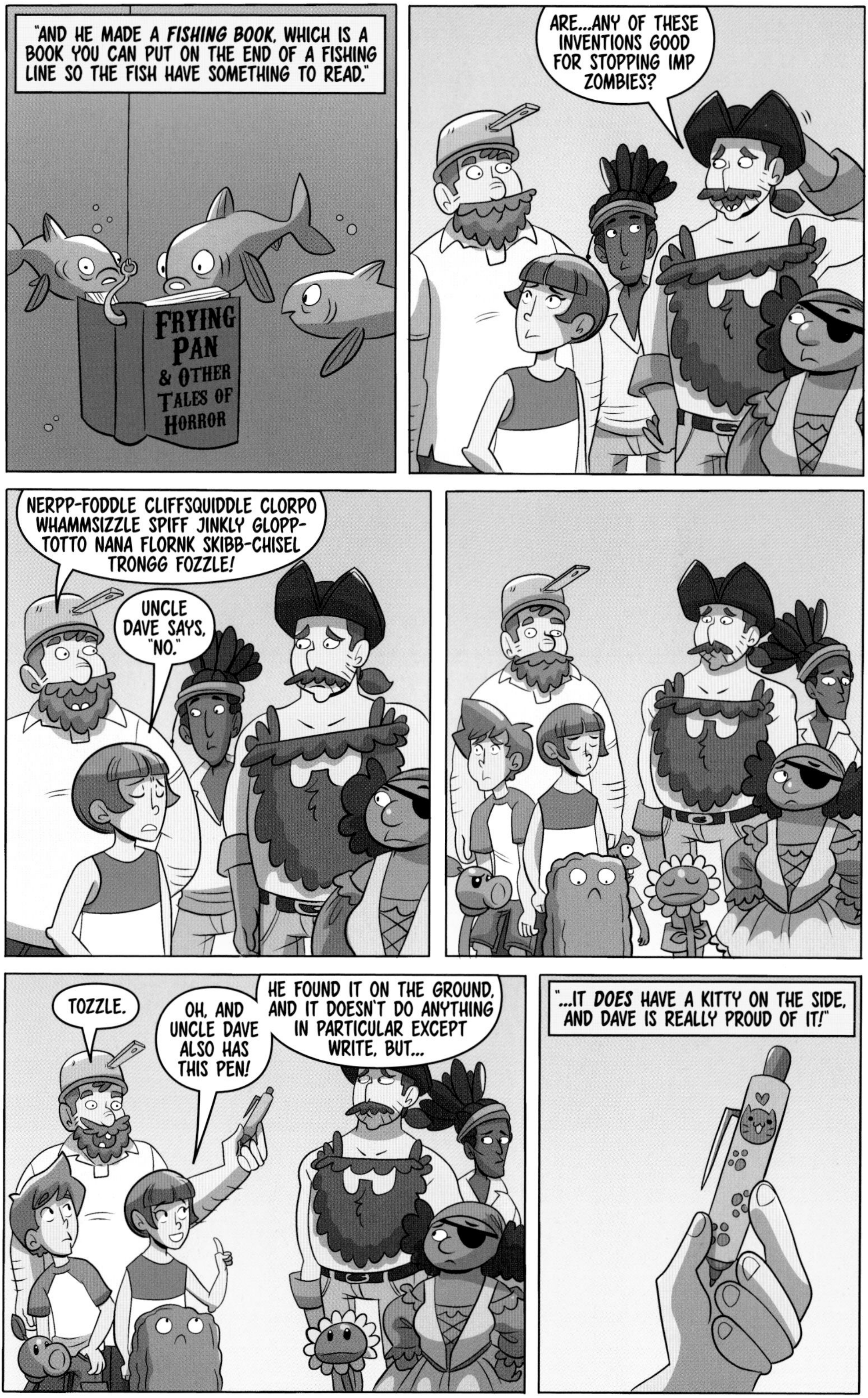
"AND HE MADE A *FISHING BOOK*, WHICH IS A BOOK YOU CAN PUT ON THE END OF A FISHING LINE SO THE FISH HAVE SOMETHING TO READ."
FRYING PAN & OTHER TALES OF HORROR
ARE...ANY OF THESE INVENTIONS GOOD FOR STOPPING IMP ZOMBIES?
NERPP-FODDLE CLIFFSQUIDDLE CLORPO WHAMMSIZZLE SPIFF JINKLY GLOPP-TOTTO NANA FLORNK SKIBB-CHISEL TRONGG FOZZLE!
UNCLE DAVE SAYS, "NO."
TOZZLE.
OH, AND UNCLE DAVE ALSO HAS THIS PEN!
HE FOUND IT ON THE GROUND, AND IT DOESN'T DO ANYTHING IN PARTICULAR EXCEPT WRITE, BUT...
"...IT *DOES* HAVE A KITTY ON THE SIDE, AND DAVE IS REALLY PROUD OF IT!"

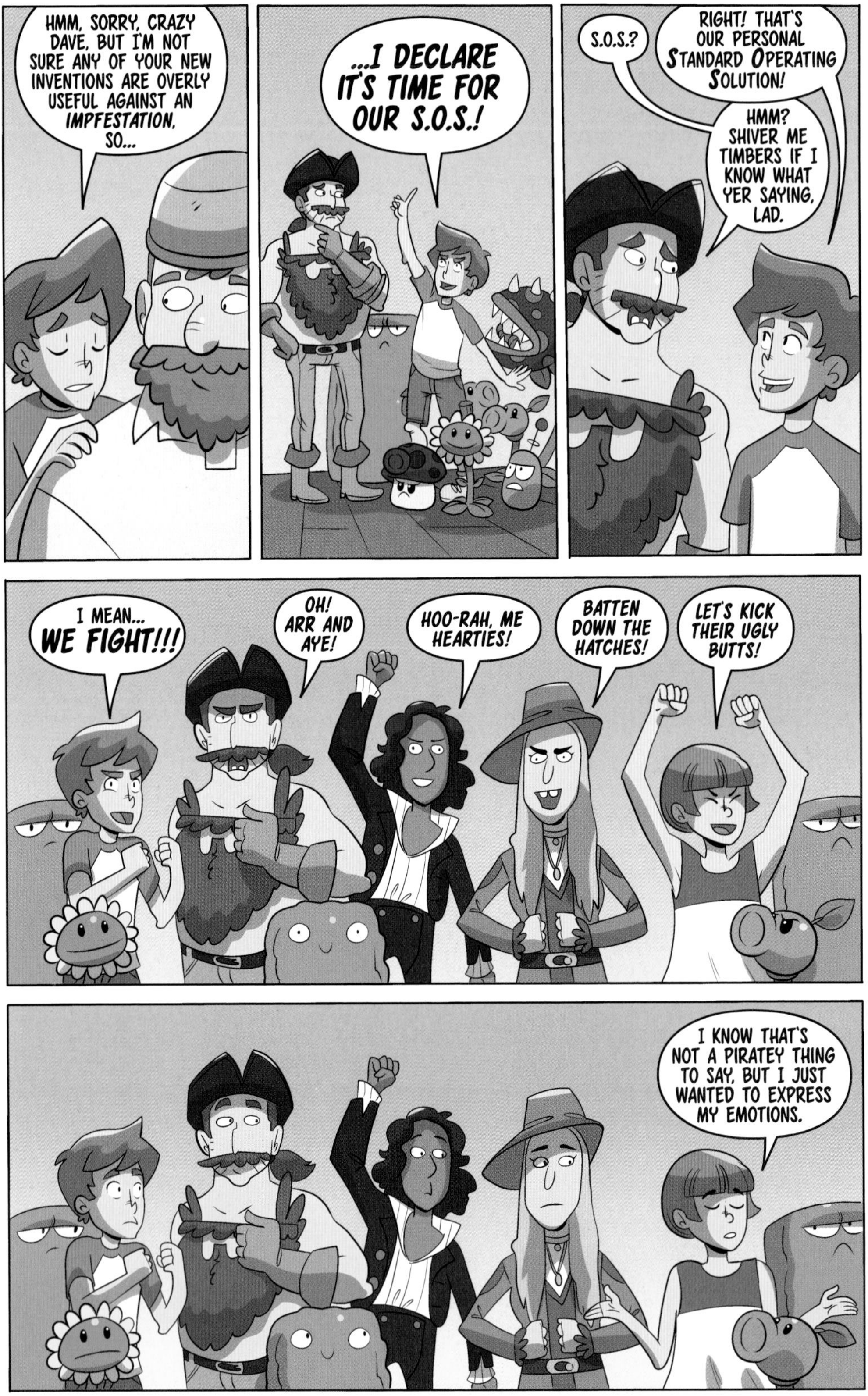
HMM, SORRY, CRAZY DAVE, BUT I'M NOT SURE ANY OF YOUR NEW INVENTIONS ARE OVERLY USEFUL AGAINST AN IMPFESTATION, SO...
...I DECLARE IT'S TIME FOR OUR S.O.S.!
S.O.S.?
RIGHT! THAT'S OUR PERSONAL STANDARD OPERATING SOLUTION!
HMM? SHIVER ME TIMBERS IF I KNOW WHAT YER SAYING, LAD.
I MEAN... WE FIGHT!!!
OH! ARR AND AYE!
HOO-RAH, ME HEARTIES!
BATTEN DOWN THE HATCHES!
LET'S KICK THEIR UGLY BUTTS!
I KNOW THAT'S NOT A PIRATEY THING TO SAY, BUT I JUST WANTED TO EXPRESS MY EMOTIONS.

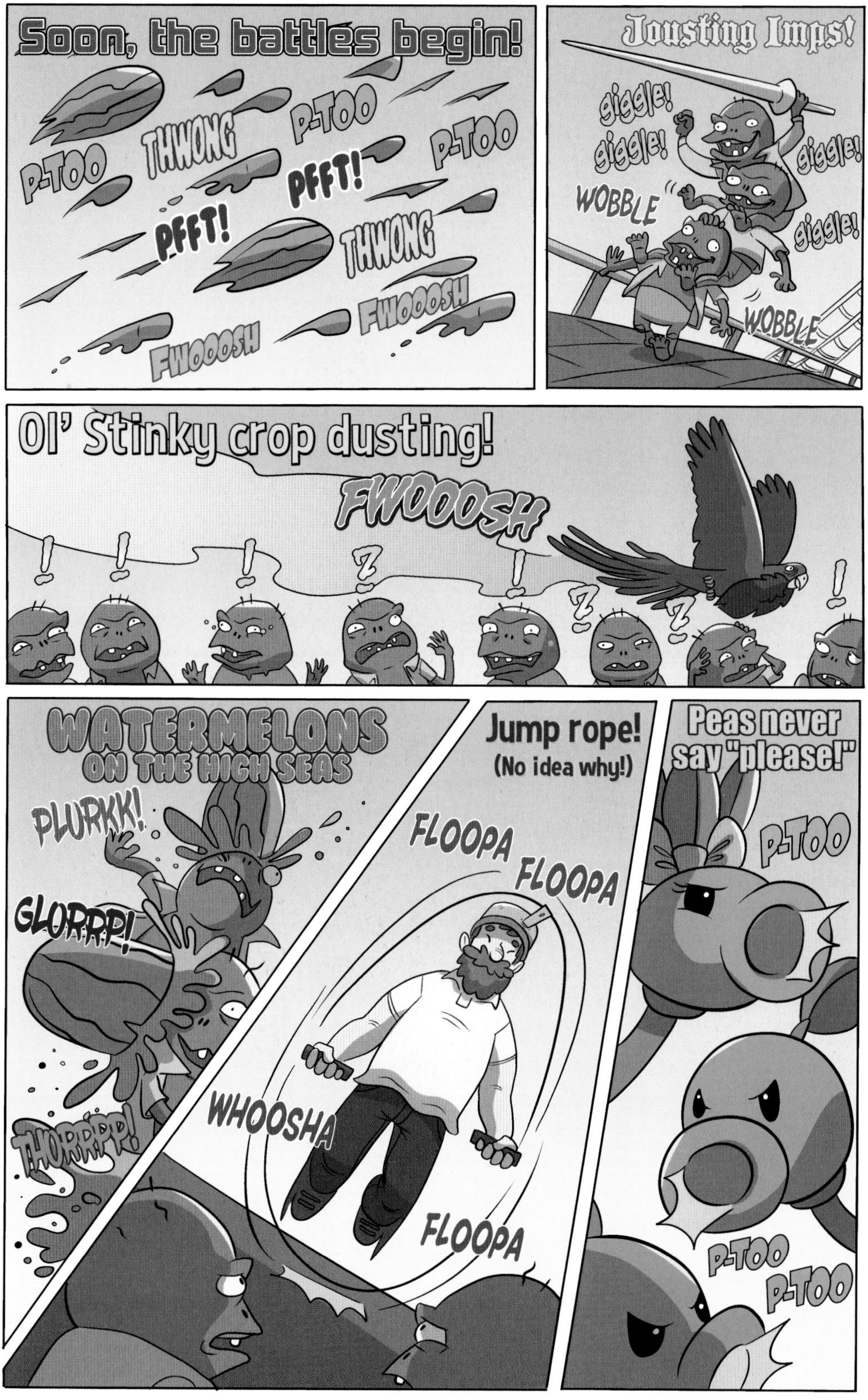
Soon, the battles begin!
P-TOO
THWONG
P-TOO
P-TOO
PFFT!
PFFT!
THWONG
FWOOOSH
FWOOOSH
Jousting Imps!
giggle!
giggle!
giggle!
giggle!
WOBBLE
WOBBLE
Ol' Stinky crop dusting!
FWOOOSH
WATERMELONS ON THE HIGH SEAS
PLURKK!
GLORRP!
THORRPP!
Jump rope!
(No idea why!)
FLOOPA
FLOOPA
WHOOSHA
FLOOPA
Peas never say "please!"
P-TOO
P-TOO
P-TOO

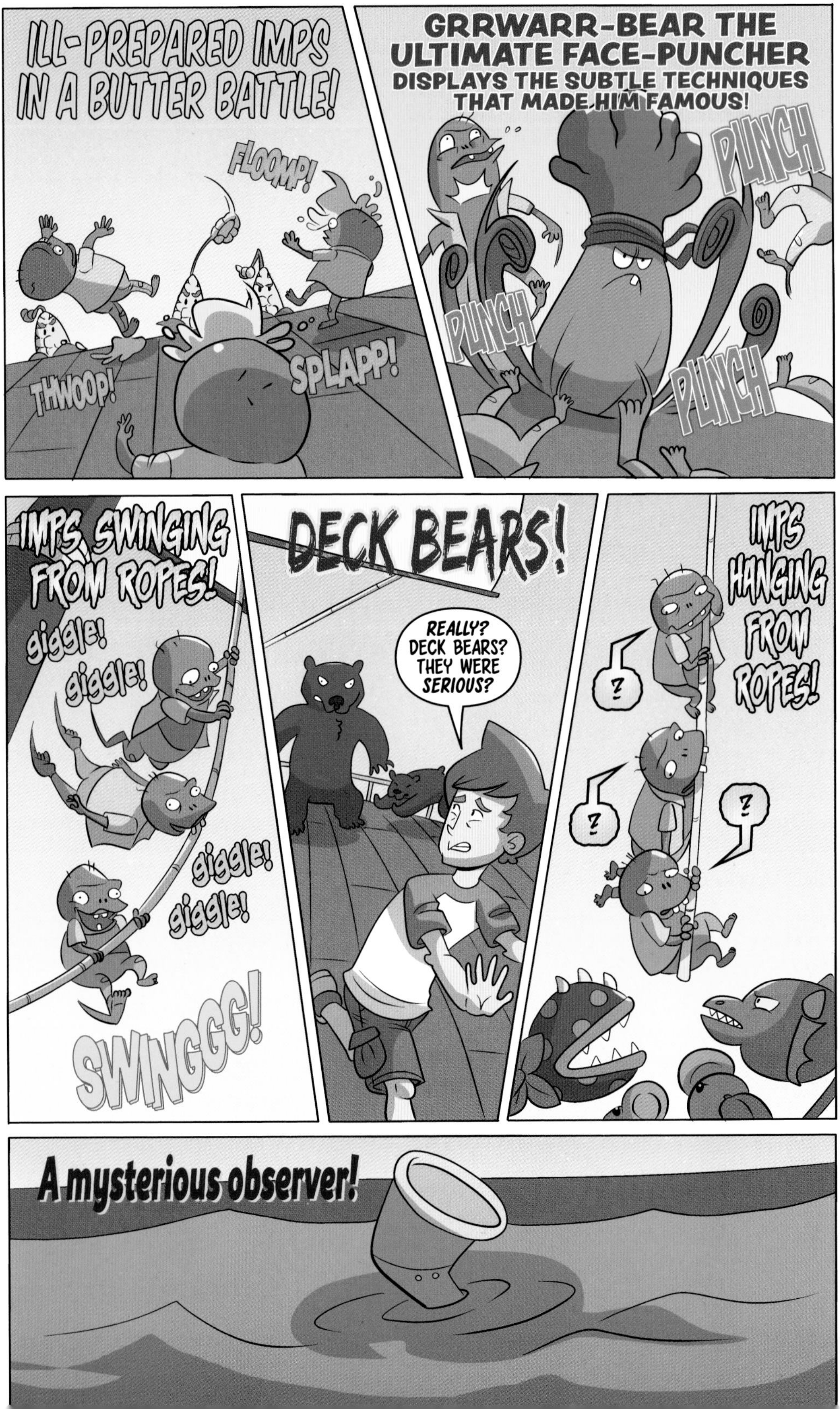
ILL-PREPARED IMPS IN A BUTTER BATTLE!
FLOOMP!
THWOOP!
SPLAPP!
GRRWARR-BEAR THE ULTIMATE FACE-PUNCHER DISPLAYS THE SUBTLE TECHNIQUES THAT MADE HIM FAMOUS!
PUNCH
PUNCH
PUNCH
IMPS SWINGING FROM ROPES!
giggle!
giggle!
giggle!
giggle!
SWINGGG!
DECK BEARS!
REALLY? DECK BEARS? THEY WERE SERIOUS?
IMPS HANGING FROM ROPES!
?
?
?
A mysterious observer!

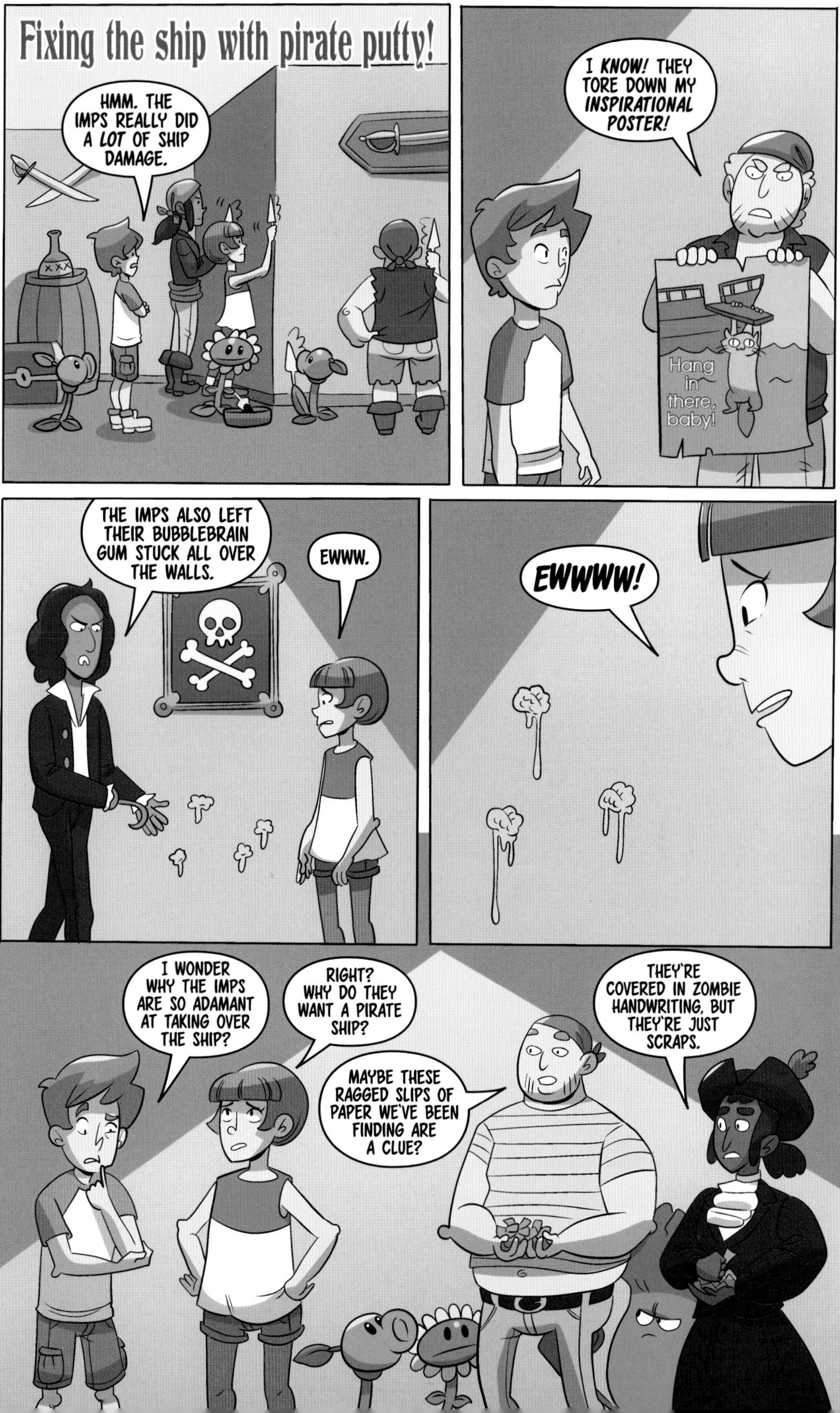
Fixing the ship with pirate putty!
HMM. THE IMPS REALLY DID A LOT OF SHIP DAMAGE.
I KNOW! THEY TORE DOWN MY INSPIRATIONAL POSTER!
Hang in there, baby!
THE IMPS ALSO LEFT THEIR BUBBLEBRAIN GUM STUCK ALL OVER THE WALLS.
EWWW.
EWWWW!
I WONDER WHY THE IMPS ARE SO ADAMANT AT TAKING OVER THE SHIP?
RIGHT? WHY DO THEY WANT A PIRATE SHIP?
MAYBE THESE RAGGED SLIPS OF PAPER WE'VE BEEN FINDING ARE A CLUE?
THEY'RE COVERED IN ZOMBIE HANDWRITING, BUT THEY'RE JUST SCRAPS.

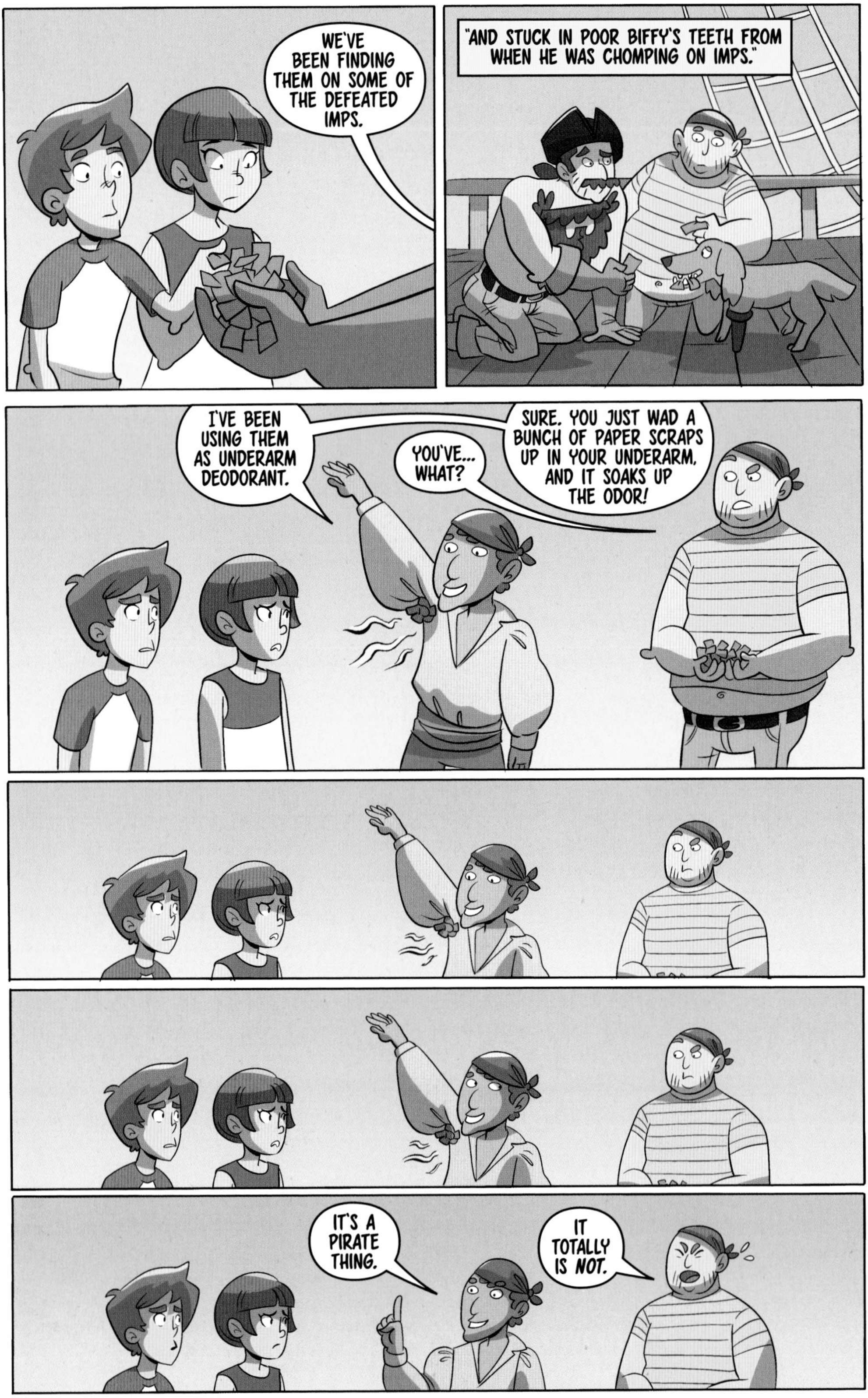
WE'VE BEEN FINDING THEM ON SOME OF THE DEFEATED IMPS.
"AND STUCK IN POOR BIFFY'S TEETH FROM WHEN HE WAS CHOMPING ON IMPS."
I'VE BEEN USING THEM AS UNDERARM DEODORANT.
YOU'VE... WHAT?
SURE. YOU JUST WAD A BUNCH OF PAPER SCRAPS UP IN YOUR UNDERARM, AND IT SOAKS UP THE ODOR!
IT'S A PIRATE THING.
IT TOTALLY IS NOT.

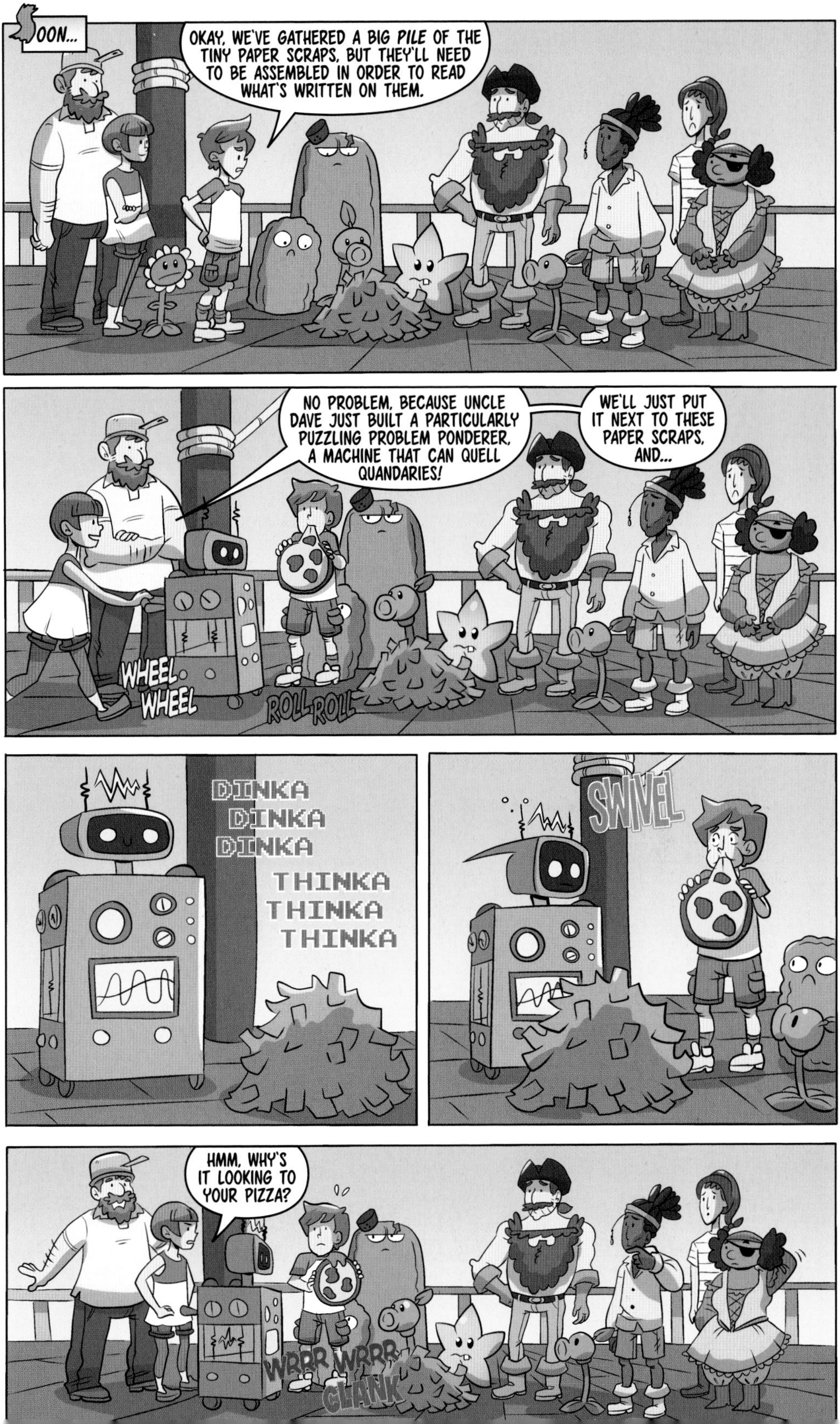
SOON...
OKAY, WE'VE GATHERED A BIG PILE OF THE TINY PAPER SCRAPS, BUT THEY'LL NEED TO BE ASSEMBLED IN ORDER TO READ WHAT'S WRITTEN ON THEM.
NO PROBLEM, BECAUSE UNCLE DAVE JUST BUILT A PARTICULARLY PUZZLING PROBLEM PONDERER, A MACHINE THAT CAN QUELL QUANDARIES!
WE'LL JUST PUT IT NEXT TO THESE PAPER SCRAPS, AND...
WHEEL WHEEL
ROLL ROLL
DINKA DINKA DINKA
THINKA THINKA THINKA
SWIVEL
HMM, WHY'S IT LOOKING TO YOUR PIZZA?
WRRR WRRR
CLANK

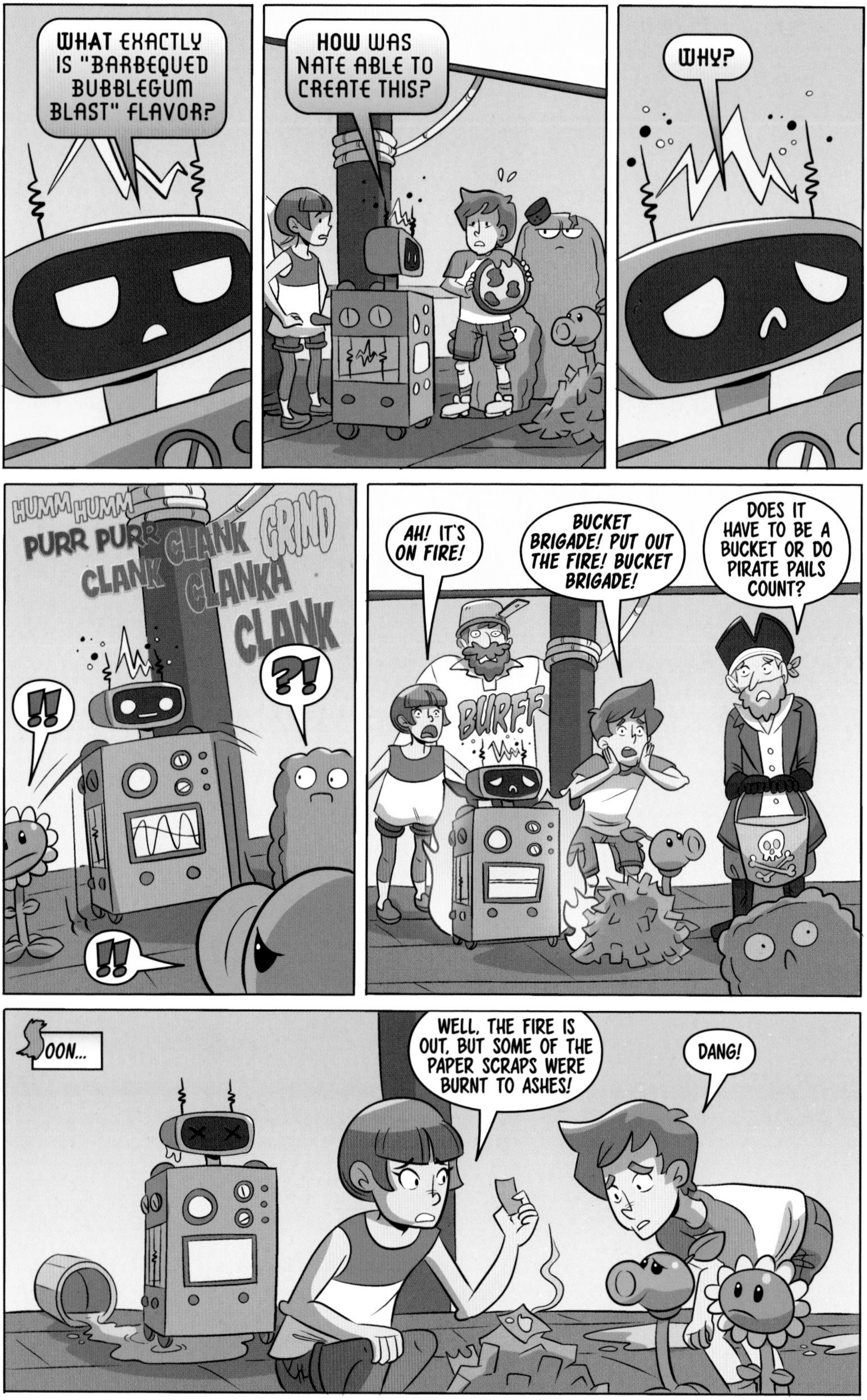
WHAT EXACTLY IS "BARBEQUED BUBBLEGUM BLAST" FLAVOR?
HOW WAS NATE ABLE TO CREATE THIS?
WHY?
HUMM HUMM
PURR PURR
CLANK
GRIND
CLANK
CLANKA
CLANK
!!
?!
!!
AH! IT'S ON FIRE!
BUCKET BRIGADE! PUT OUT THE FIRE! BUCKET BRIGADE!
BURFF
DOES IT HAVE TO BE A BUCKET OR DO PIRATE PAILS COUNT?
SOON...
WELL, THE FIRE IS OUT, BUT SOME OF THE PAPER SCRAPS WERE BURNT TO ASHES!
DANG!

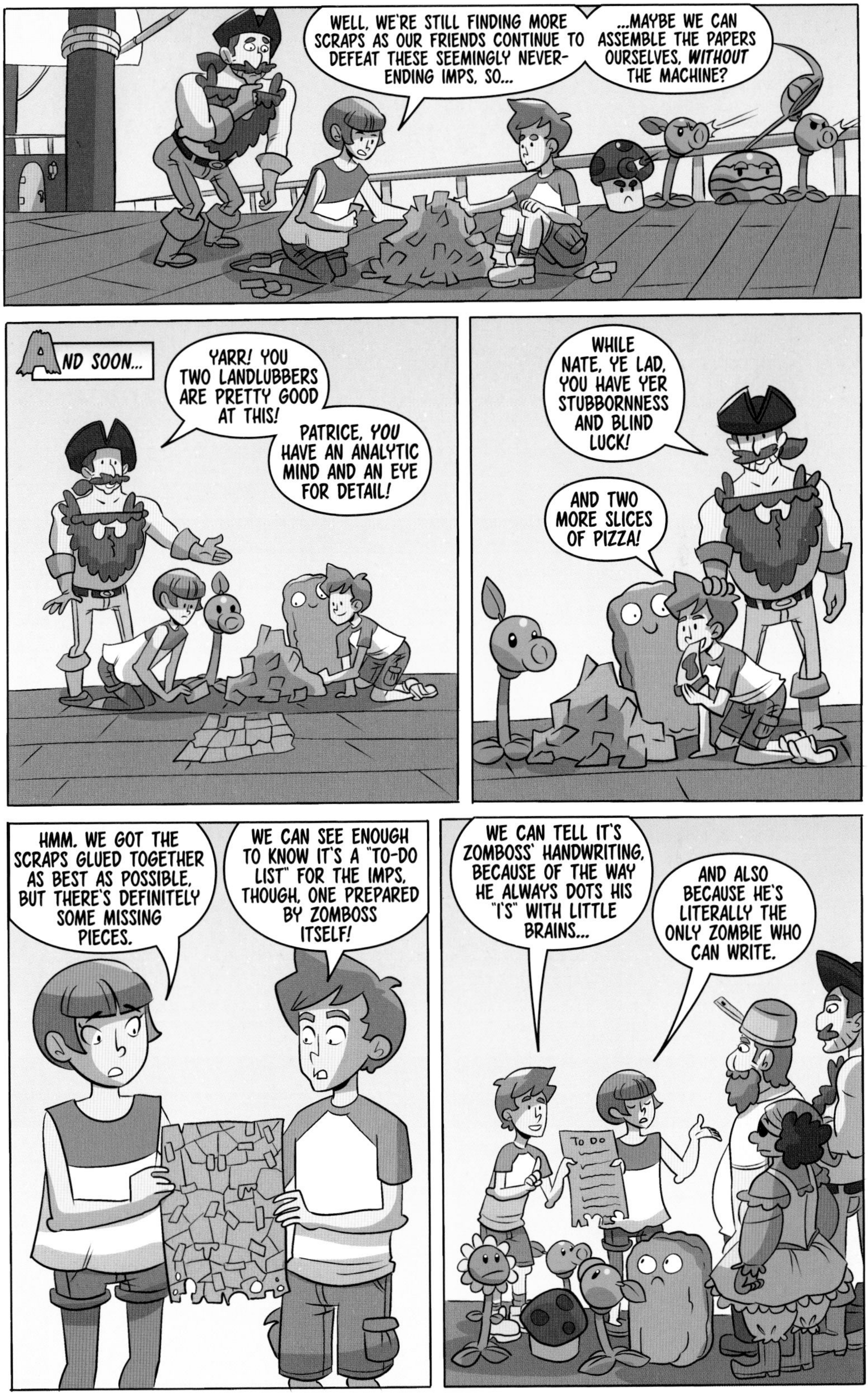
WELL, WE'RE STILL FINDING MORE SCRAPS AS OUR FRIENDS CONTINUE TO DEFEAT THESE SEEMINGLY NEVER-ENDING IMPS, SO...
...MAYBE WE CAN ASSEMBLE THE PAPERS OURSELVES, *WITHOUT* THE MACHINE?
AND SOON...
YARR! YOU TWO LANDLUBBERS ARE PRETTY GOOD AT THIS!
PATRICE, *YOU* HAVE AN ANALYTIC MIND AND AN EYE FOR DETAIL!
WHILE NATE, YE LAD, YOU HAVE YER STUBBORNNESS AND BLIND LUCK!
AND TWO MORE SLICES OF PIZZA!
HMM. WE GOT THE SCRAPS GLUED TOGETHER AS BEST AS POSSIBLE, BUT THERE'S DEFINITELY SOME MISSING PIECES.
WE CAN SEE ENOUGH TO KNOW IT'S A "TO-DO LIST" FOR THE IMPS, THOUGH, ONE PREPARED BY ZOMBOSS ITSELF!
WE CAN TELL IT'S ZOMBOSS' HANDWRITING, BECAUSE OF THE WAY HE ALWAYS DOTS HIS "I'S" WITH LITTLE BRAINS...
AND ALSO BECAUSE HE'S LITERALLY THE ONLY ZOMBIE WHO CAN WRITE.
TO DO

"THE LIST IS... 'PICK UP THE POSTER-SIZE PRINTS OF ZOMBOSS IN HIS FAVORITE DISCO SWIMSUITS.'

"BUY A BIRTHDAY CAKE FOR TUGBOAT!

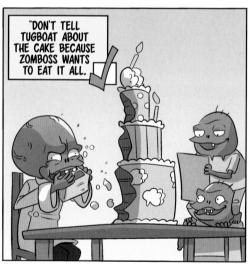

"DON'T TELL TUGBOAT ABOUT THE CAKE BECAUSE ZOMBOSS WANTS TO EAT IT ALL.

"INFEST PIRATE SHIP.

"BALLOT STUFFING FOR EINSTEIN-FLAVORED POP SMARTS IN ELECTION FOR A NEW POP SMARTS FLAVOR."

POP-SMARTS HEADQUARTERS!

BALLOT BOX!

STUFF

STUFF

VOTE HERE!

giggle!

giggle!

giggle!

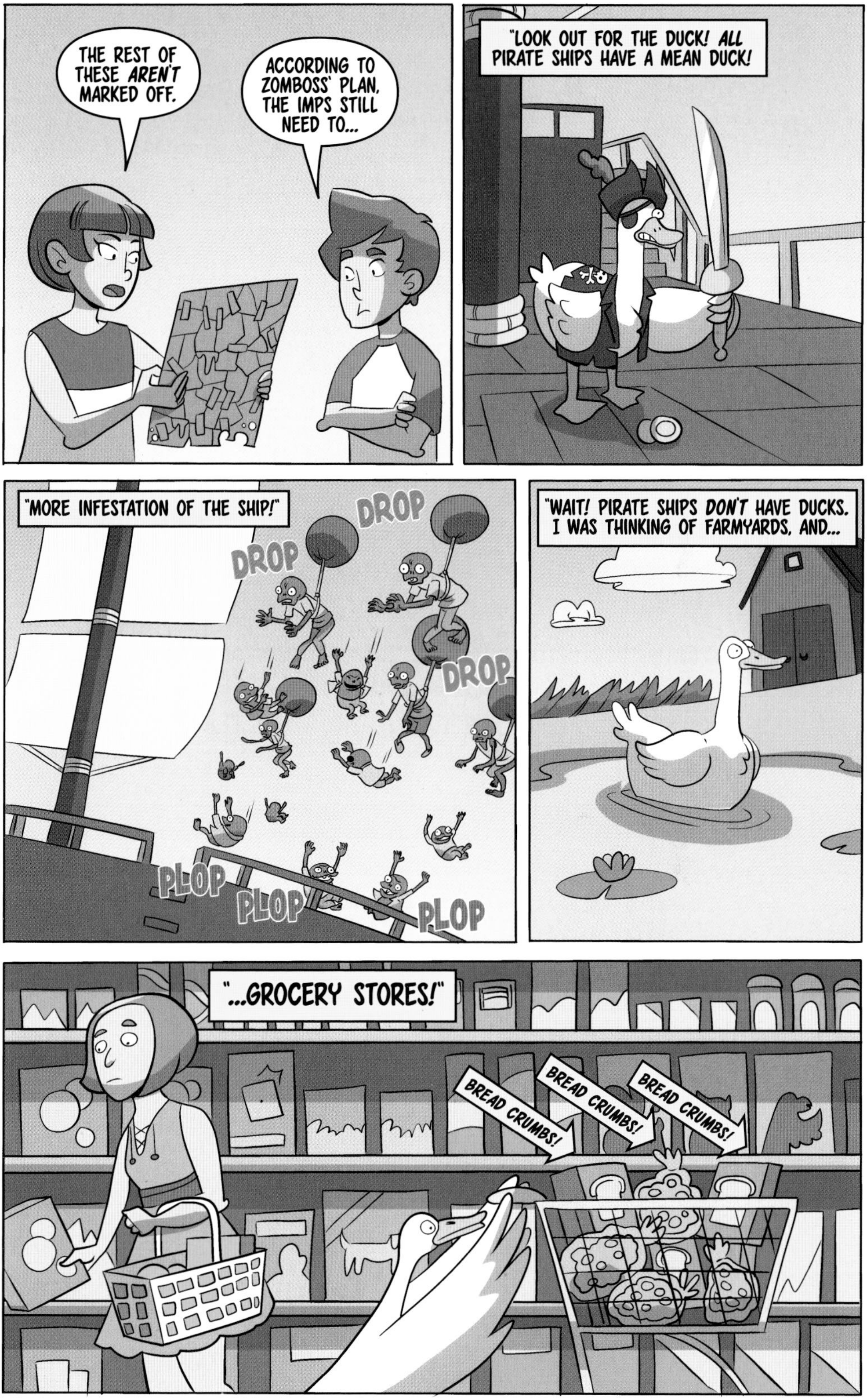
THE REST OF THESE AREN'T MARKED OFF.
ACCORDING TO ZOMBOSS' PLAN, THE IMPS STILL NEED TO...
"LOOK OUT FOR THE DUCK! ALL PIRATE SHIPS HAVE A MEAN DUCK!
"MORE INFESTATION OF THE SHIP!"
DROP
DROP
DROP
PLOP
PLOP
PLOP
"WAIT! PIRATE SHIPS DON'T HAVE DUCKS. I WAS THINKING OF FARMYARDS, AND...
"...GROCERY STORES!"
BREAD CRUMBS!
BREAD CRUMBS!
BREAD CRUMBS!

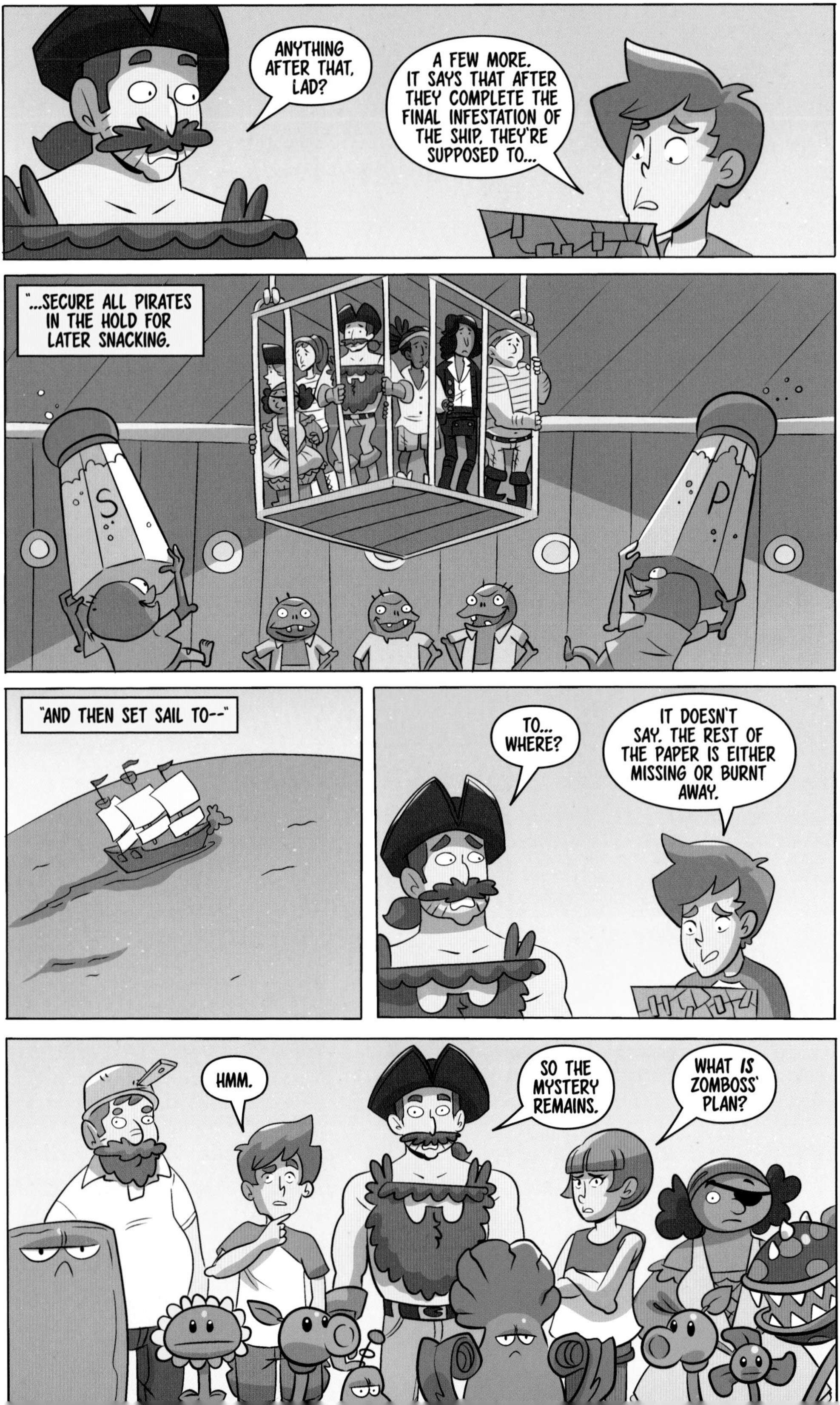
ANYTHING AFTER THAT, LAD?
A FEW MORE. IT SAYS THAT AFTER THEY COMPLETE THE FINAL INFESTATION OF THE SHIP, THEY'RE SUPPOSED TO...
"...SECURE ALL PIRATES IN THE HOLD FOR LATER SNACKING.
S
P
"AND THEN SET SAIL TO--"
TO... WHERE?
IT DOESN'T SAY. THE REST OF THE PAPER IS EITHER MISSING OR BURNT AWAY.
HMM.
SO THE MYSTERY REMAINS.
WHAT *IS* ZOMBOSS' PLAN?

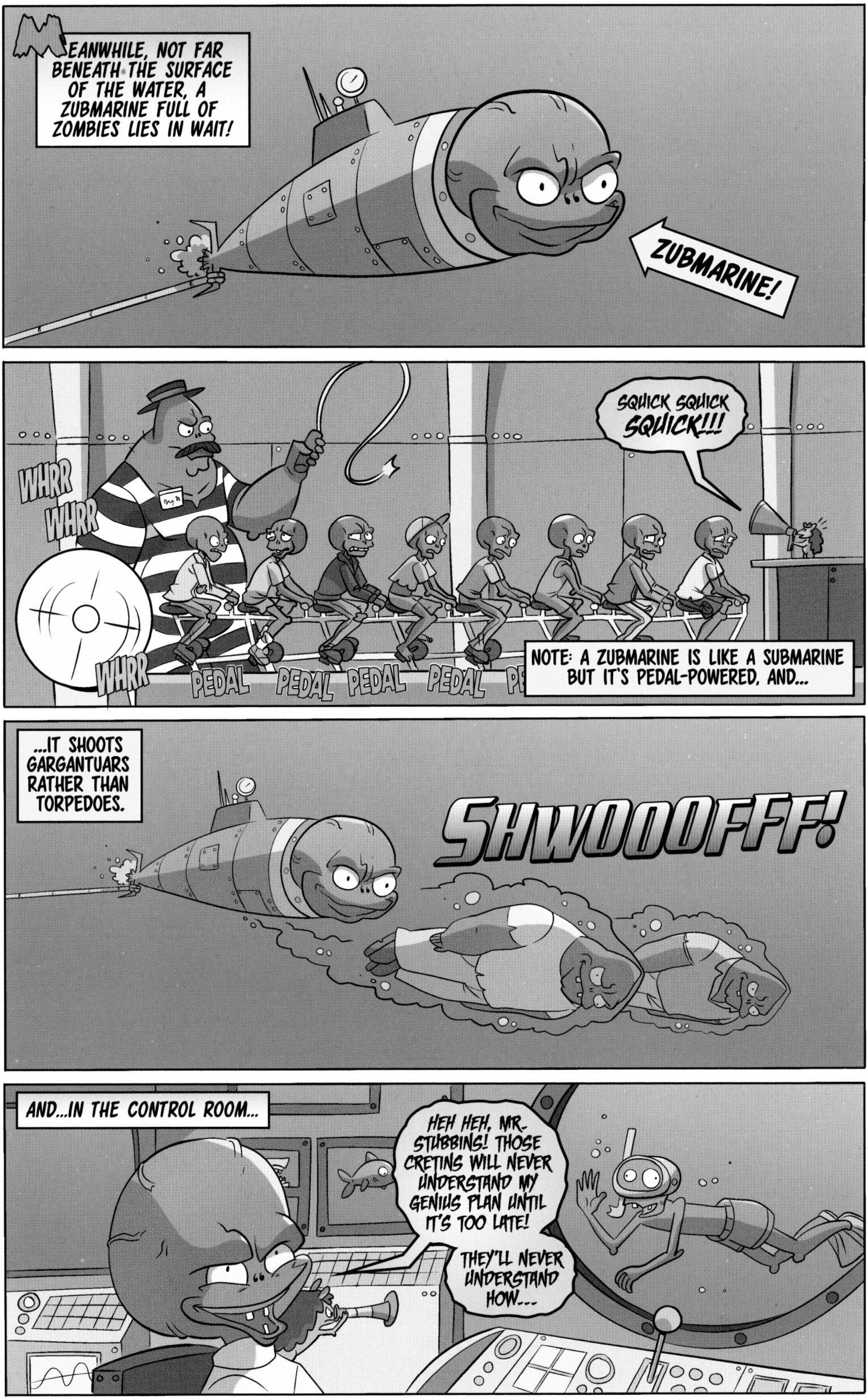
MEANWHILE, NOT FAR BENEATH THE SURFACE OF THE WATER, A ZUBMARINE FULL OF ZOMBIES LIES IN WAIT!
ZUBMARINE!
WHRR
WHRR
WHRR
SQUICK SQUICK SQUICK!!!
PEDAL
PEDAL
PEDAL
PEDAL
NOTE: A ZUBMARINE IS LIKE A SUBMARINE BUT IT'S PEDAL-POWERED, AND...
...IT SHOOTS GARGANTUARS RATHER THAN TORPEDOES.
SHWOOOFFF!
AND...IN THE CONTROL ROOM...
HEH HEH, MR. STUBBINS! THOSE CRETINS WILL NEVER UNDERSTAND MY GENIUS PLAN UNTIL IT'S TOO LATE!
THEY'LL NEVER UNDERSTAND HOW...

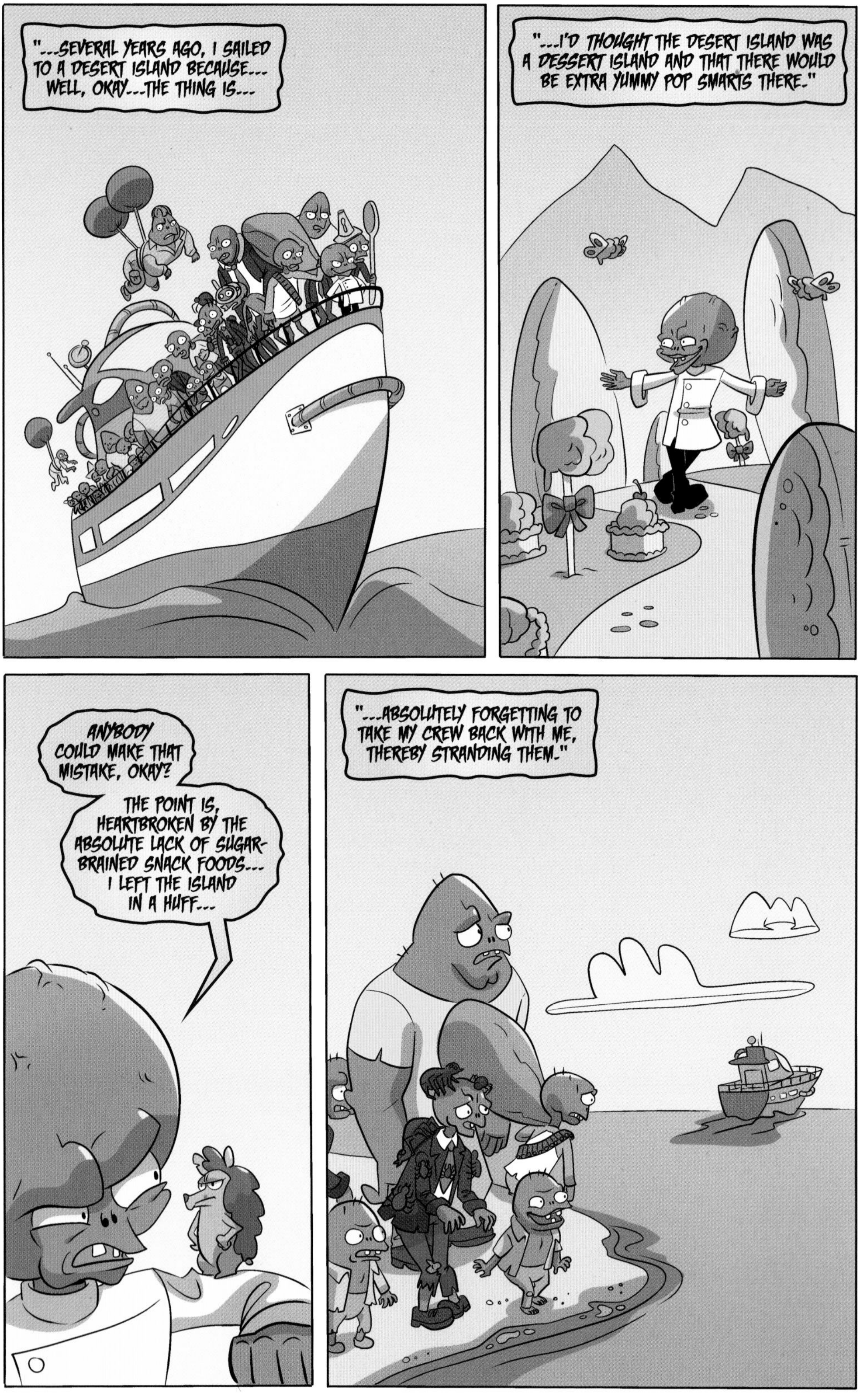
"...SEVERAL YEARS AGO, I SAILED TO A DESERT ISLAND BECAUSE... WELL, OKAY...THE THING IS...
"...I'D THOUGHT THE DESERT ISLAND WAS A DESSERT ISLAND AND THAT THERE WOULD BE EXTRA YUMMY POP SMARTS THERE."
ANYBODY COULD MAKE THAT MISTAKE, OKAY?
THE POINT IS, HEARTBROKEN BY THE ABSOLUTE LACK OF SUGAR-BRAINED SNACK FOODS... I LEFT THE ISLAND IN A HUFF...
"...ABSOLUTELY FORGETTING TO TAKE MY CREW BACK WITH ME, THEREBY STRANDING THEM."

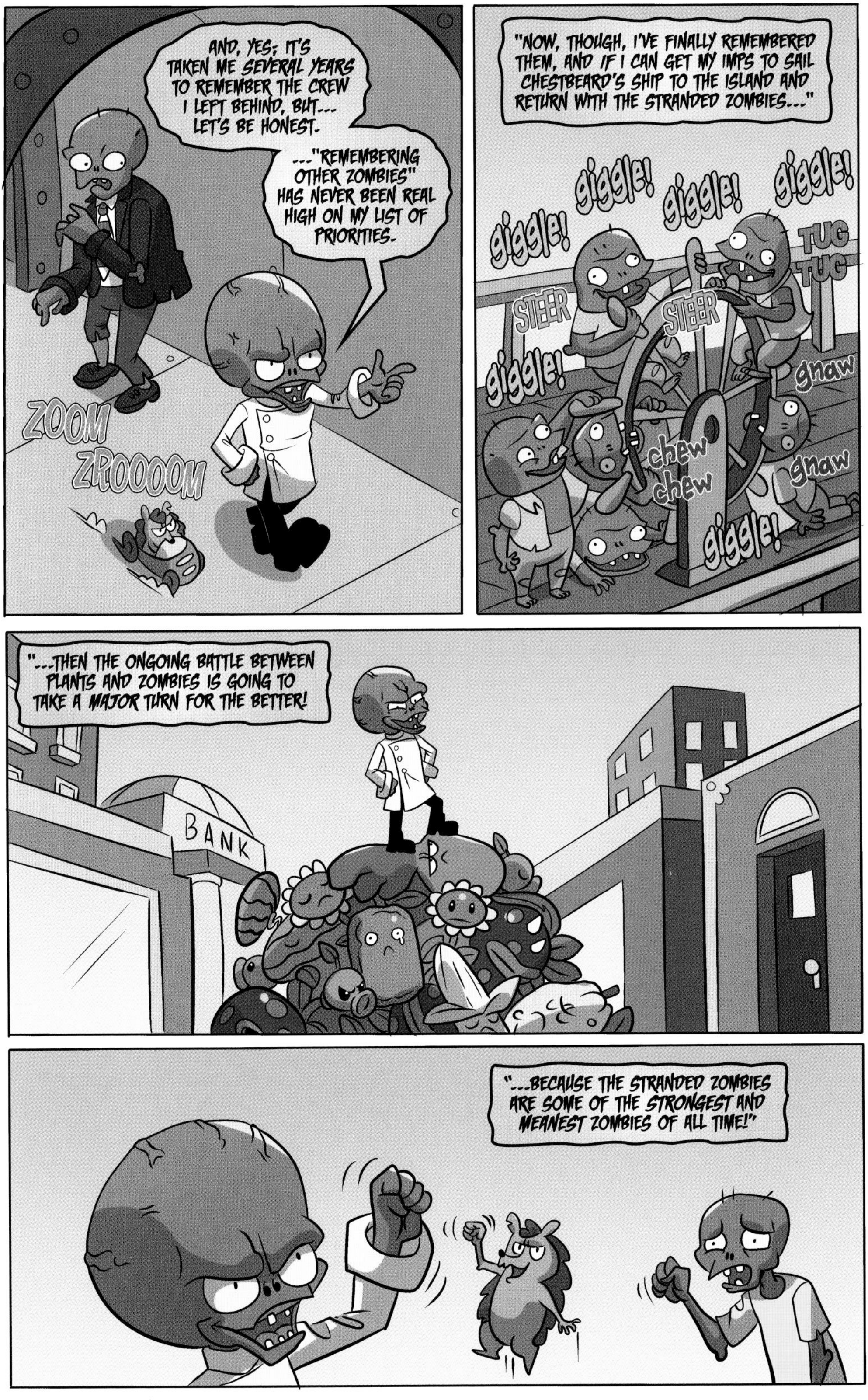
AND, YES; IT'S TAKEN ME SEVERAL YEARS TO REMEMBER THE CREW I LEFT BEHIND, BUT... LET'S BE HONEST.
..."REMEMBERING OTHER ZOMBIES" HAS NEVER BEEN REAL HIGH ON MY LIST OF PRIORITIES.
ZOOM
ZROOOOM
"NOW, THOUGH, I'VE FINALLY REMEMBERED THEM, AND IF I CAN GET MY IMPS TO SAIL CHESTBEARD'S SHIP TO THE ISLAND AND RETURN WITH THE STRANDED ZOMBIES..."
giggle!
giggle!
giggle!
giggle!
TUG
TUG
STEER
STEER
giggle!
gnaw
chew
chew
gnaw
giggle!
"...THEN THE ONGOING BATTLE BETWEEN PLANTS AND ZOMBIES IS GOING TO TAKE A MAJOR TURN FOR THE BETTER!
BANK
"...BECAUSE THE STRANDED ZOMBIES ARE SOME OF THE STRONGEST AND MEANEST ZOMBIES OF ALL TIME!"

STRANDED ZOMBIE Trading Card Set

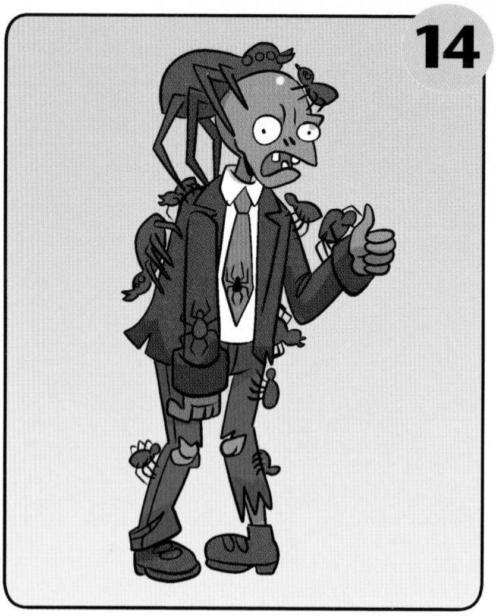

14

SPIDER FAN!

- **Major Achievements:** Gold Badge for Scaring Children
- **Hobbies:** Scaring children
- **Favorite music:** The sound of 2,000 spiders creeping through someone's hair
- **Power level:** Immense
- **Motto:** Gnarrr!

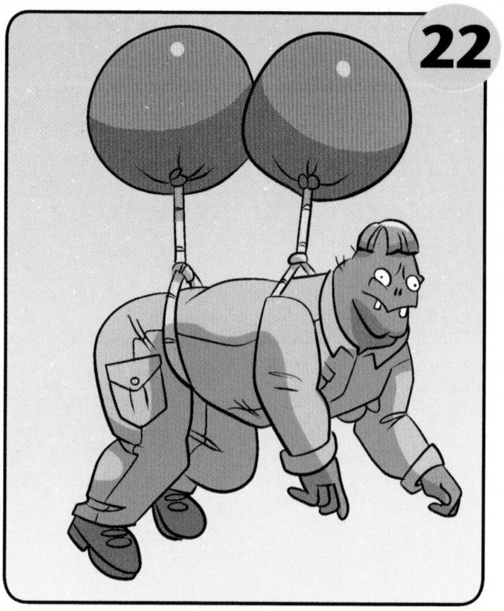

22

JUNEBUG!

- **Major Achievements:** Accidentally ate a van
- **Hobbies:** Staring at things without blinking
- **Favorite music:** Car alarms
- **Power level:** Startling
- **Motto:** Grahh?

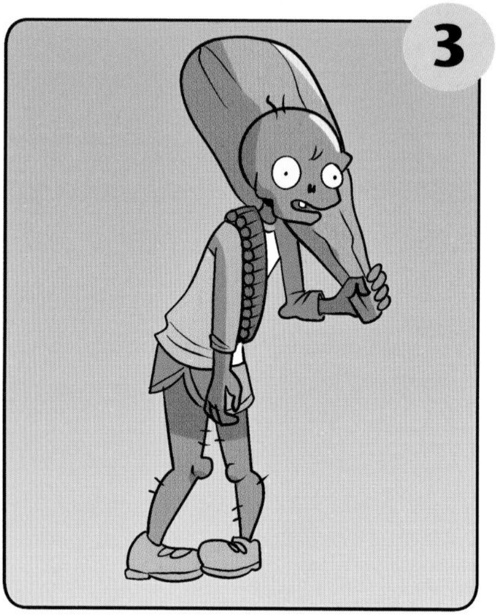

3

MILO BONKBRAIN

- **Major Achievements:** Bronze Badge of Bonking
- **Hobbies:** Studying the ancient art of Hitting Things Really Hard
- **Favorite music:** *The Wit and Wisdom of Zomboss* live album (with extended gloating remix)
- **Power level:** Gargantuan
- **Motto:** Brains!

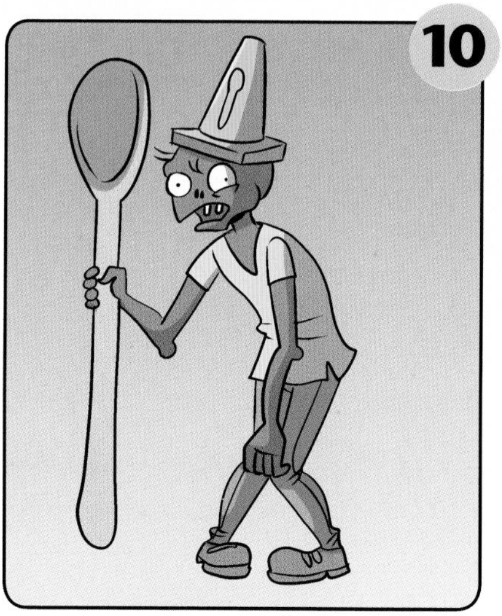

10

SPOON!

- **Major Achievements:** Has that spoon
- **Hobbies:** Spoon-related rodeo
- **Favorite music:** Spoon-chimes
- **Power level:** S Level
- **Motto:** Spoooon?

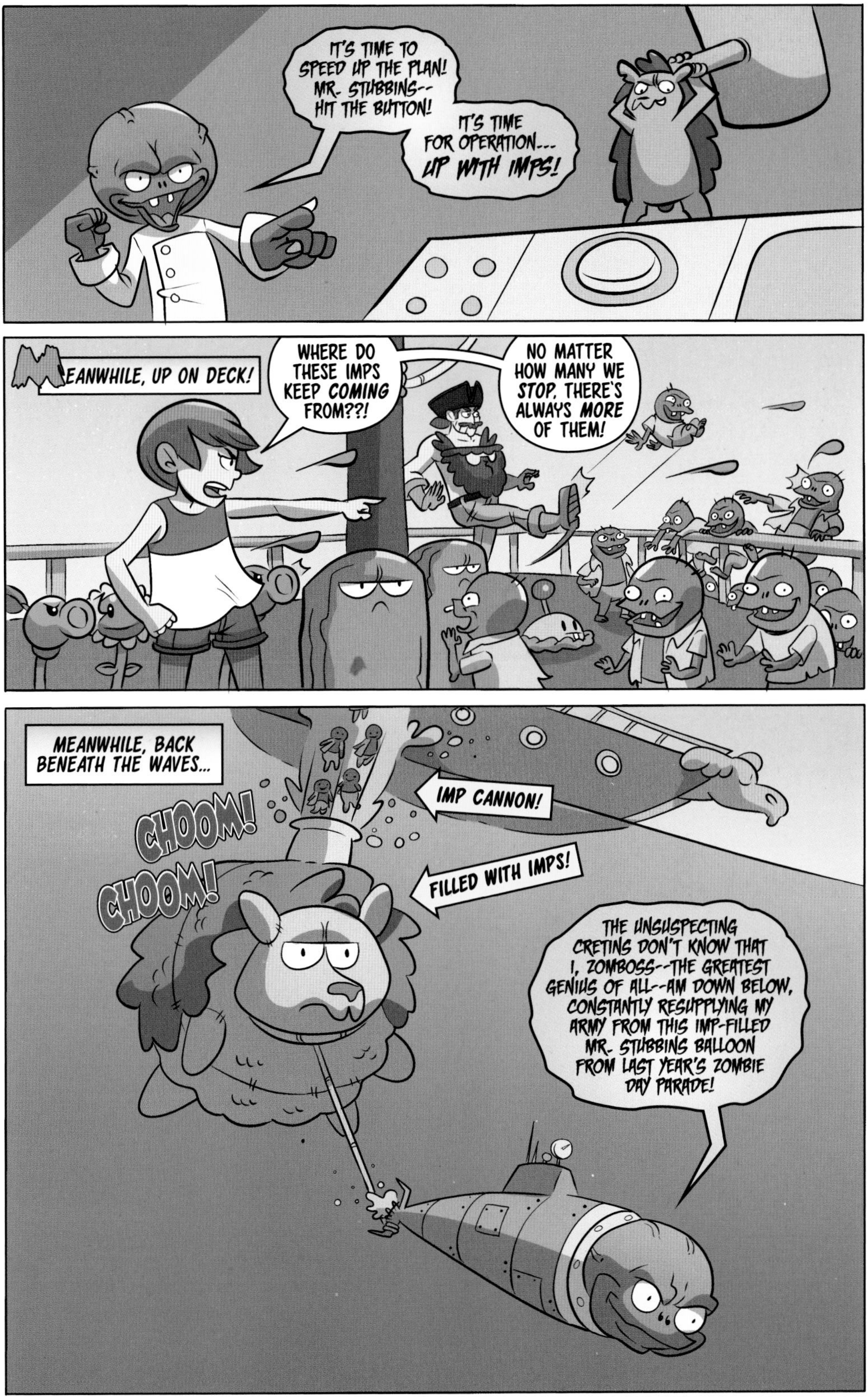
IT'S TIME TO SPEED UP THE PLAN! MR. STUBBINS-- HIT THE BUTTON!
IT'S TIME FOR OPERATION... UP WITH IMPS!
MEANWHILE, UP ON DECK!
WHERE DO THESE IMPS KEEP COMING FROM??!
NO MATTER HOW MANY WE STOP, THERE'S ALWAYS MORE OF THEM!
MEANWHILE, BACK BENEATH THE WAVES...
IMP CANNON!
CHOOM!
CHOOM!
FILLED WITH IMPS!
THE UNSUSPECTING CRETINS DON'T KNOW THAT I, ZOMBOSS--THE GREATEST GENIUS OF ALL--AM DOWN BELOW, CONSTANTLY RESUPPLYING MY ARMY FROM THIS IMP-FILLED MR. STUBBINS BALLOON FROM LAST YEAR'S ZOMBIE DAY PARADE!

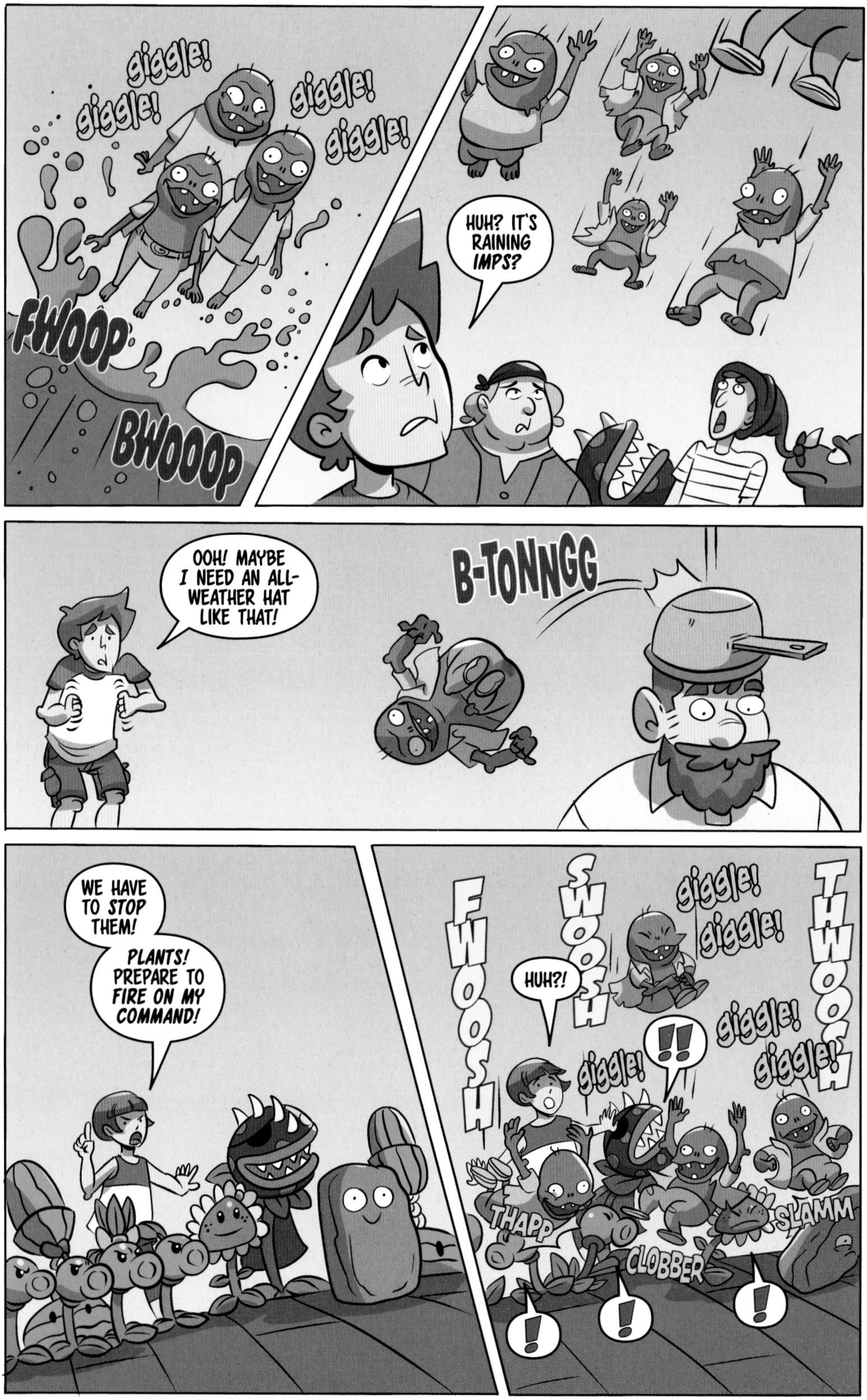
giggle!
giggle!
giggle!
giggle!
FWOOP
BWOOOP
HUH? IT'S RAINING IMPS?
OOH! MAYBE I NEED AN ALL-WEATHER HAT LIKE THAT!
B-TONNGG
WE HAVE TO STOP THEM!
PLANTS! PREPARE TO FIRE ON MY COMMAND!
FWOOSH
SWOOSH
giggle!
giggle!
THWOOSH
HUH?!
giggle!
!!
giggle!
giggle!
THAPP
CLOBBER
SLAMM
!
!
!

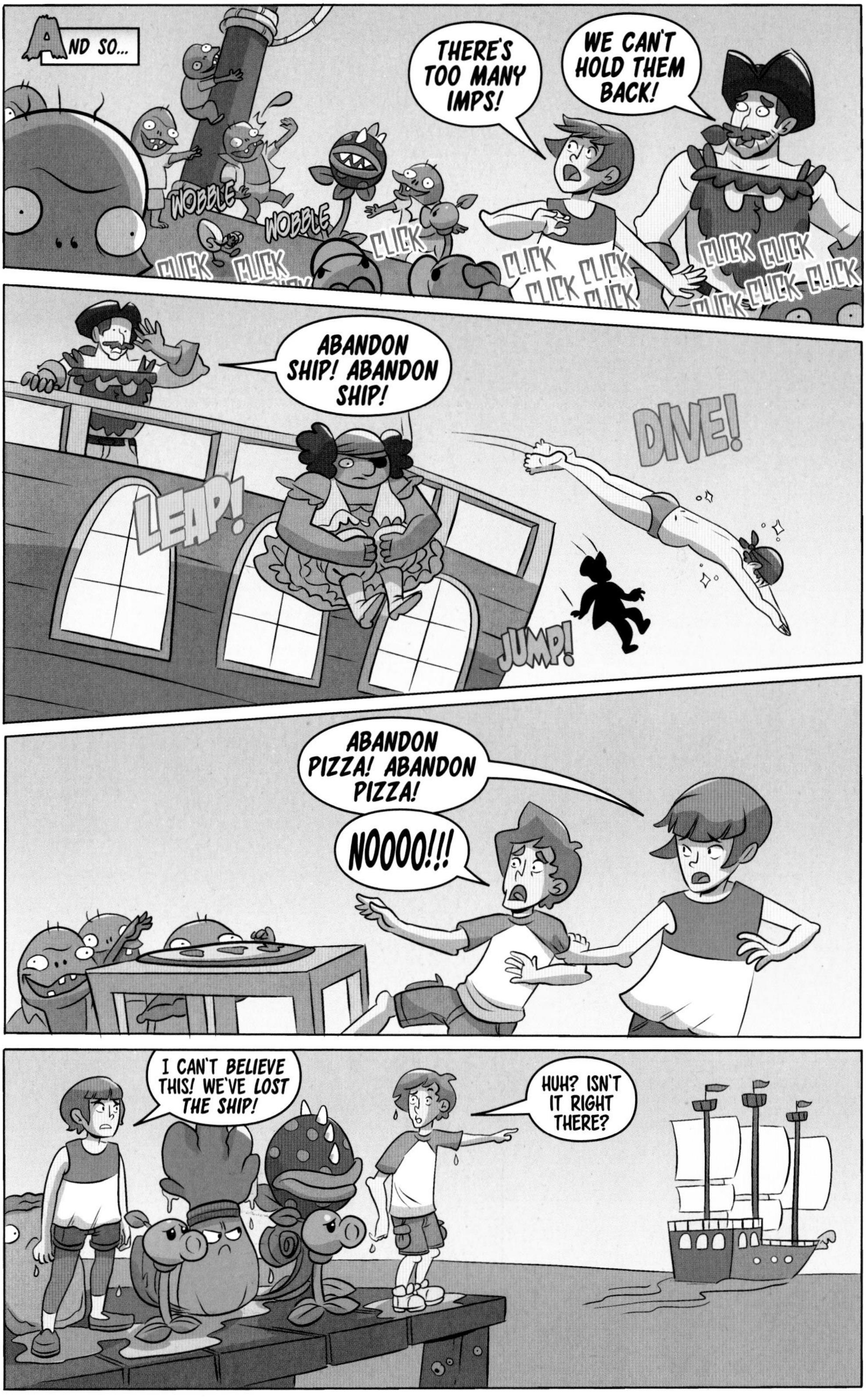
AND SO...
THERE'S TOO MANY IMPS!
WE CAN'T HOLD THEM BACK!
WOBBLE
WOBBLE
CLICK CLICK CLICK CLICK CLICK CLICK CLICK CLICK CLICK CLICK
ABANDON SHIP! ABANDON SHIP!
DIVE!
LEAP!
JUMP!
ABANDON PIZZA! ABANDON PIZZA!
NOOOO!!!
I CAN'T BELIEVE THIS! WE'VE LOST THE SHIP!
HUH? ISN'T IT RIGHT THERE?

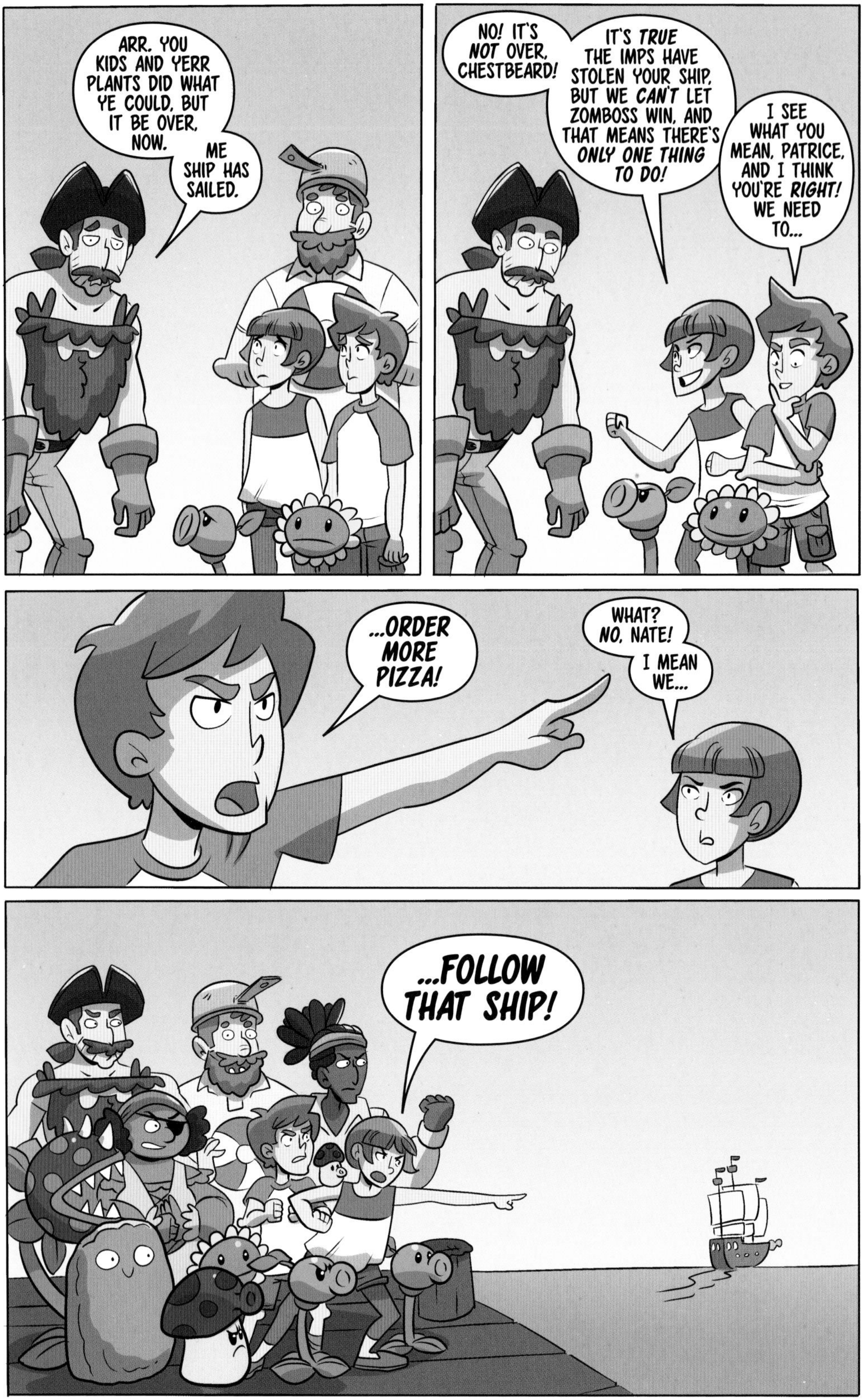
ARR. YOU KIDS AND YERR PLANTS DID WHAT YE COULD, BUT IT BE OVER, NOW.
ME SHIP HAS SAILED.
NO! IT'S NOT OVER, CHESTBEARD!
IT'S TRUE THE IMPS HAVE STOLEN YOUR SHIP, BUT WE CAN'T LET ZOMBOSS WIN, AND THAT MEANS THERE'S ONLY ONE THING TO DO!
I SEE WHAT YOU MEAN, PATRICE, AND I THINK YOU'RE RIGHT! WE NEED TO...
...ORDER MORE PIZZA!
WHAT? NO, NATE!
I MEAN WE...
...FOLLOW THAT SHIP!

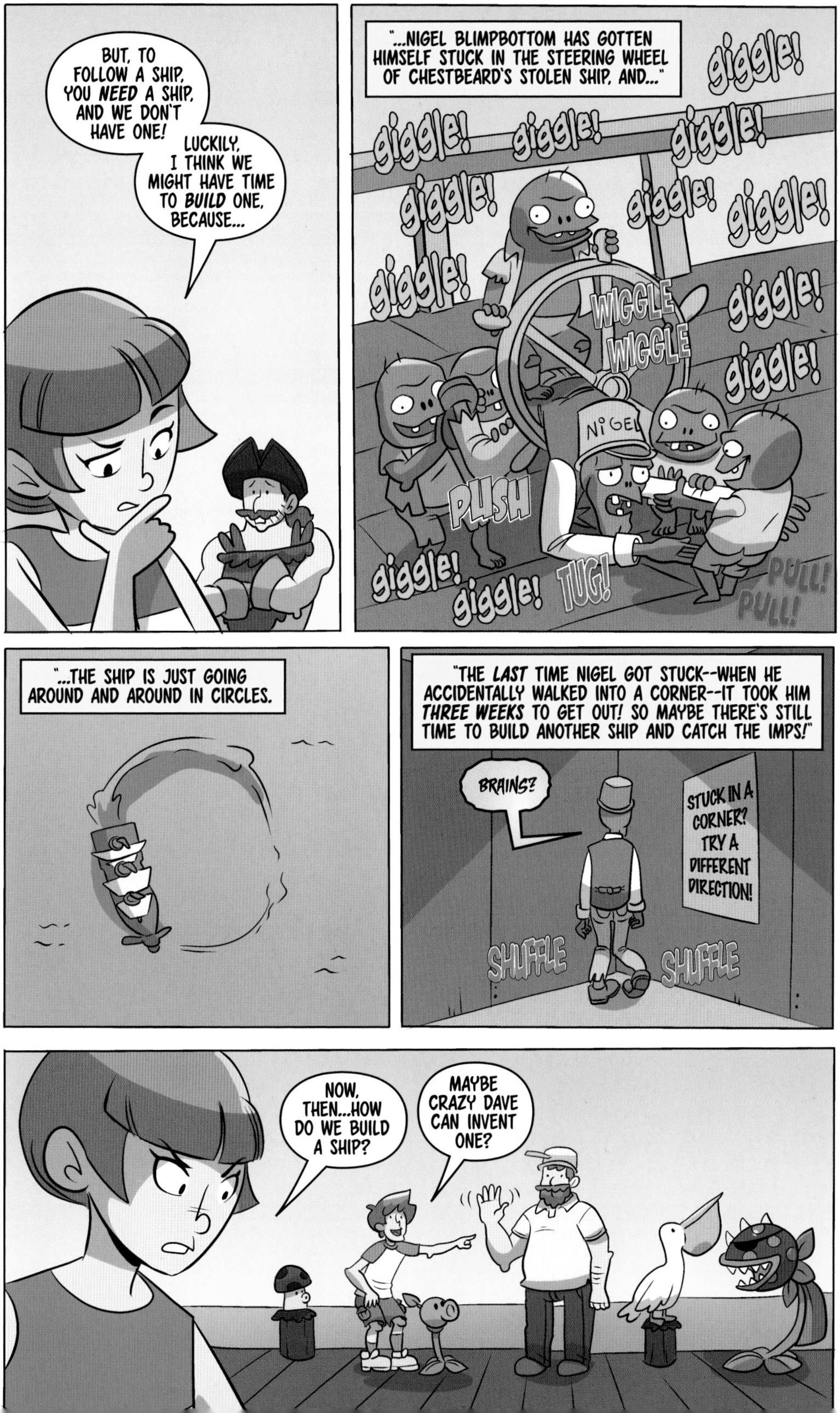
BUT, TO FOLLOW A SHIP, YOU NEED A SHIP, AND WE DON'T HAVE ONE!
LUCKILY, I THINK WE MIGHT HAVE TIME TO BUILD ONE, BECAUSE...
"...NIGEL BLIMPBOTTOM HAS GOTTEN HIMSELF STUCK IN THE STEERING WHEEL OF CHESTBEARD'S STOLEN SHIP, AND..."
giggle!
giggle! giggle! giggle!
giggle! giggle! giggle!
giggle!
WIGGLE WIGGLE
giggle!
giggle!
NiGEL
PUSH
giggle! giggle! TUG!
PULL! PULL!
"...THE SHIP IS JUST GOING AROUND AND AROUND IN CIRCLES.
"THE LAST TIME NIGEL GOT STUCK--WHEN HE ACCIDENTALLY WALKED INTO A CORNER--IT TOOK HIM THREE WEEKS TO GET OUT! SO MAYBE THERE'S STILL TIME TO BUILD ANOTHER SHIP AND CATCH THE IMPS!"
BRAINS?
STUCK IN A CORNER? TRY A DIFFERENT DIRECTION!
SHUFFLE SHUFFLE
NOW, THEN...HOW DO WE BUILD A SHIP?
MAYBE CRAZY DAVE CAN INVENT ONE?

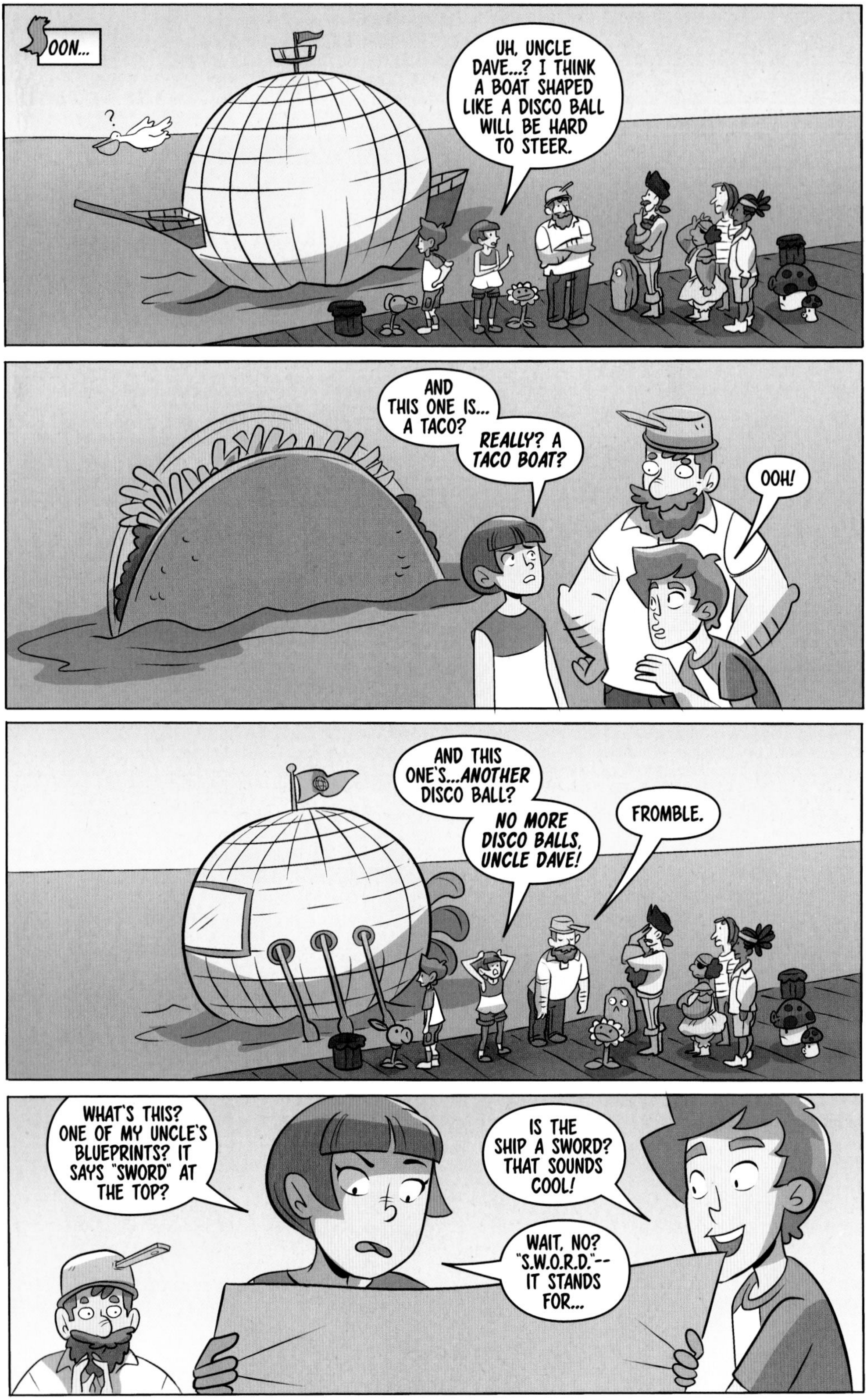
SOON...
UH, UNCLE DAVE...? I THINK A BOAT SHAPED LIKE A DISCO BALL WILL BE HARD TO STEER.
AND THIS ONE IS... A TACO?
REALLY? A TACO BOAT?
OOH!
AND THIS ONE'S...ANOTHER DISCO BALL?
NO MORE DISCO BALLS, UNCLE DAVE!
FROMBLE.
WHAT'S THIS? ONE OF MY UNCLE'S BLUEPRINTS? IT SAYS "SWORD" AT THE TOP?
IS THE SHIP A SWORD? THAT SOUNDS COOL!
WAIT, NO? "S.W.O.R.D."-- IT STANDS FOR...

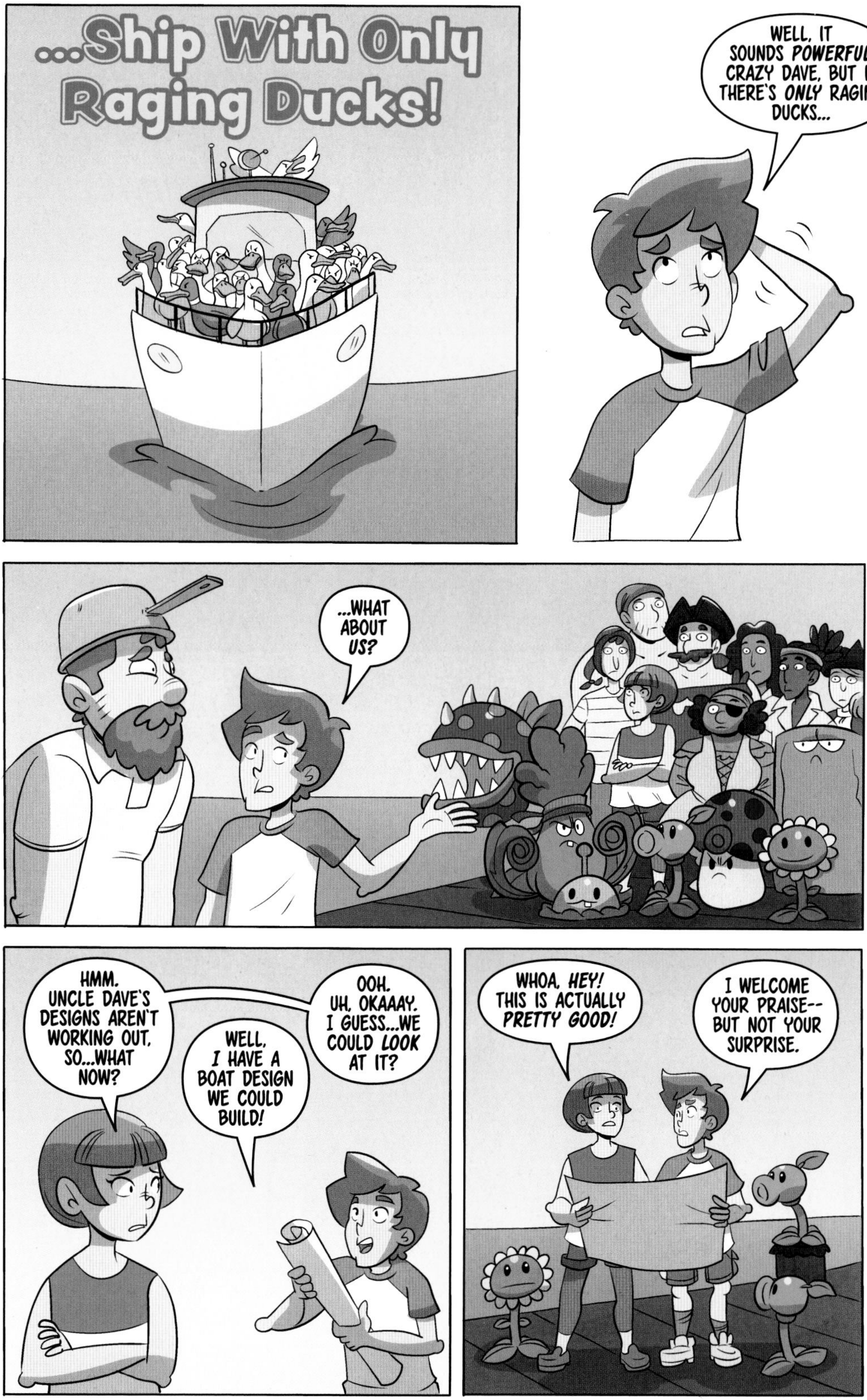
...Ship With Only Raging Ducks!
WELL, IT SOUNDS POWERFUL, CRAZY DAVE, BUT IF THERE'S ONLY RAGING DUCKS...
...WHAT ABOUT US?
HMM. UNCLE DAVE'S DESIGNS AREN'T WORKING OUT, SO...WHAT NOW?
WELL, I HAVE A BOAT DESIGN WE COULD BUILD!
OOH. UH, OKAAAY. I GUESS...WE COULD LOOK AT IT?
WHOA, HEY! THIS IS ACTUALLY PRETTY GOOD!
I WELCOME YOUR PRAISE--BUT NOT YOUR SURPRISE.

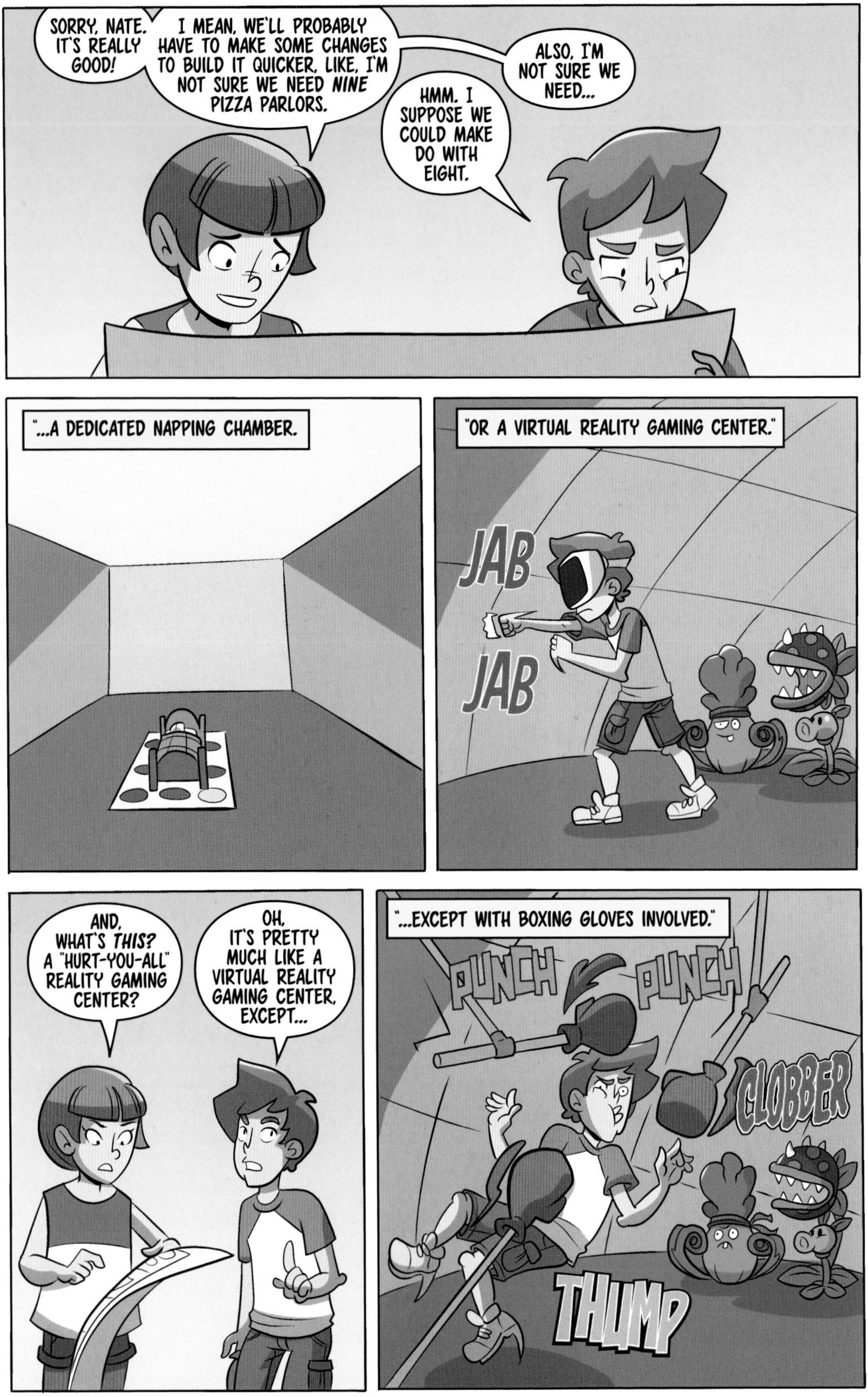
SORRY, NATE. IT'S REALLY GOOD!
I MEAN, WE'LL PROBABLY HAVE TO MAKE SOME CHANGES TO BUILD IT QUICKER, LIKE, I'M NOT SURE WE NEED *NINE* PIZZA PARLORS.
HMM. I SUPPOSE WE COULD MAKE DO WITH EIGHT.
ALSO, I'M NOT SURE WE NEED...
"...A DEDICATED NAPPING CHAMBER.
"OR A VIRTUAL REALITY GAMING CENTER."
JAB
JAB
AND, WHAT'S *THIS*? A "HURT-YOU-ALL" REALITY GAMING CENTER?
OH, IT'S PRETTY MUCH LIKE A VIRTUAL REALITY GAMING CENTER, EXCEPT...
"...EXCEPT WITH BOXING GLOVES INVOLVED."
PUNCH
PUNCH
CLOBBER
THUMP

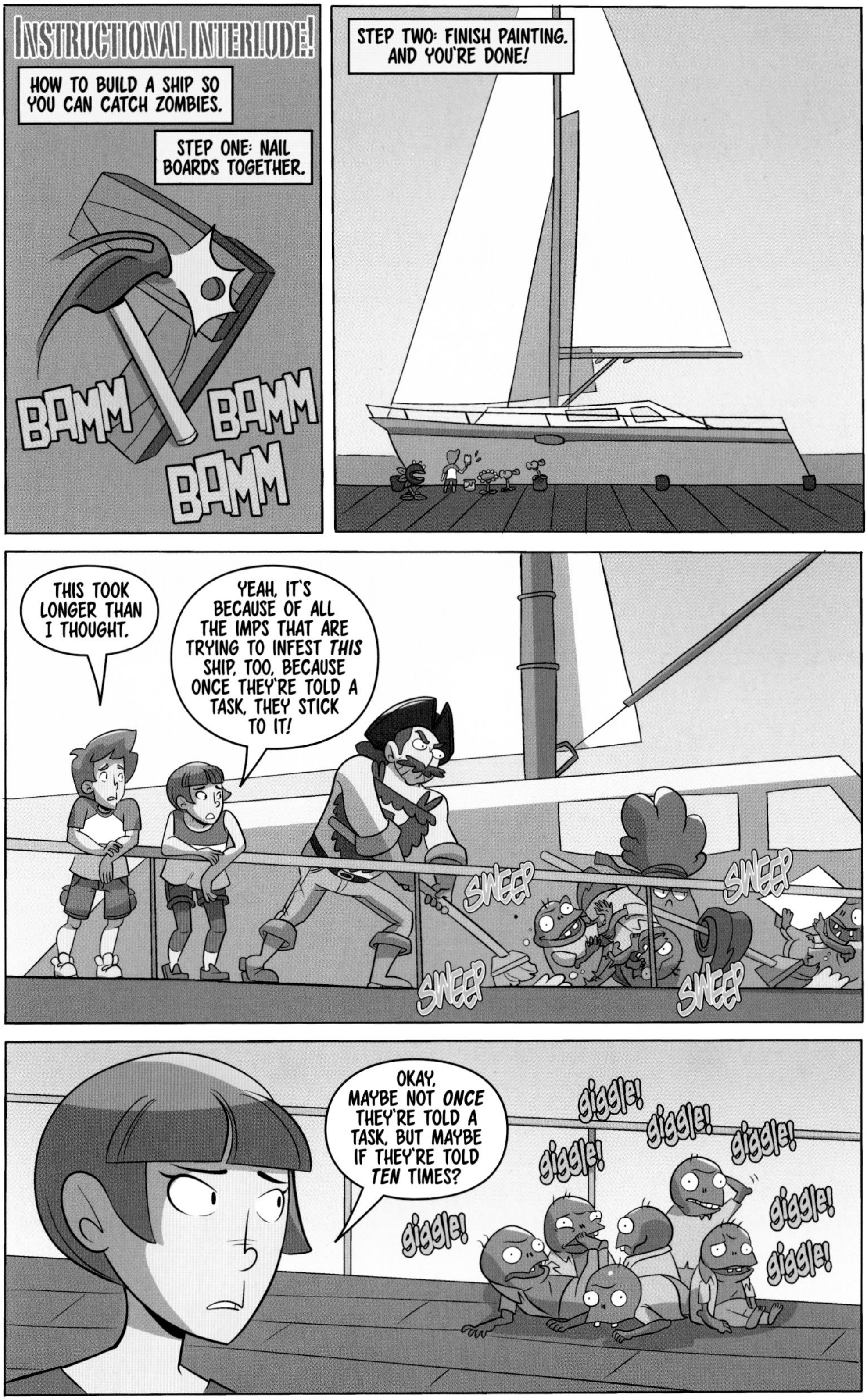
INSTRUCTIONAL INTERLUDE!
HOW TO BUILD A SHIP SO YOU CAN CATCH ZOMBIES.
STEP ONE: NAIL BOARDS TOGETHER.
BAMM BAMM BAMM
STEP TWO: FINISH PAINTING. AND YOU'RE DONE!
THIS TOOK LONGER THAN I THOUGHT.
YEAH, IT'S BECAUSE OF ALL THE IMPS THAT ARE TRYING TO INFEST *THIS* SHIP, TOO, BECAUSE ONCE THEY'RE TOLD A TASK, THEY STICK TO IT!
SWEEP SWEEP SWEEP SWEEP
OKAY, MAYBE NOT *ONCE* THEY'RE TOLD A TASK, BUT MAYBE IF THEY'RE TOLD *TEN* TIMES?
giggle! giggle! giggle! giggle! giggle! giggle! giggle!

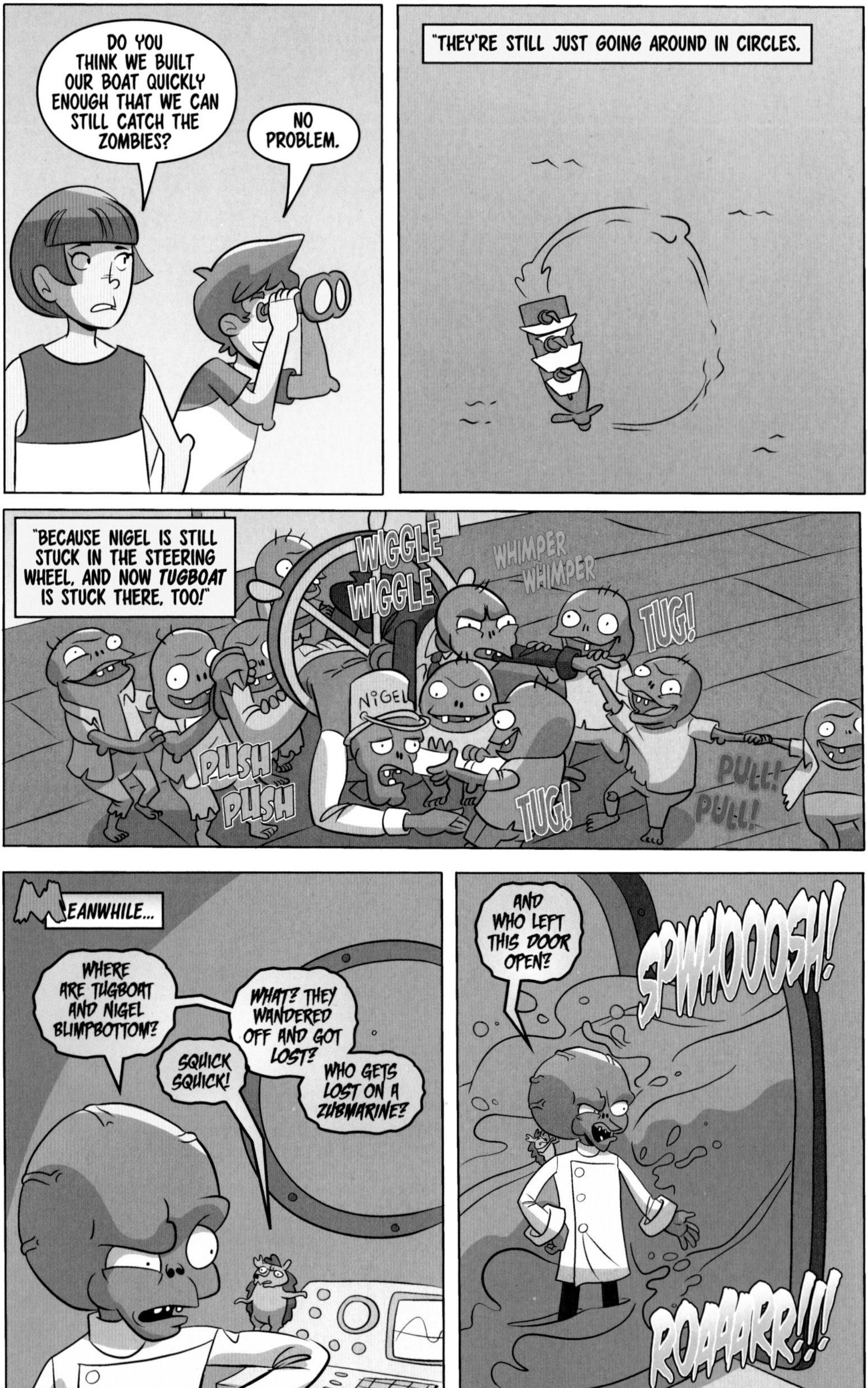
DO YOU THINK WE BUILT OUR BOAT QUICKLY ENOUGH THAT WE CAN STILL CATCH THE ZOMBIES?
NO PROBLEM.
"THEY'RE STILL JUST GOING AROUND IN CIRCLES.
"BECAUSE NIGEL IS STILL STUCK IN THE STEERING WHEEL, AND NOW TUGBOAT IS STUCK THERE, TOO!"
WIGGLE WIGGLE
WHIMPER WHIMPER
TUG!
NIGEL
PUSH PUSH
TUG!
PULL! PULL!
MEANWHILE...
WHERE ARE TUGBOAT AND NIGEL BLIMPBOTTOM?
WHAT? THEY WANDERED OFF AND GOT LOST?
SQUICK SQUICK!
WHO GETS LOST ON A ZUBMARINE?
AND WHO LEFT THIS DOOR OPEN?
SPWHOOOSH!
ROAAARR!!!

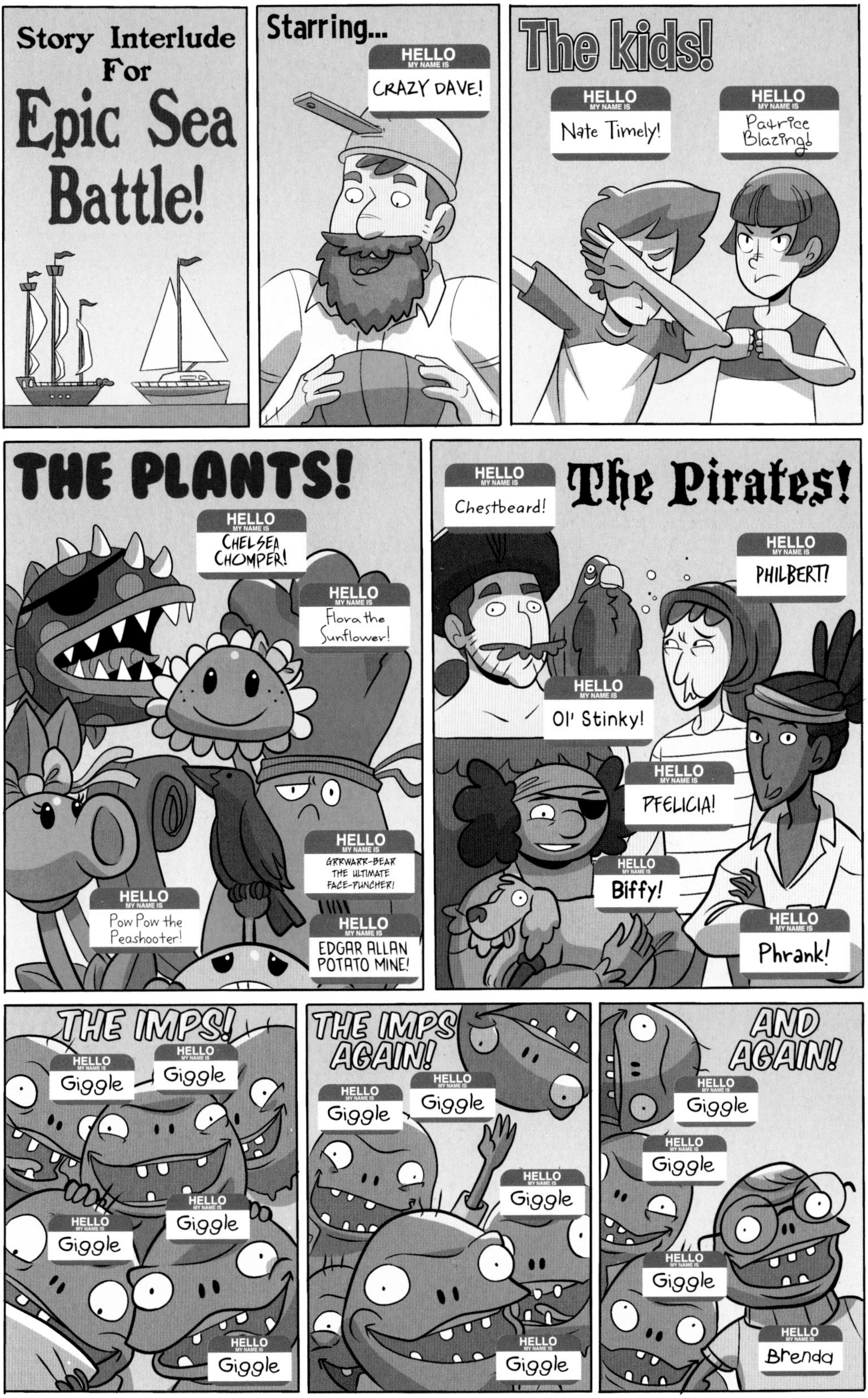
Story Interlude For Epic Sea Battle!
Starring...
HELLO MY NAME IS CRAZY DAVE!
The kids!
HELLO MY NAME IS Nate Timely!
HELLO MY NAME IS Patrice Blazing!
THE PLANTS!
HELLO MY NAME IS CHELSEA CHOMPER!
HELLO MY NAME IS Flora the Sunflower!
HELLO MY NAME IS GRRWARR-BEAR THE ULTIMATE FACE-PUNCHER!
HELLO MY NAME IS Pow Pow the Peashooter!
HELLO MY NAME IS EDGAR ALLAN POTATO MINE!
HELLO MY NAME IS Chestbeard!
The Pirates!
HELLO MY NAME IS PHILBERT!
HELLO MY NAME IS Ol' Stinky!
HELLO MY NAME IS PFELICIA!
HELLO MY NAME IS Biffy!
HELLO MY NAME IS Phrank!
THE IMPS!
HELLO MY NAME IS Giggle
HELLO MY NAME IS Giggle
HELLO MY NAME IS Giggle
HELLO MY NAME IS Giggle
HELLO MY NAME IS Giggle
THE IMPS AGAIN!
HELLO MY NAME IS Giggle
HELLO MY NAME IS Giggle
HELLO MY NAME IS Giggle
HELLO MY NAME IS Giggle
AND AGAIN!
HELLO MY NAME IS Giggle
HELLO MY NAME IS Giggle
HELLO MY NAME IS Giggle
HELLO MY NAME IS Brenda

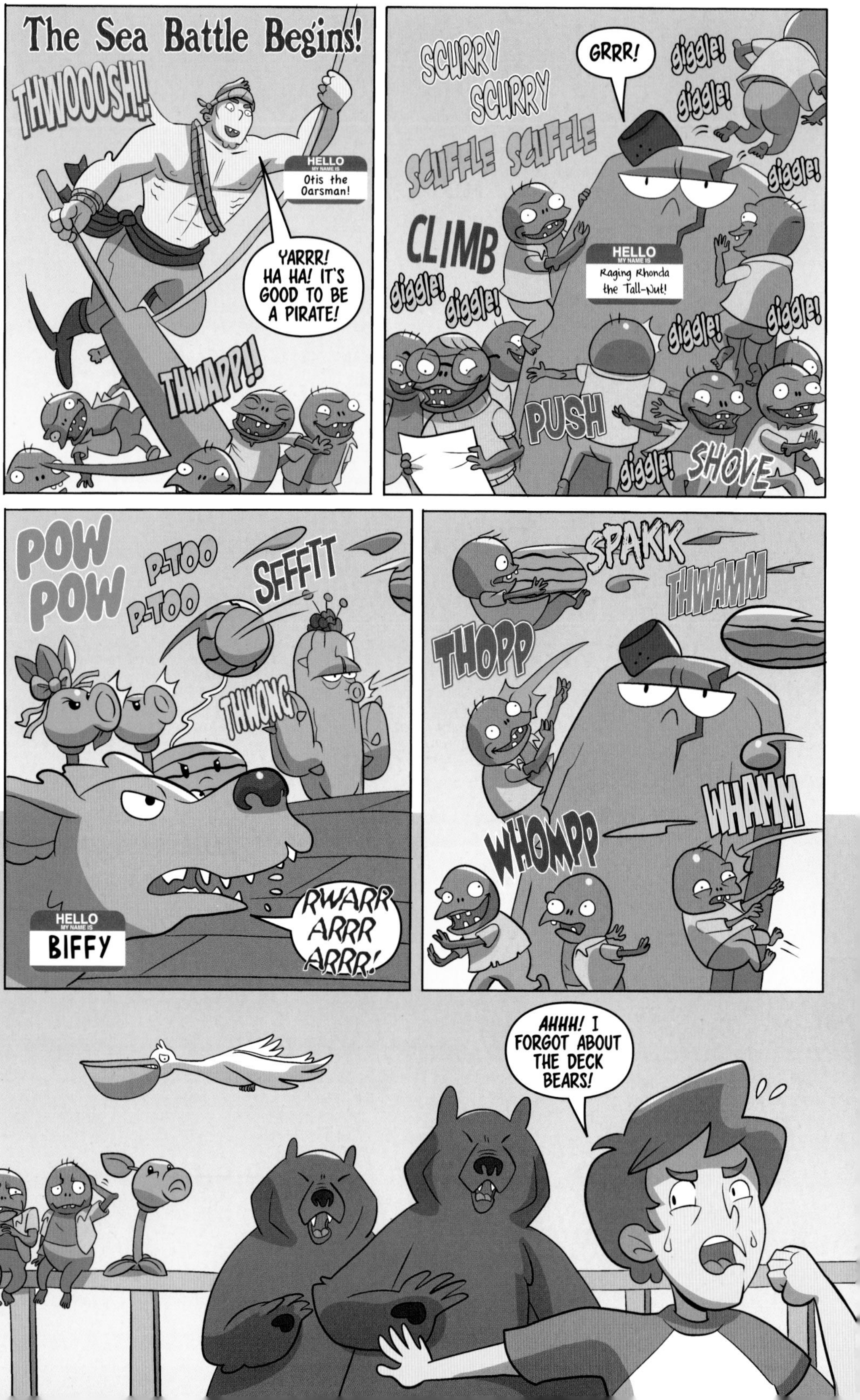

The Sea Battle Begins!
THWOOOSH!!
HELLO MY NAME IS Otis the Oarsman!
YARRR! HA HA! IT'S GOOD TO BE A PIRATE!
THWAPP!!
SCURRY SCURRY
SCUFFLE SCUFFLE
GRRR!
giggle! giggle!
giggle!
CLIMB
HELLO MY NAME IS Raging Rhonda the Tall-Nut!
giggle! giggle!
giggle!
giggle!
PUSH
giggle!
SHOVE
POW POW
P-TOO P-TOO
SFFFIT
THWONG
HELLO MY NAME IS BIFFY
RWARR ARRR ARRR!
SPAKK
THWAMM
THOPP
WHAMM
WHOMPP
AHHH! I FORGOT ABOUT THE DECK BEARS!

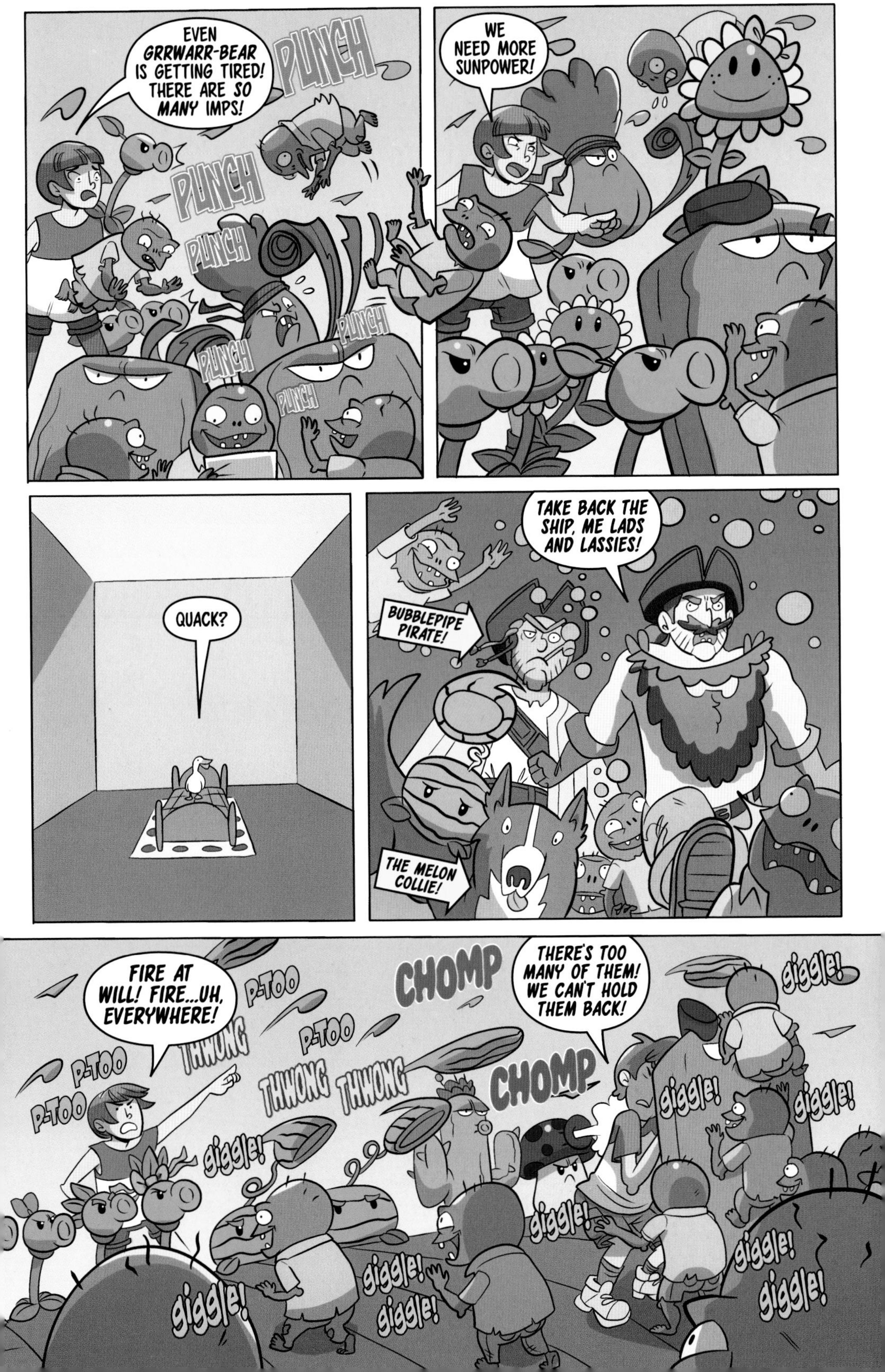
EVEN GRRWARR-BEAR IS GETTING TIRED! THERE ARE SO MANY IMPS!
PUNCH
PUNCH
PUNCH
PUNCH
PUNCH
PUNCH
WE NEED MORE SUNPOWER!
QUACK?
TAKE BACK THE SHIP, ME LADS AND LASSIES!
BUBBLEPIPE PIRATE!
THE MELON COLLIE!
FIRE AT WILL! FIRE...UH, EVERYWHERE!
P-TOO
P-TOO
P-TOO
P-TOO
THWONG
THWONG
THWONG
CHOMP
THERE'S TOO MANY OF THEM! WE CAN'T HOLD THEM BACK!
CHOMP
giggle!
giggle!
giggle!
giggle!
giggle!
giggle!
giggle!
giggle!
giggle!
giggle!
giggle!

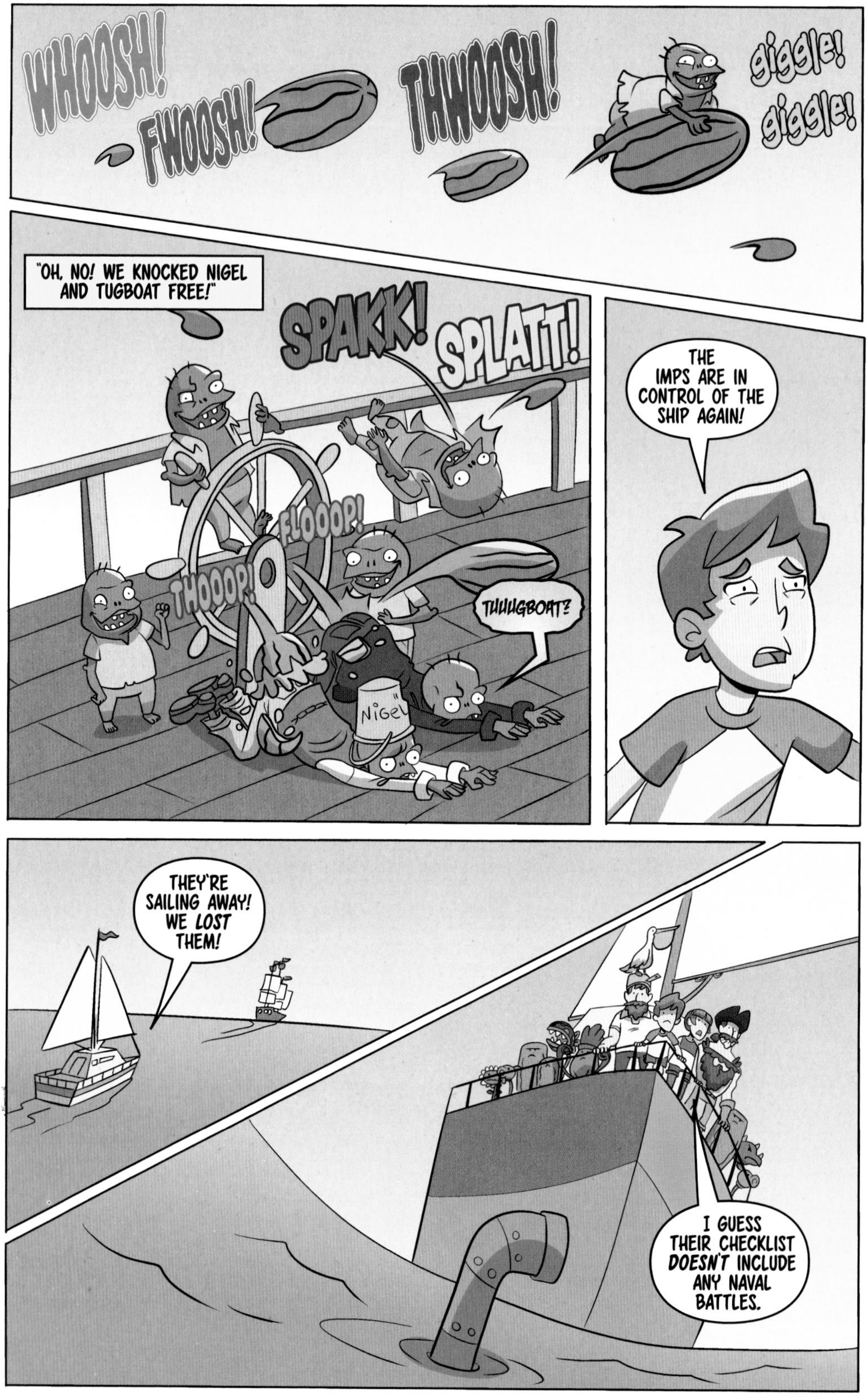
WHOOSH!
FWOOSH!
THWOOSH!
giggle! giggle!
"OH, NO! WE KNOCKED NIGEL AND TUGBOAT FREE!"
SPAKK!
SPLATT!
FLOOOP!
THOOOP!
THUUUGBOAT?
NIGEL
THE IMPS ARE IN CONTROL OF THE SHIP AGAIN!
THEY'RE SAILING AWAY! WE *LOST* THEM!
I GUESS THEIR CHECKLIST *DOESN'T* INCLUDE ANY NAVAL BATTLES.

HEH HEH, EXACTLY TRUE.

ALTHOUGH THE IMPS' "TO-DO" LIST DOES INCLUDE....

"...STOPPING OFF AT A Z-MART, THE CONVENIENCE STORE FOR ALL ZOMBIE NEEDS, SO THEY CAN PICK UP SOME MORE POP SMARTS FOR ME!"

OUT OF STOCK

"AND A FEW ZOTTO TICKETS, THE LOTTERY WHERE YOU CAN WIN BRAINS INSTEAD OF MONEY!"

Three Tasty BRAINS!

Win up to 3 brains!

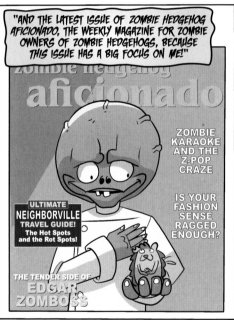

"AND THE LATEST ISSUE OF ZOMBIE HEDGEHOG AFICIONADO, THE WEEKLY MAGAZINE FOR ZOMBIE OWNERS OF ZOMBIE HEDGEHOGS, BECAUSE THIS ISSUE HAS A BIG FOCUS ON ME!"

zombie hedgehog
aficionado

ZOMBIE KARAOKE AND THE Z-POP CRAZE

IS YOUR FASHION SENSE RAGGED ENOUGH?

ULTIMATE NEIGHBORVILLE TRAVEL GUIDE! The Hot Spots and the Rot Spots!

THE TENDER SIDE OF EDGAR ZOMBOSS

WELL, ACTUALLY, ALL ISSUES HAVE A FOCUS ON ME, BECAUSE I'M THE ONLY ZOMBIE WHO OWNS A ZOMBIE HEDGEHOG.

zombie hedgehog aficionado

LUCKILY, MY IMPS WON'T HAVE TO TRAVEL TOO FAR OUT OF THEIR WAY TO GO TO A Z-MART, BECAUSE...

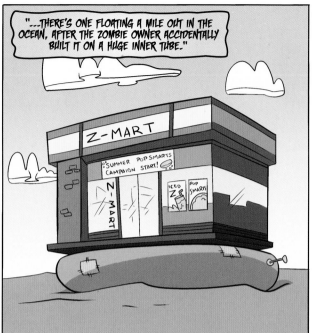

"...THERE'S ONE FLOATING A MILE OUT IN THE OCEAN, AFTER THE ZOMBIE OWNER ACCIDENTALLY BUILT IT ON A HUGE INNER TUBE."

Z-MART

SUMMER POP SMARTS CAMPAIGN START!

MEANWHILE...

ARE THEY... STOPPING AT A STORE?

AYE! THIS GIVES US A CHANCE TO CATCH UP WITH ME PIRATE SHIP!

THE RACE IS ON!

BUT WE STILL DON'T KNOW WHERE THEY'RE GOING! OR WHY!

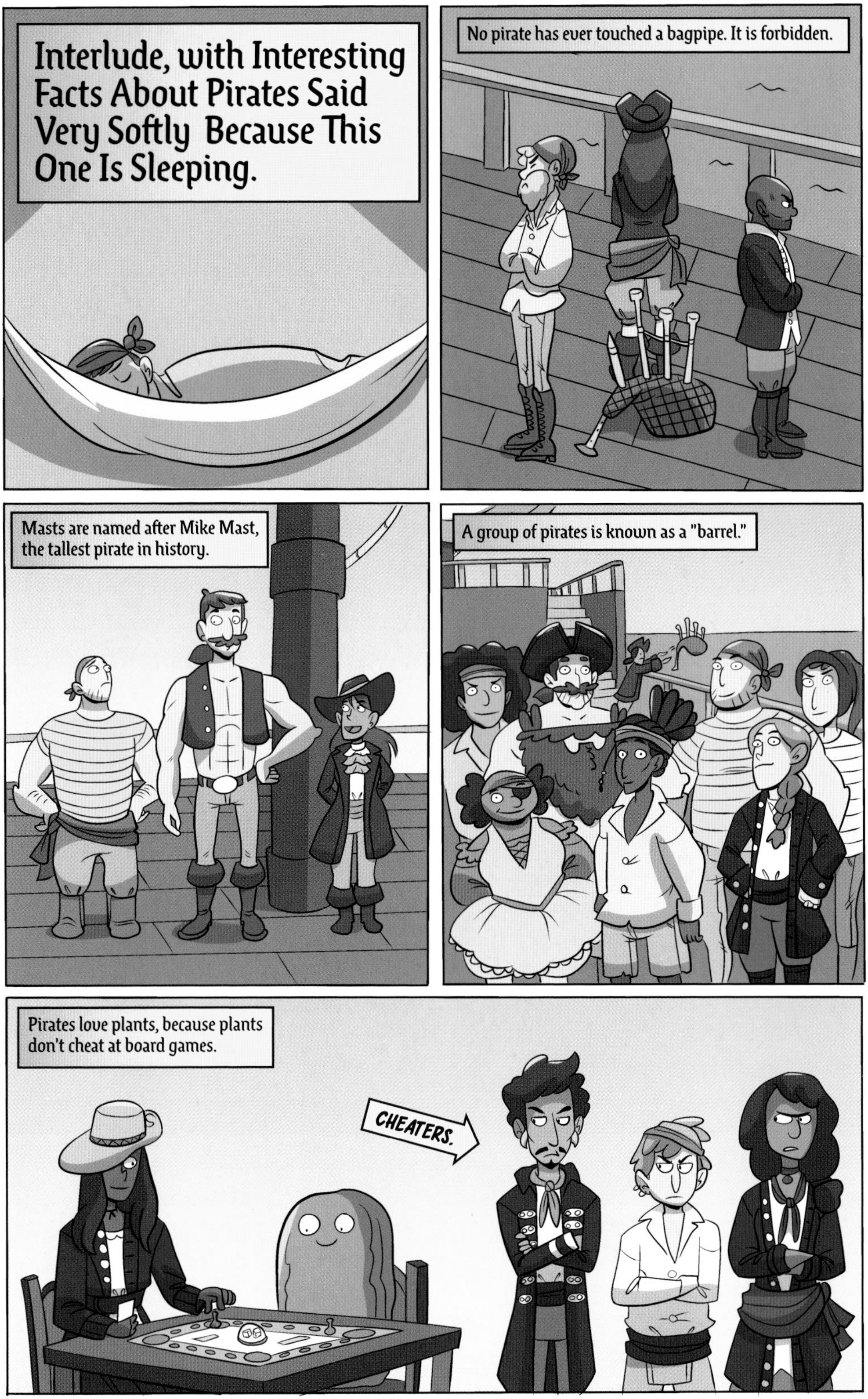
Interlude, with Interesting Facts About Pirates Said Very Softly Because This One Is Sleeping.
No pirate has ever touched a bagpipe. It is forbidden.
Masts are named after Mike Mast, the tallest pirate in history.
A group of pirates is known as a "barrel."
Pirates love plants, because plants don't cheat at board games.
CHEATERS.

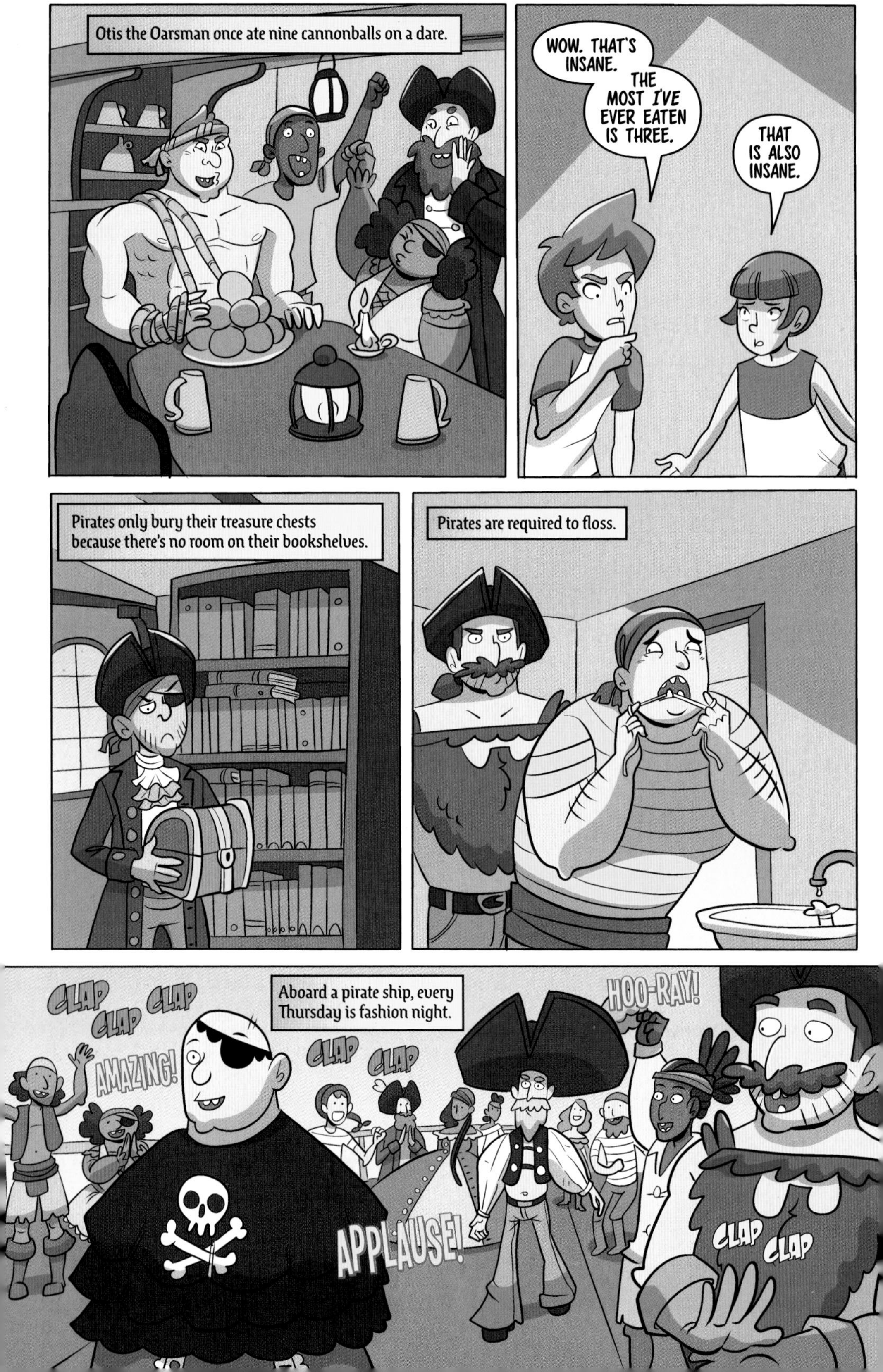

Otis the Oarsman once ate nine cannonballs on a dare.
WOW. THAT'S INSANE.
THE MOST I'VE EVER EATEN IS THREE.
THAT IS ALSO INSANE.
Pirates only bury their treasure chests because there's no room on their bookshelves.
Pirates are required to floss.
Aboard a pirate ship, every Thursday is fashion night.
CLAP
CLAP
CLAP
AMAZING!
CLAP
CLAP
HOO-RAY!
APPLAUSE!
CLAP
CLAP

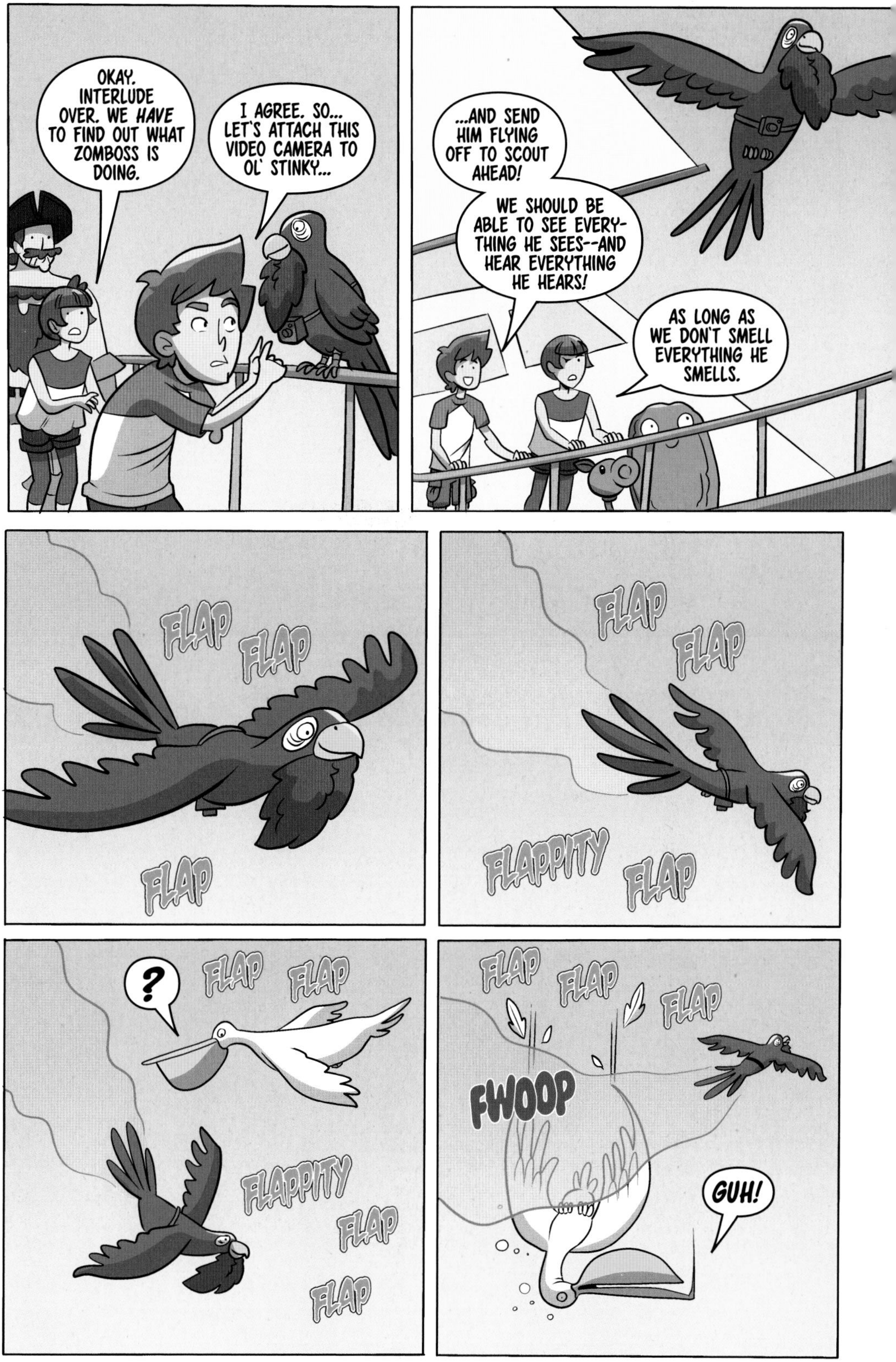
OKAY. INTERLUDE OVER. WE HAVE TO FIND OUT WHAT ZOMBOSS IS DOING.
I AGREE. SO... LET'S ATTACH THIS VIDEO CAMERA TO OL' STINKY...
...AND SEND HIM FLYING OFF TO SCOUT AHEAD!
WE SHOULD BE ABLE TO SEE EVERYTHING HE SEES--AND HEAR EVERYTHING HE HEARS!
AS LONG AS WE DON'T SMELL EVERYTHING HE SMELLS.
FLAP
FLAP
FLAP
FLAP
FLAP
FLAPPITY
FLAP
?
FLAP
FLAP
FLAPPITY
FLAP
FLAP
FLAP
FLAP
FLAP
FWOOP
GUH!

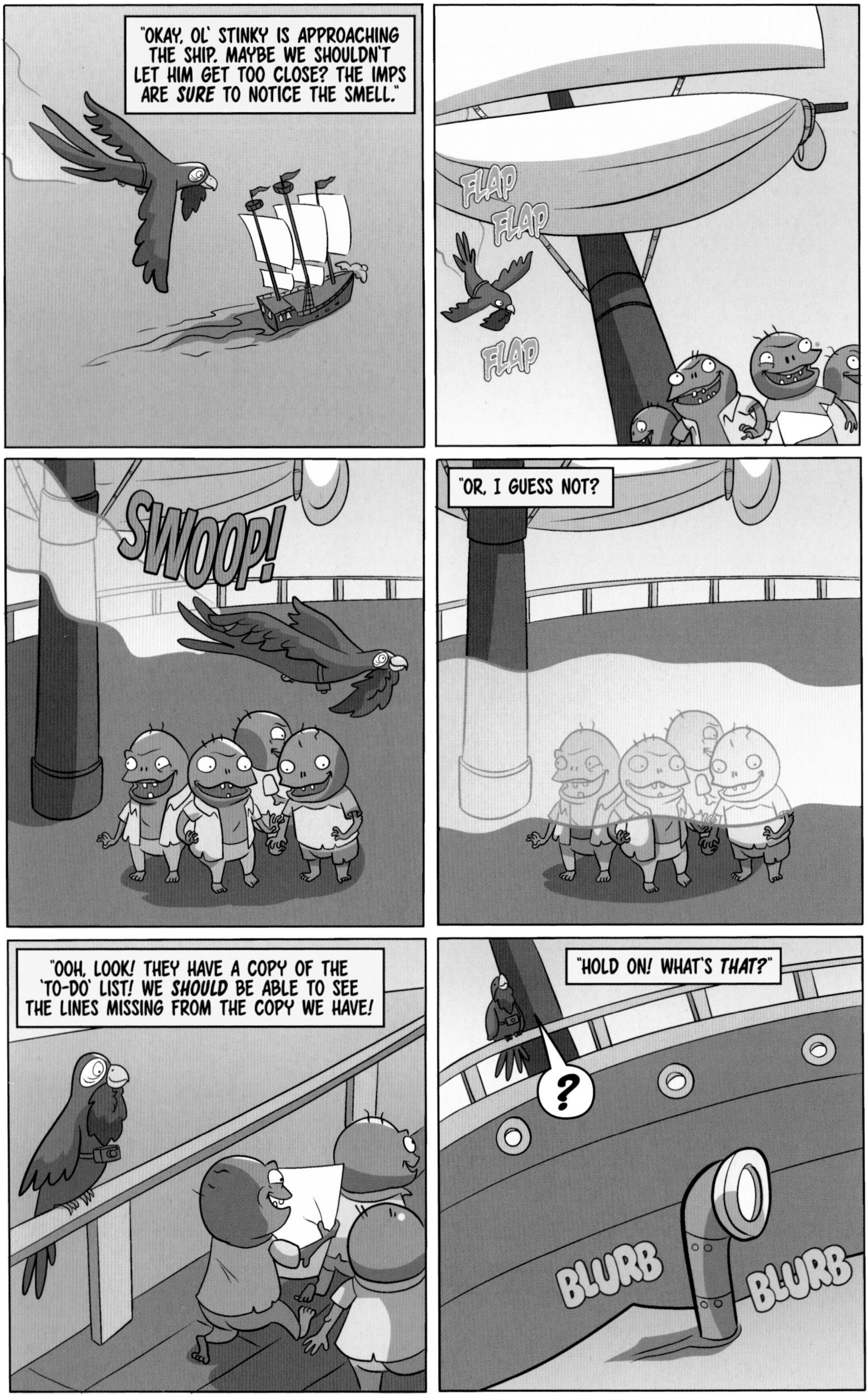
"OKAY, OL' STINKY IS APPROACHING THE SHIP. MAYBE WE SHOULDN'T LET HIM GET TOO CLOSE? THE IMPS ARE *SURE* TO NOTICE THE SMELL."
FLAP
FLAP
FLAP
SWOOP!
"OR, I GUESS NOT?
"OOH, LOOK! THEY HAVE A COPY OF THE 'TO-DO' LIST! WE *SHOULD* BE ABLE TO SEE THE LINES MISSING FROM THE COPY WE HAVE!
"HOLD ON! WHAT'S *THAT?*"
?
BLURB
BLURB

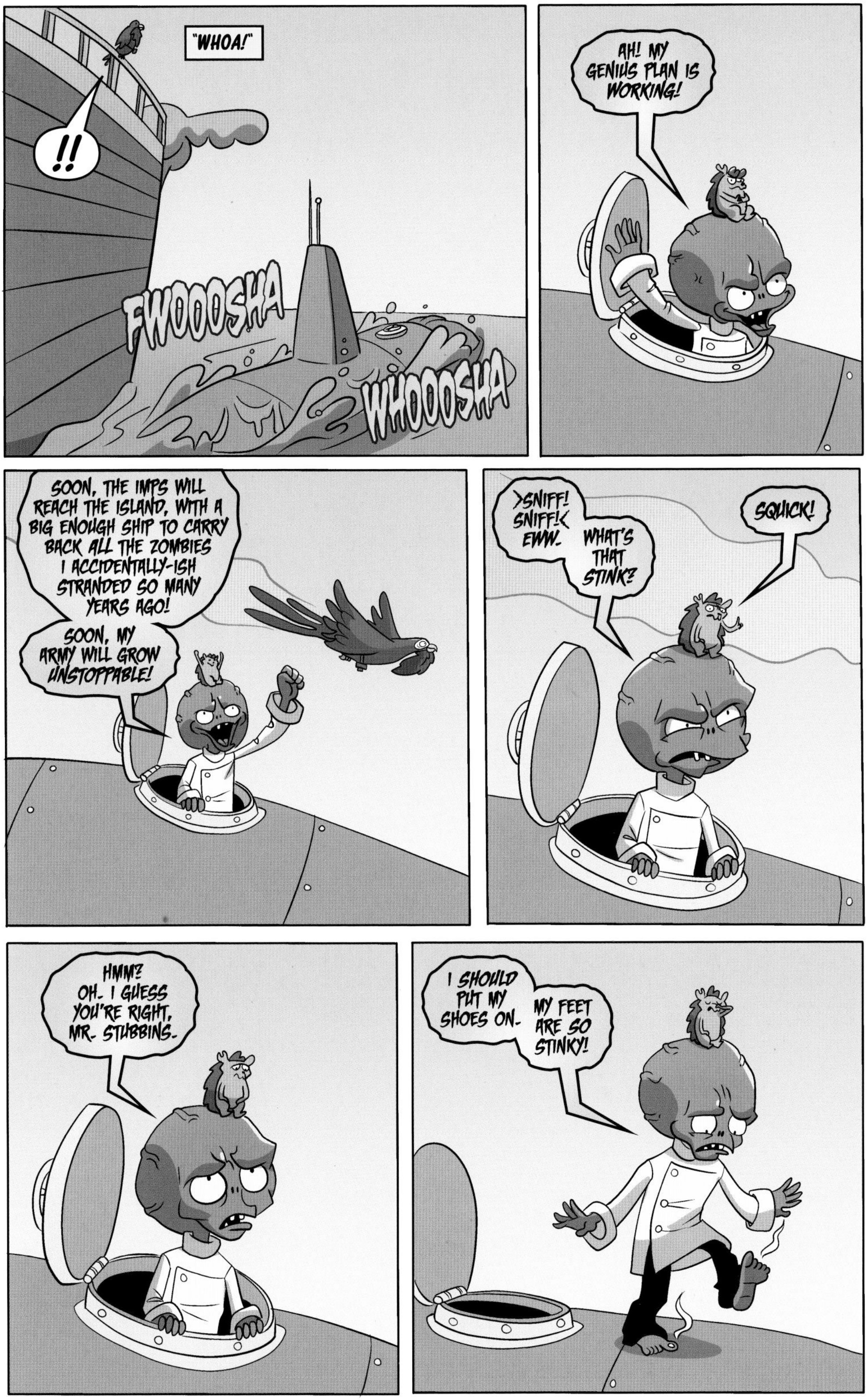
"WHOA!"
!!
FWOOOSHA
WHOOOSHA
AH! MY GENIUS PLAN IS WORKING!
SOON, THE IMPS WILL REACH THE ISLAND, WITH A BIG ENOUGH SHIP TO CARRY BACK ALL THE ZOMBIES I ACCIDENTALLY-ISH STRANDED SO MANY YEARS AGO!
SOON, MY ARMY WILL GROW UNSTOPPABLE!
>SNIFF! SNIFF!< EWW.
WHAT'S THAT STINK?
SQUICK!
HMM? OH. I GUESS YOU'RE RIGHT, MR. STUBBINS.
I SHOULD PUT MY SHOES ON.
MY FEET ARE SO STINKY!

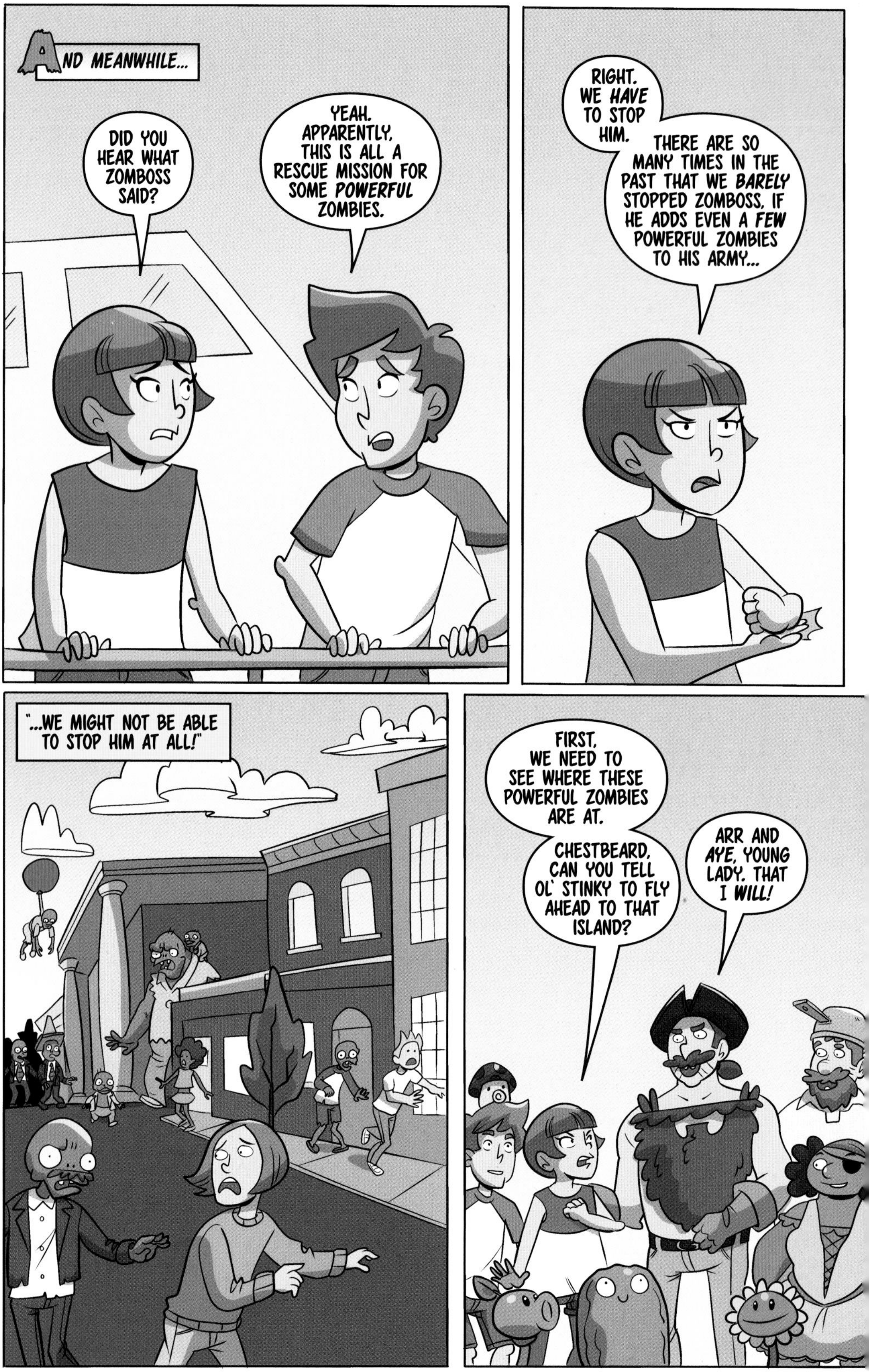
AND MEANWHILE...
DID YOU HEAR WHAT ZOMBOSS SAID?
YEAH. APPARENTLY, THIS IS ALL A RESCUE MISSION FOR SOME POWERFUL ZOMBIES.
RIGHT. WE HAVE TO STOP HIM.
THERE ARE SO MANY TIMES IN THE PAST THAT WE BARELY STOPPED ZOMBOSS. IF HE ADDS EVEN A FEW POWERFUL ZOMBIES TO HIS ARMY...
"...WE MIGHT NOT BE ABLE TO STOP HIM AT ALL!"
FIRST, WE NEED TO SEE WHERE THESE POWERFUL ZOMBIES ARE AT.
CHESTBEARD, CAN YOU TELL OL' STINKY TO FLY AHEAD TO THAT ISLAND?
ARR AND AYE, YOUNG LADY. THAT I WILL!

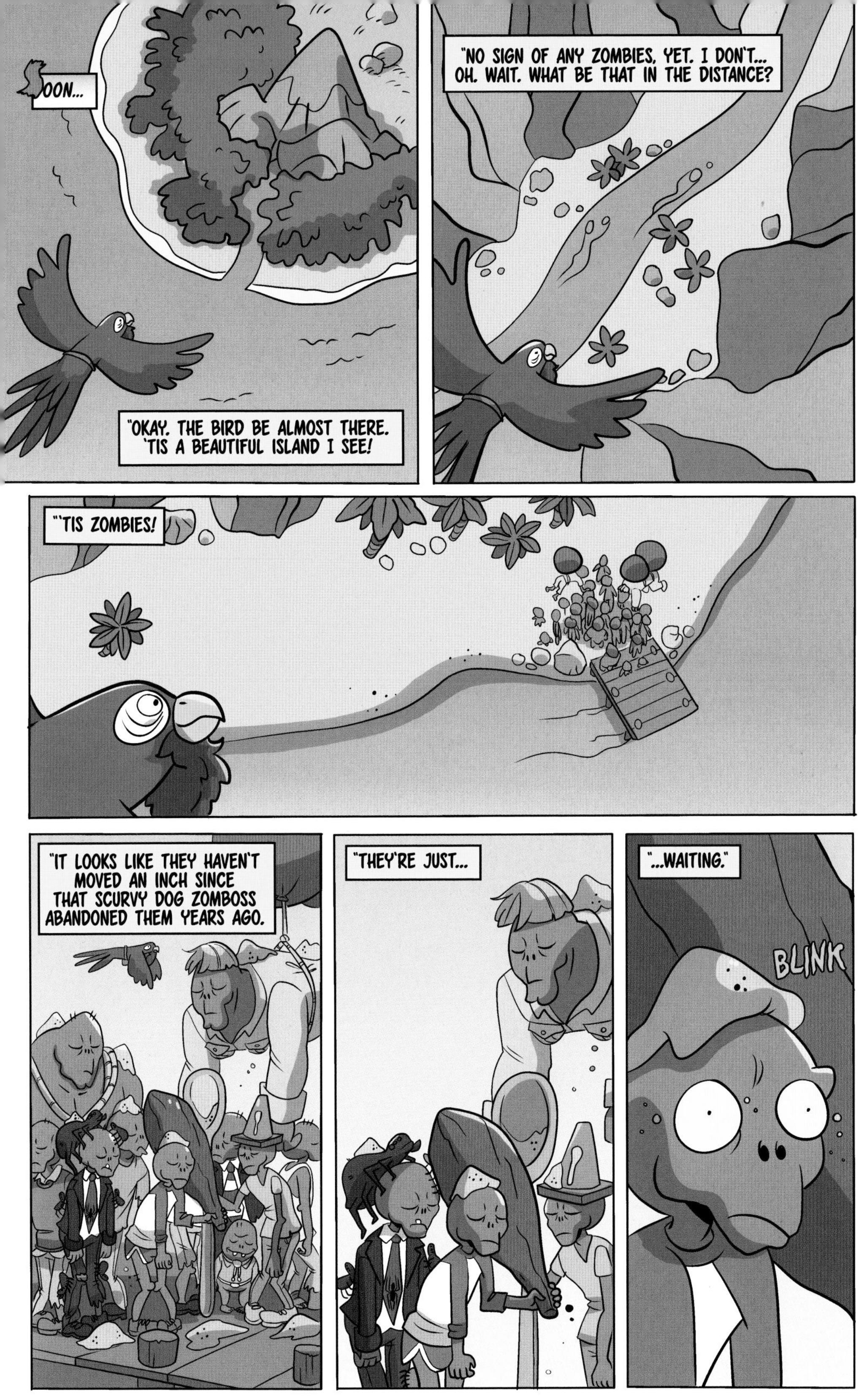
SOON...
"OKAY. THE BIRD BE ALMOST THERE. 'TIS A BEAUTIFUL ISLAND I SEE!
"NO SIGN OF ANY ZOMBIES, YET. I DON'T... OH. WAIT. WHAT BE THAT IN THE DISTANCE?
"'TIS ZOMBIES!
"IT LOOKS LIKE THEY HAVEN'T MOVED AN INCH SINCE THAT SCURVY DOG ZOMBOSS ABANDONED THEM YEARS AGO.
"THEY'RE JUST...
"...WAITING."
BLINK

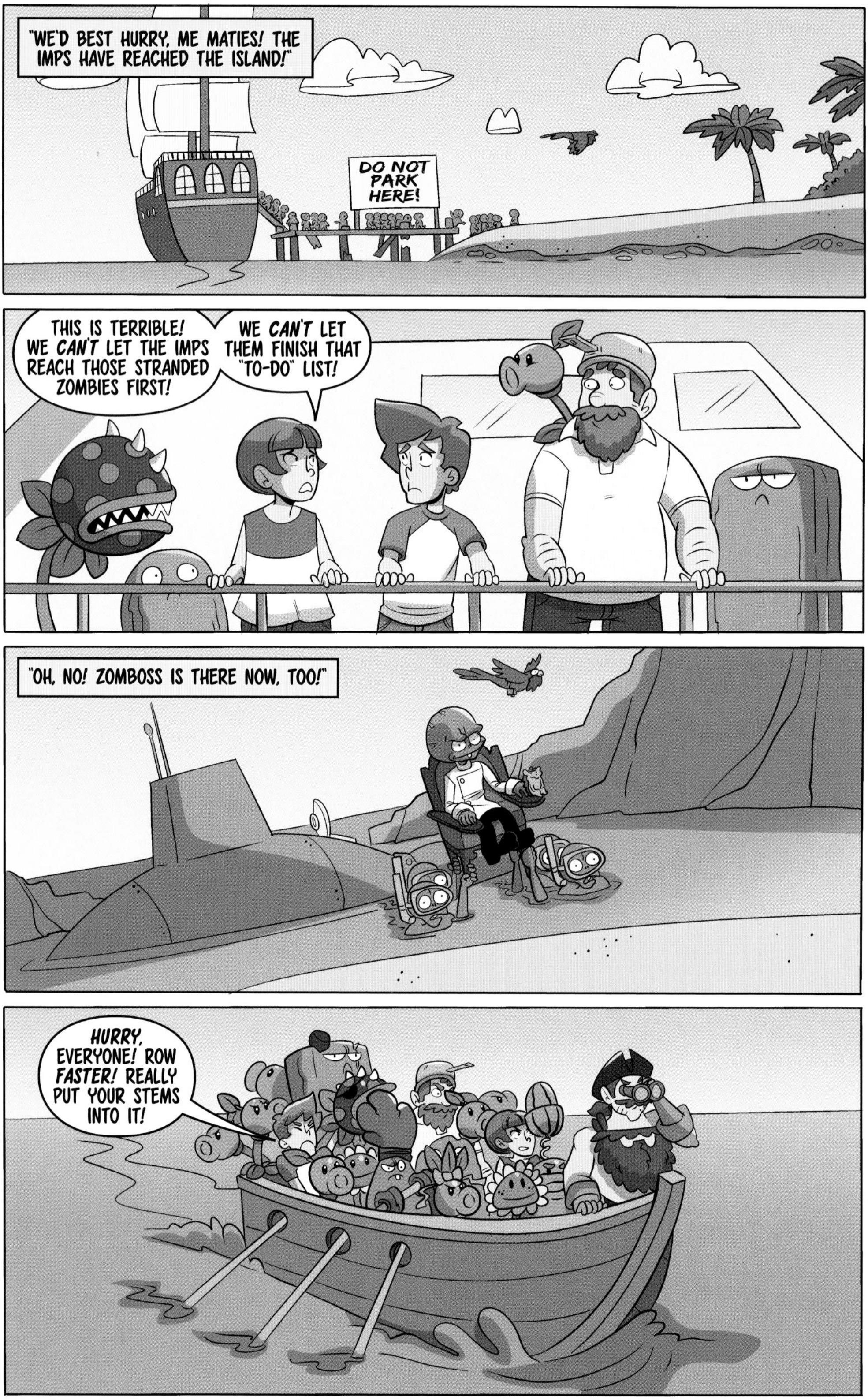
"WE'D BEST HURRY, ME MATIES! THE IMPS HAVE REACHED THE ISLAND!"
DO NOT PARK HERE!
THIS IS TERRIBLE! WE CAN'T LET THE IMPS REACH THOSE STRANDED ZOMBIES FIRST!
WE CAN'T LET THEM FINISH THAT "TO-DO" LIST!
"OH, NO! ZOMBOSS IS THERE NOW, TOO!"
HURRY, EVERYONE! ROW FASTER! REALLY PUT YOUR STEMS INTO IT!

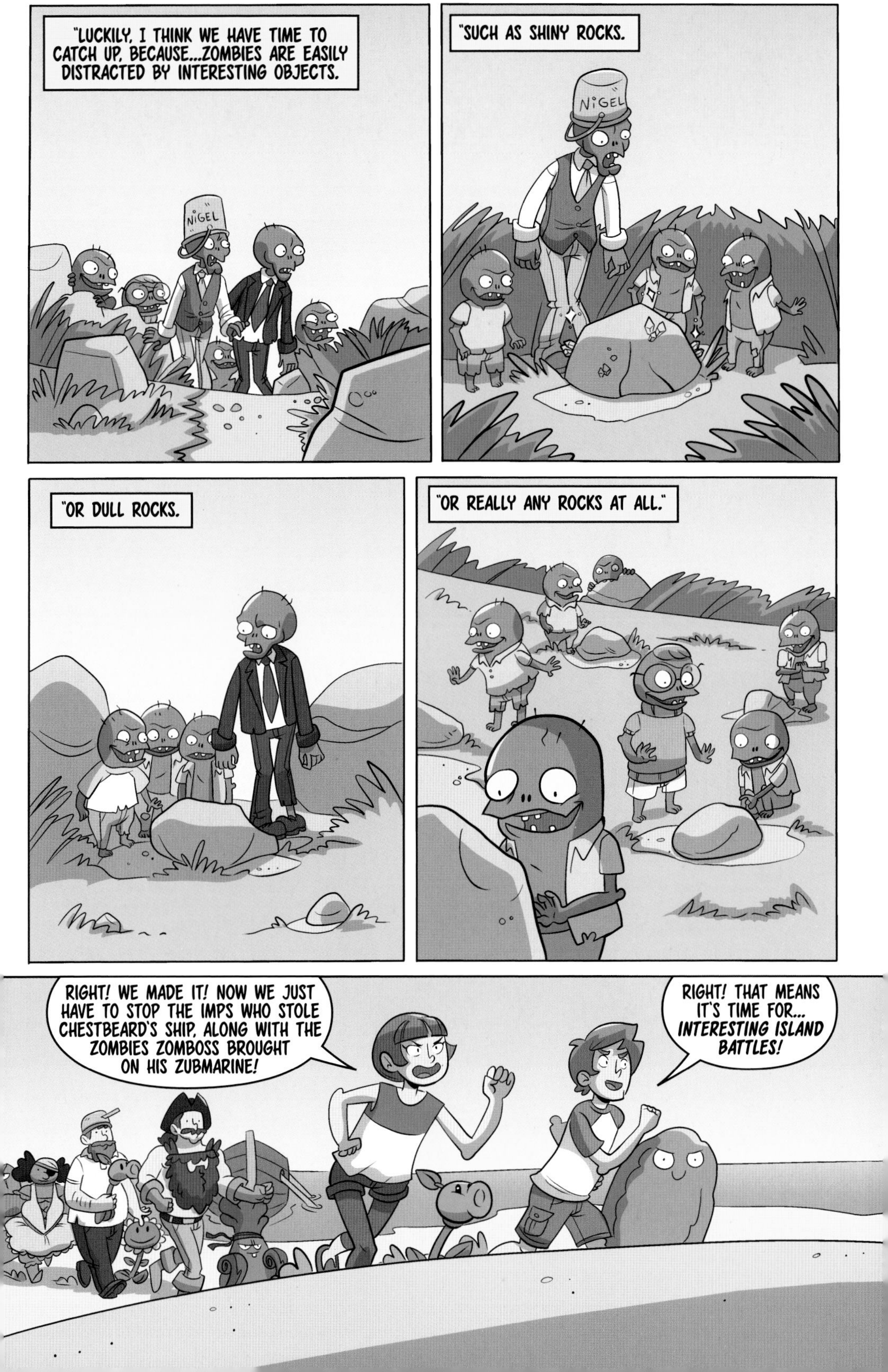
"LUCKILY, I THINK WE HAVE TIME TO CATCH UP, BECAUSE...ZOMBIES ARE EASILY DISTRACTED BY INTERESTING OBJECTS.
NIGEL
"SUCH AS SHINY ROCKS.
NIGEL
"OR DULL ROCKS.
"OR REALLY ANY ROCKS AT ALL."
RIGHT! WE MADE IT! NOW WE JUST HAVE TO STOP THE IMPS WHO STOLE CHESTBEARD'S SHIP, ALONG WITH THE ZOMBIES ZOMBOSS BROUGHT ON HIS ZUBMARINE!
RIGHT! THAT MEANS IT'S TIME FOR... *INTERESTING ISLAND BATTLES!*

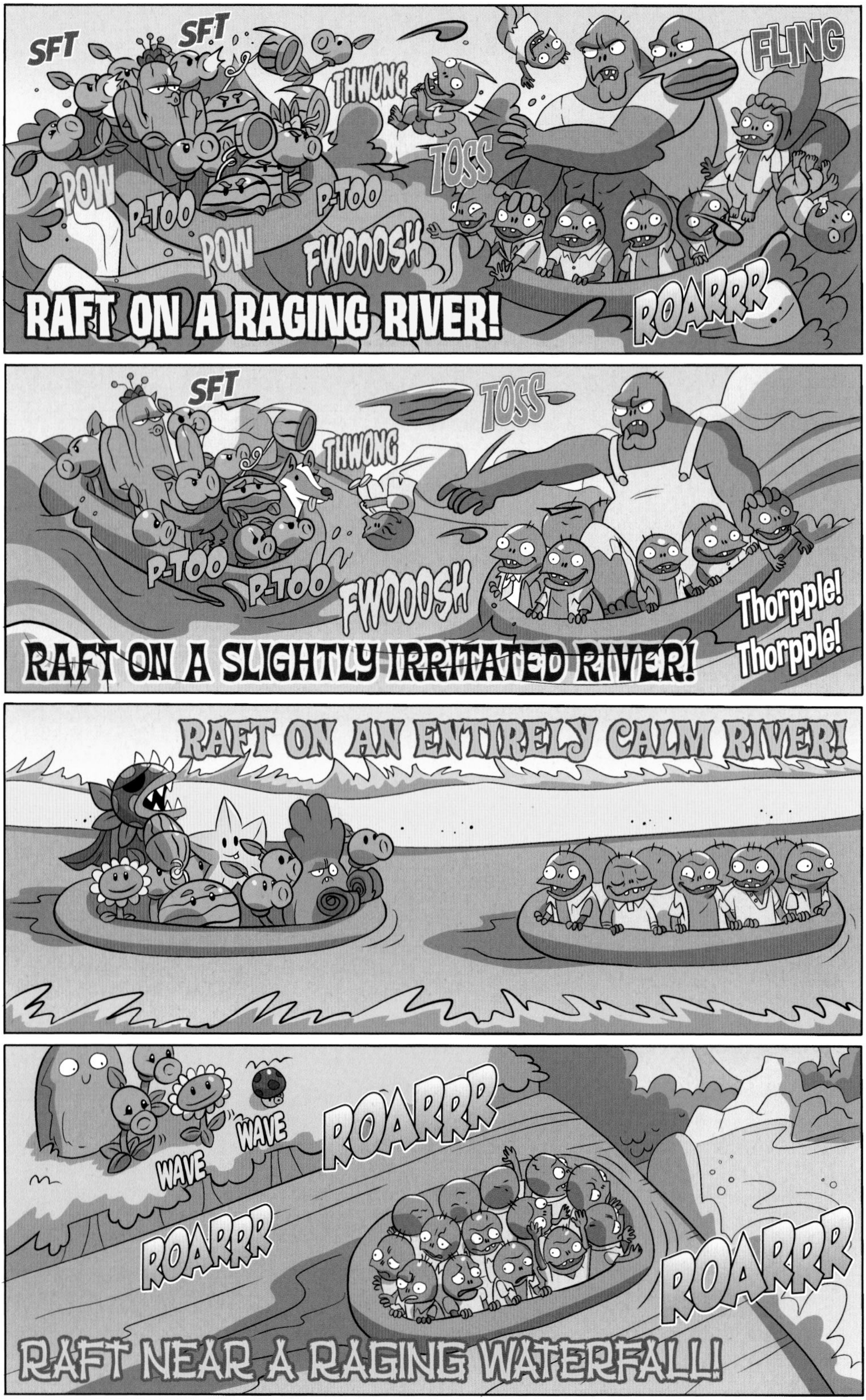
SFT
SFT
THWONG
FLING
TOSS
POW
P-TOO
P-TOO
POW
FWOOOSH
RAFT ON A RAGING RIVER!
ROARRR
SFT
TOSS
THWONG
P-TOO
P-TOO
FWOOOSH
Thorpple! Thorpple!
RAFT ON A SLIGHTLY IRRITATED RIVER!
RAFT ON AN ENTIRELY CALM RIVER!
WAVE
WAVE
ROARRR
ROARRR
ROARRR
RAFT NEAR A RAGING WATERFALL!

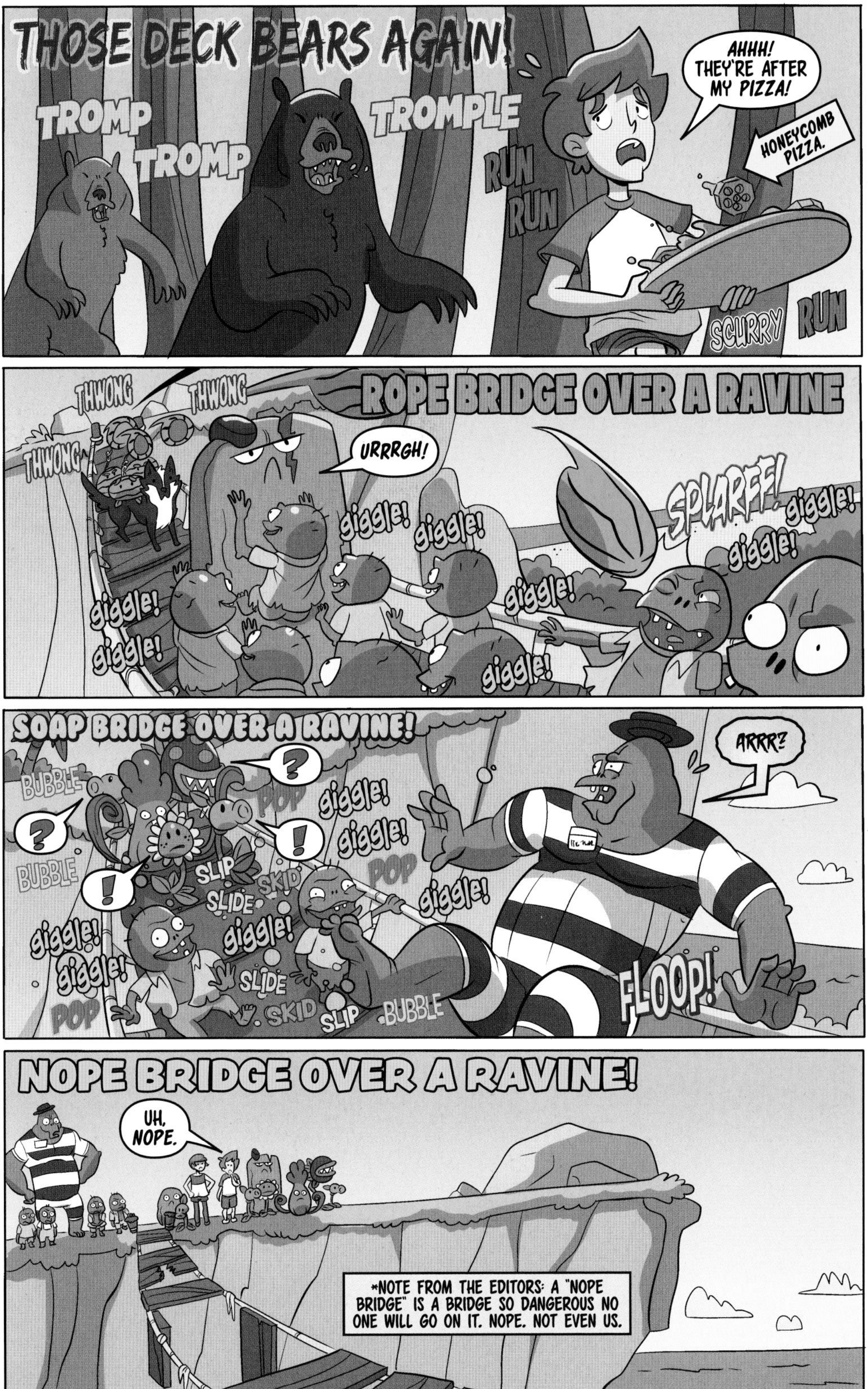
THOSE DECK BEARS AGAIN!
TROMP
TROMP
TROMPLE
RUN
RUN
AHHH! THEY'RE AFTER MY PIZZA!
HONEYCOMB PIZZA.
SCURRY
RUN
ROPE BRIDGE OVER A RAVINE
THWONG
THWONG
THWONG
URRRGH!
giggle!
giggle!
SPLARFF!
giggle!
giggle!
giggle!
giggle!
giggle!
giggle!
SOAP BRIDGE OVER A RAVINE!
BUBBLE
?
?
POP
giggle!
giggle!
!
BUBBLE
!
SLIP
SKID
POP
SLIDE
giggle!
ARRR?
giggle!
giggle!
giggle!
SLIDE
POP
SKID
SLIP
BUBBLE
FLOOP!
NOPE BRIDGE OVER A RAVINE!
UH, NOPE.
*NOTE FROM THE EDITORS: A "NOPE BRIDGE" IS A BRIDGE SO DANGEROUS NO ONE WILL GO ON IT. NOPE. NOT EVEN US.

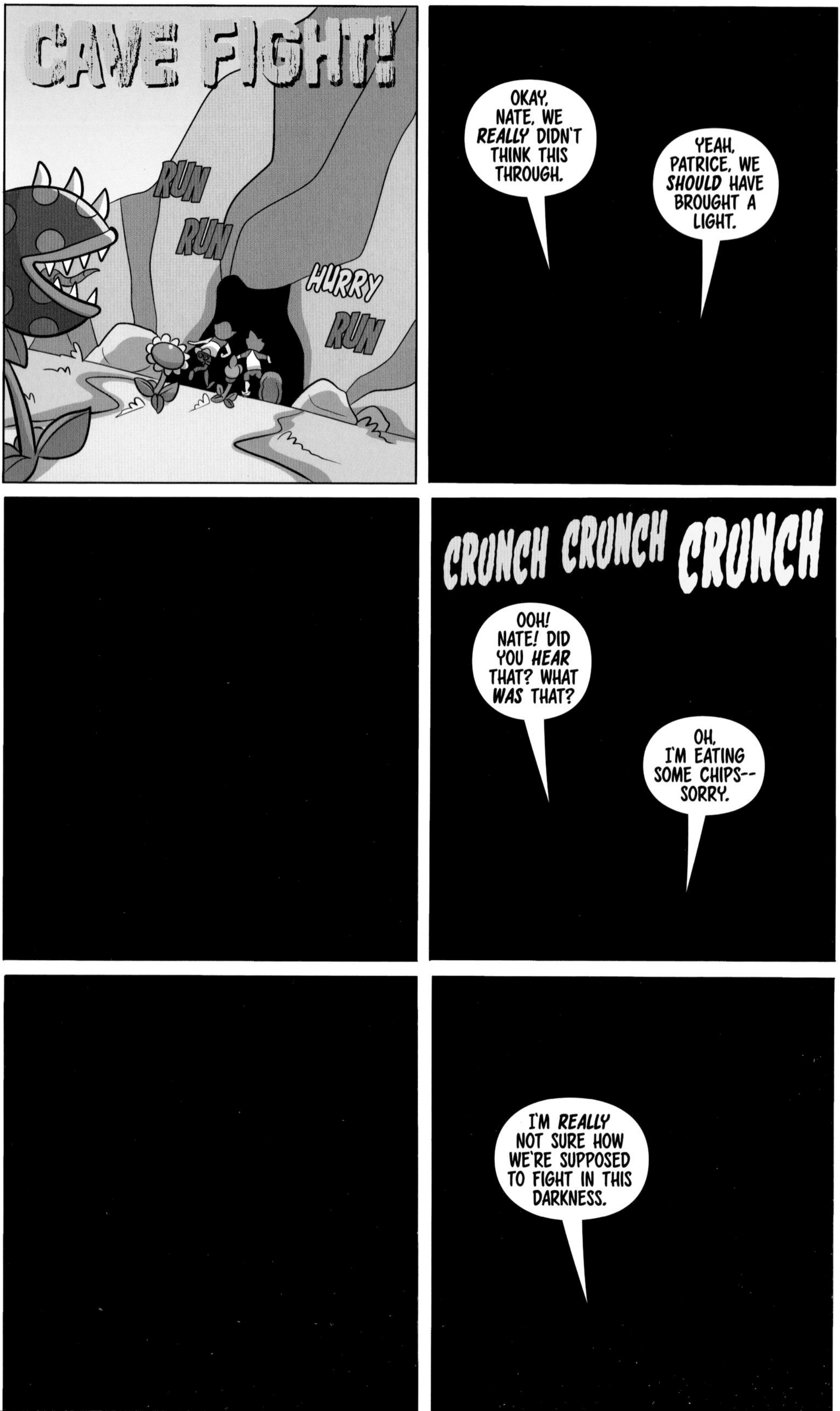
CAVE FIGHT!
RUN
RUN
HURRY
RUN
OKAY, NATE, WE REALLY DIDN'T THINK THIS THROUGH.
YEAH, PATRICE, WE SHOULD HAVE BROUGHT A LIGHT.
CRUNCH CRUNCH CRUNCH
OOH! NATE! DID YOU HEAR THAT? WHAT WAS THAT?
OH, I'M EATING SOME CHIPS-- SORRY.
I'M REALLY NOT SURE HOW WE'RE SUPPOSED TO FIGHT IN THIS DARKNESS.

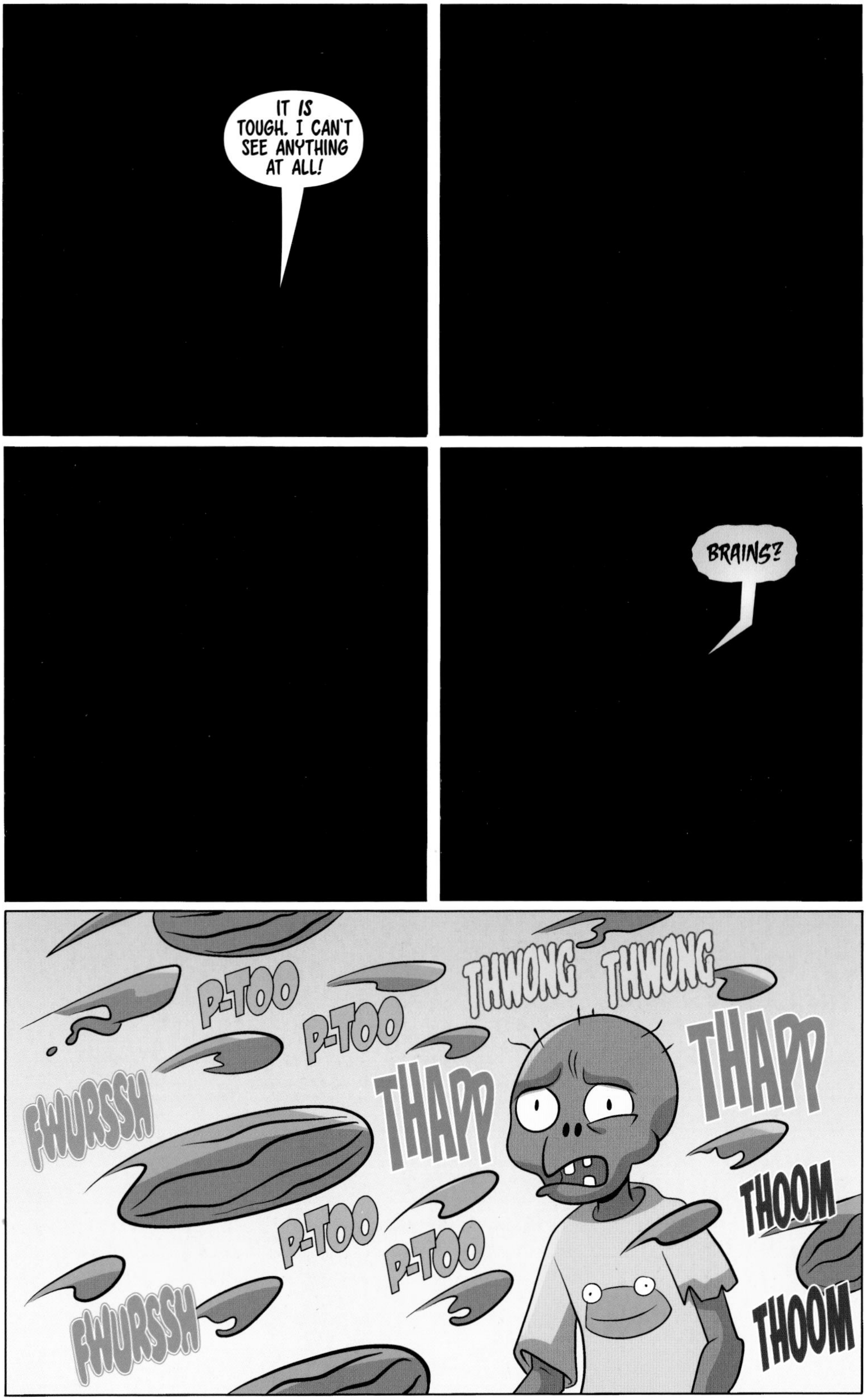
IT IS TOUGH. I CAN'T SEE ANYTHING AT ALL!
BRAINS?
P-TOO
P-TOO
THWONG
THWONG
FWURSSH
THAPP
THAPP
THOOM
P-TOO
P-TOO
THOOM
FWURSSH

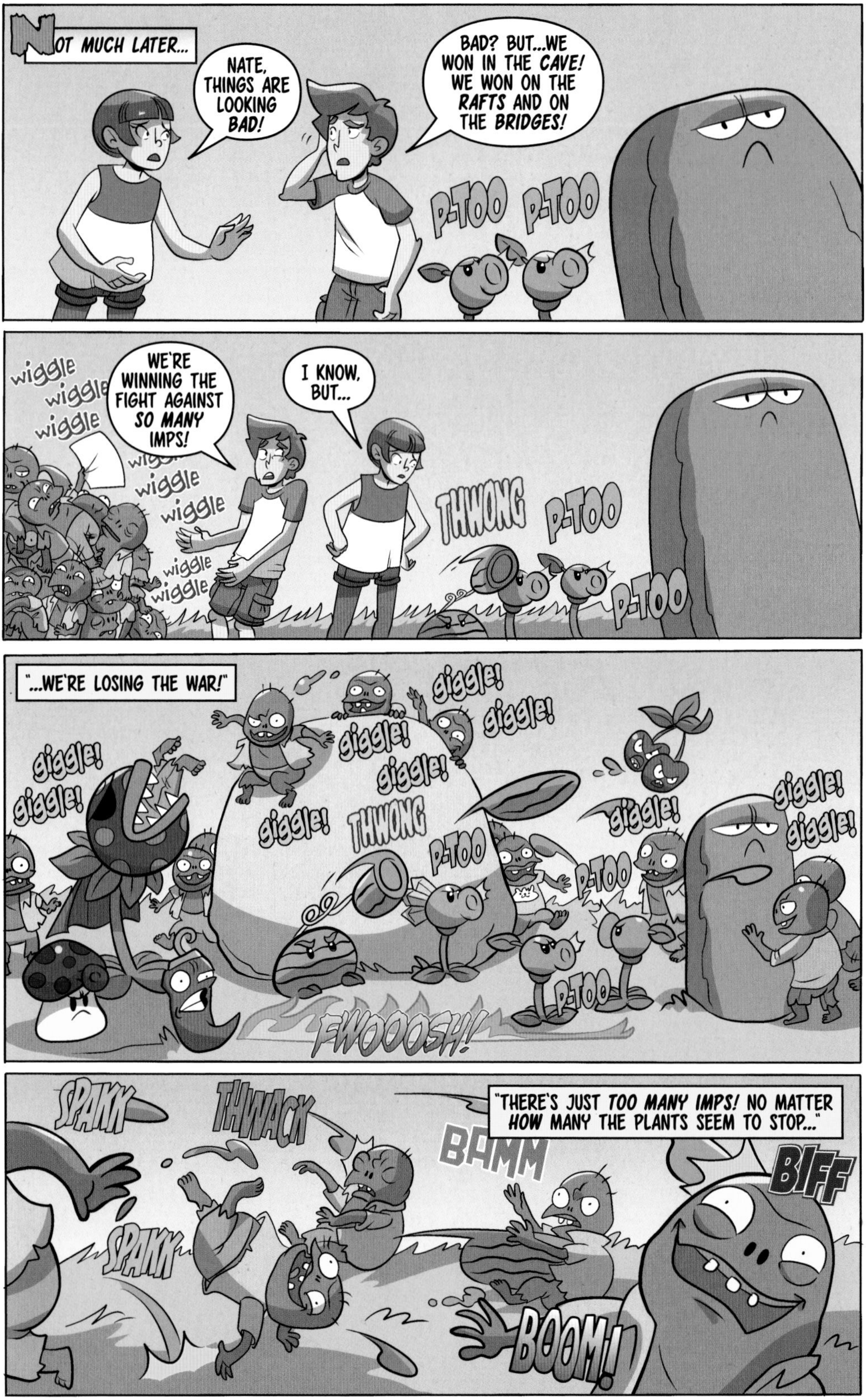
NOT MUCH LATER...
NATE, THINGS ARE LOOKING BAD!
BAD? BUT...WE WON IN THE CAVE! WE WON ON THE RAFTS AND ON THE BRIDGES!
P-TOO P-TOO
wiggle wiggle wiggle
WE'RE WINNING THE FIGHT AGAINST SO MANY IMPS!
I KNOW, BUT...
wiggle wiggle wiggle
wiggle wiggle
THWONG P-TOO
P-TOO
"...WE'RE LOSING THE WAR!"
giggle! giggle!
giggle! giggle!
giggle! giggle!
giggle! THWONG
P-TOO
giggle!
giggle! giggle!
P-TOO
P-TOO
FWOOOSH!
SPAKK THWACK
"THERE'S JUST TOO MANY IMPS! NO MATTER HOW MANY THE PLANTS SEEM TO STOP..."
BAMM BIFF
SPAKK
BOOM!

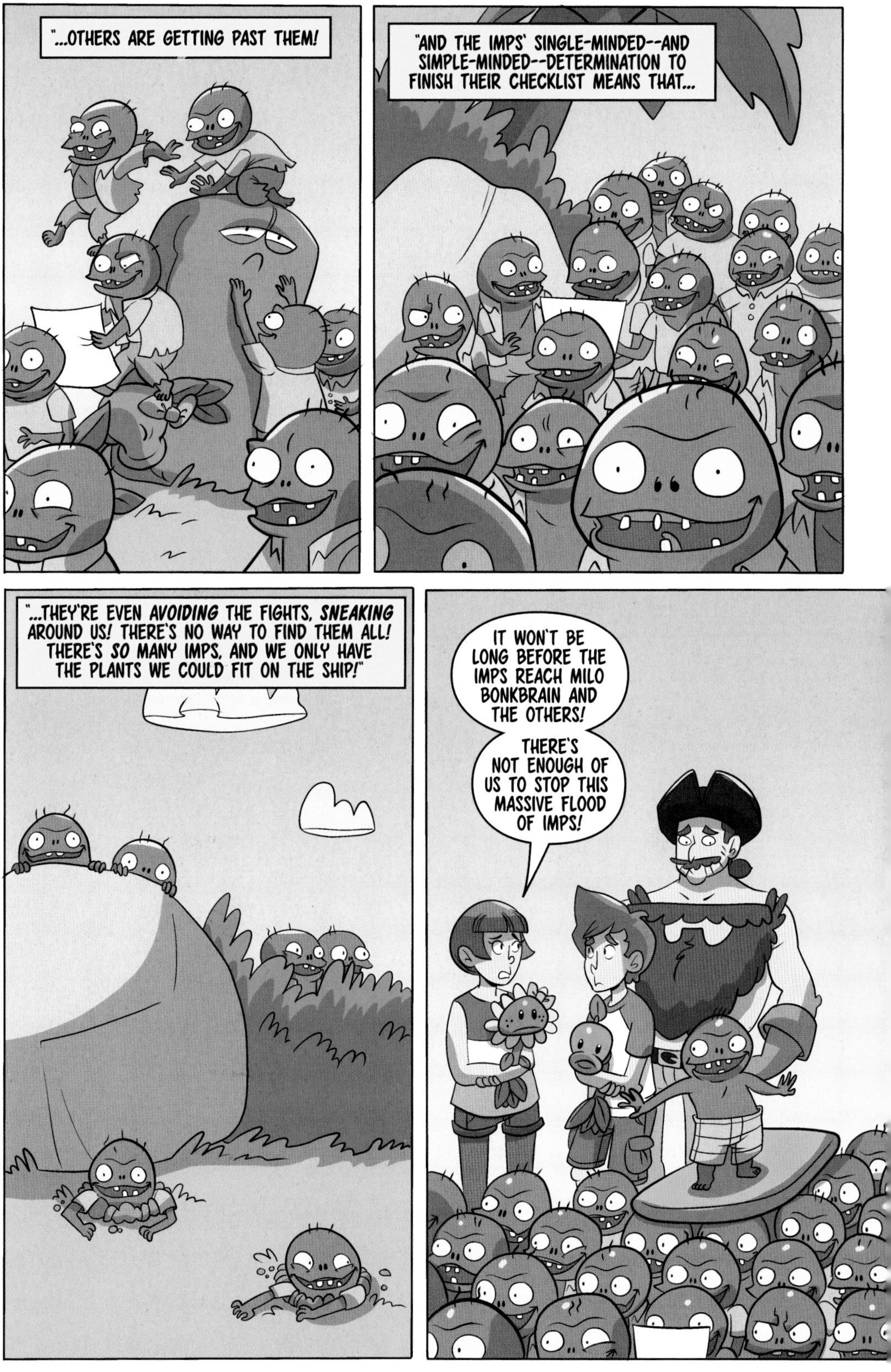
"...OTHERS ARE GETTING PAST THEM!
"AND THE IMPS' SINGLE-MINDED--AND SIMPLE-MINDED--DETERMINATION TO FINISH THEIR CHECKLIST MEANS THAT...
"...THEY'RE EVEN *AVOIDING* THE FIGHTS, *SNEAKING* AROUND US! THERE'S NO WAY TO FIND THEM ALL! THERE'S *SO* MANY IMPS, AND WE ONLY HAVE THE PLANTS WE COULD FIT ON THE SHIP!"
IT WON'T BE LONG BEFORE THE IMPS REACH MILO BONKBRAIN AND THE OTHERS!
THERE'S NOT ENOUGH OF US TO STOP THIS MASSIVE FLOOD OF IMPS!

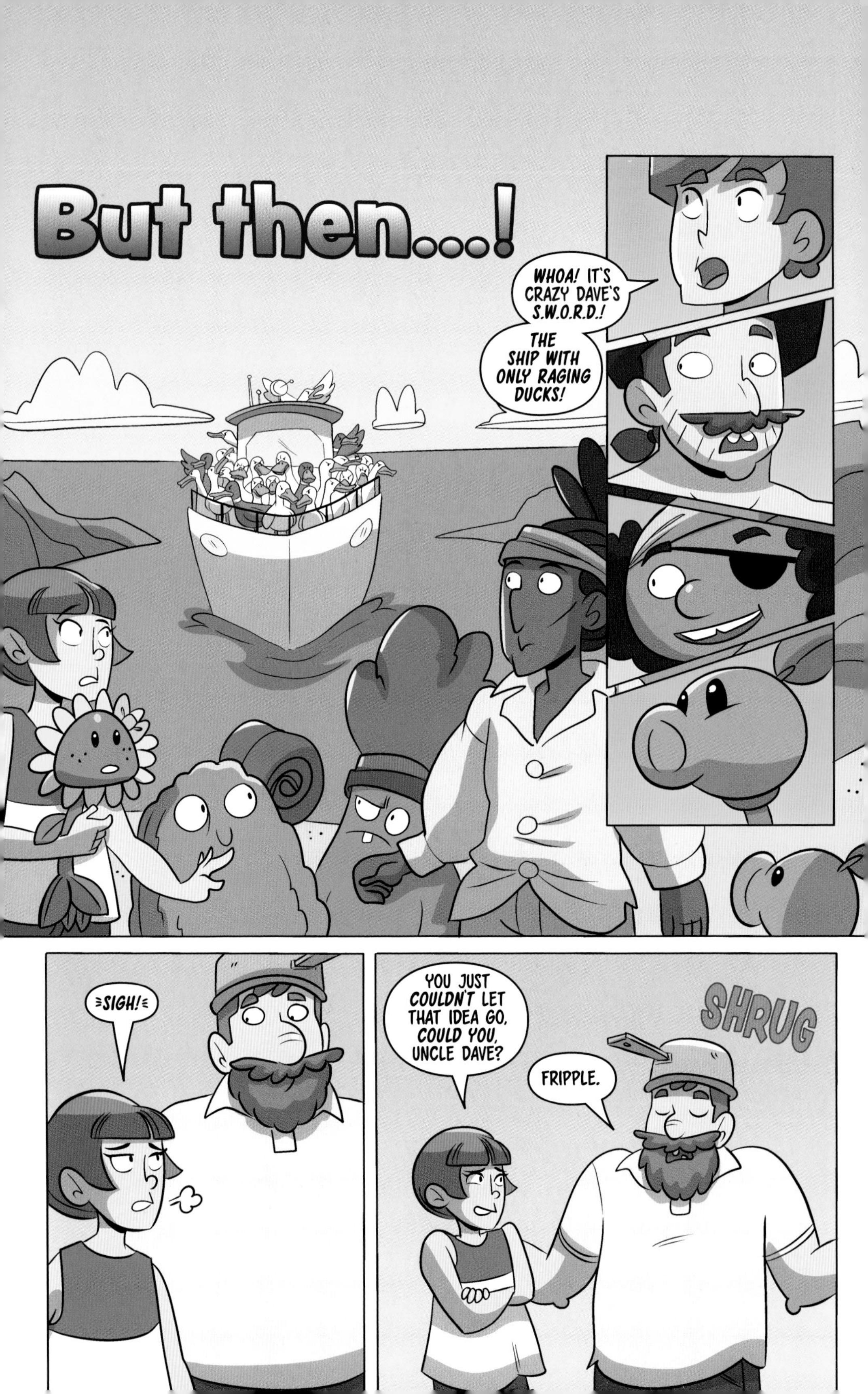
But then...!
WHOA! IT'S CRAZY DAVE'S S.W.O.R.D.!
THE SHIP WITH ONLY RAGING DUCKS!
≡SIGH!≡
YOU JUST COULDN'T LET THAT IDEA GO, COULD YOU, UNCLE DAVE?
SHRUG
FRIPPLE.

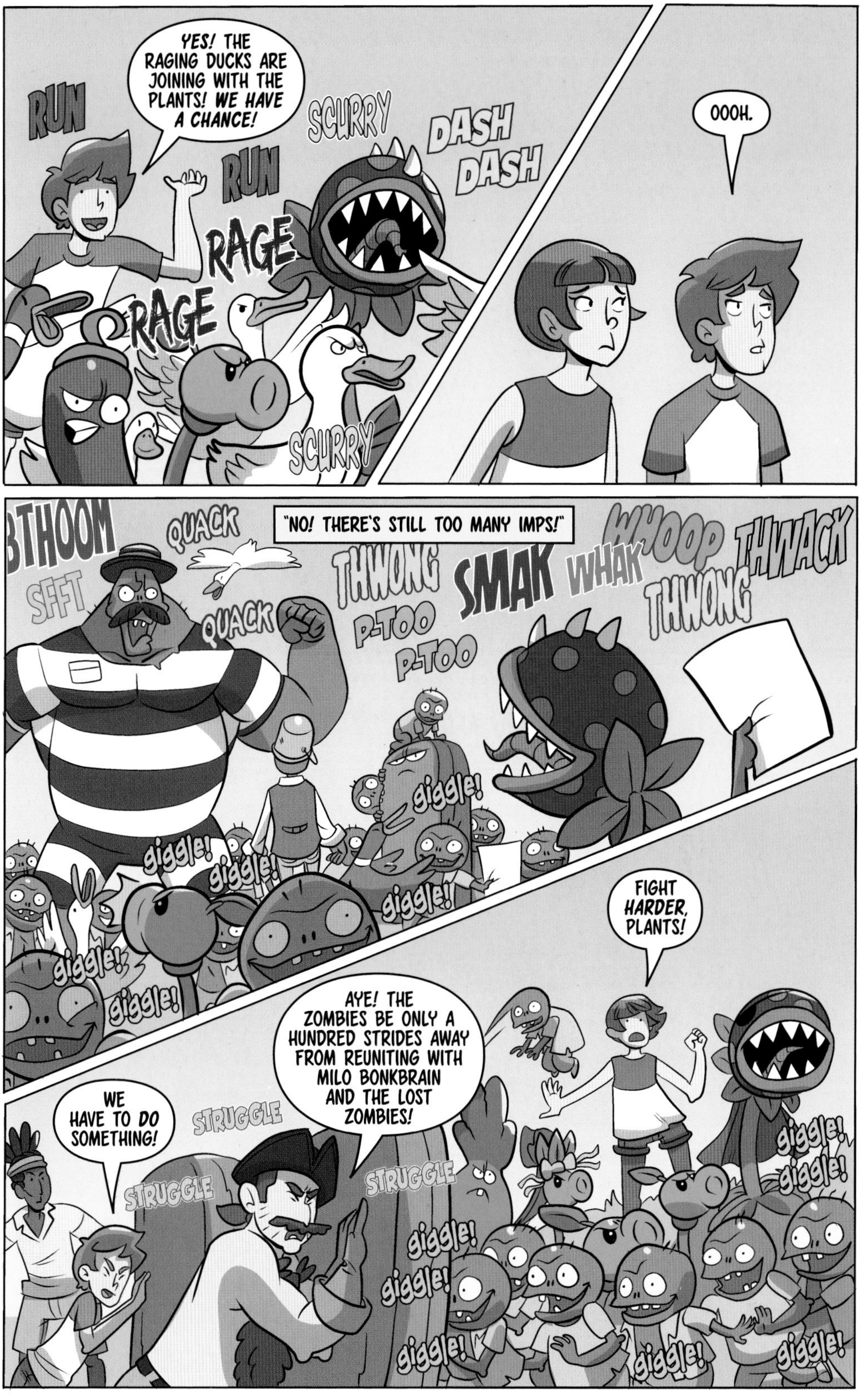
RUN
YES! THE RAGING DUCKS ARE JOINING WITH THE PLANTS! WE HAVE A CHANCE!
SCURRY
RUN
DASH
DASH
RAGE
RAGE
SCURRY
OOOH.
BTHOOM
QUACK
"NO! THERE'S STILL TOO MANY IMPS!"
WHOOP
THWACK
SFFT
THWONG
SMAK
WHAK
THWONG
QUACK
P-TOO
P-TOO
giggle!
giggle!
giggle!
giggle!
giggle!
giggle!
FIGHT HARDER, PLANTS!
AYE! THE ZOMBIES BE ONLY A HUNDRED STRIDES AWAY FROM REUNITING WITH MILO BONKBRAIN AND THE LOST ZOMBIES!
WE HAVE TO DO SOMETHING!
STRUGGLE
STRUGGLE
STRUGGLE
giggle!
giggle!
giggle!
giggle!
giggle!
giggle!
giggle!

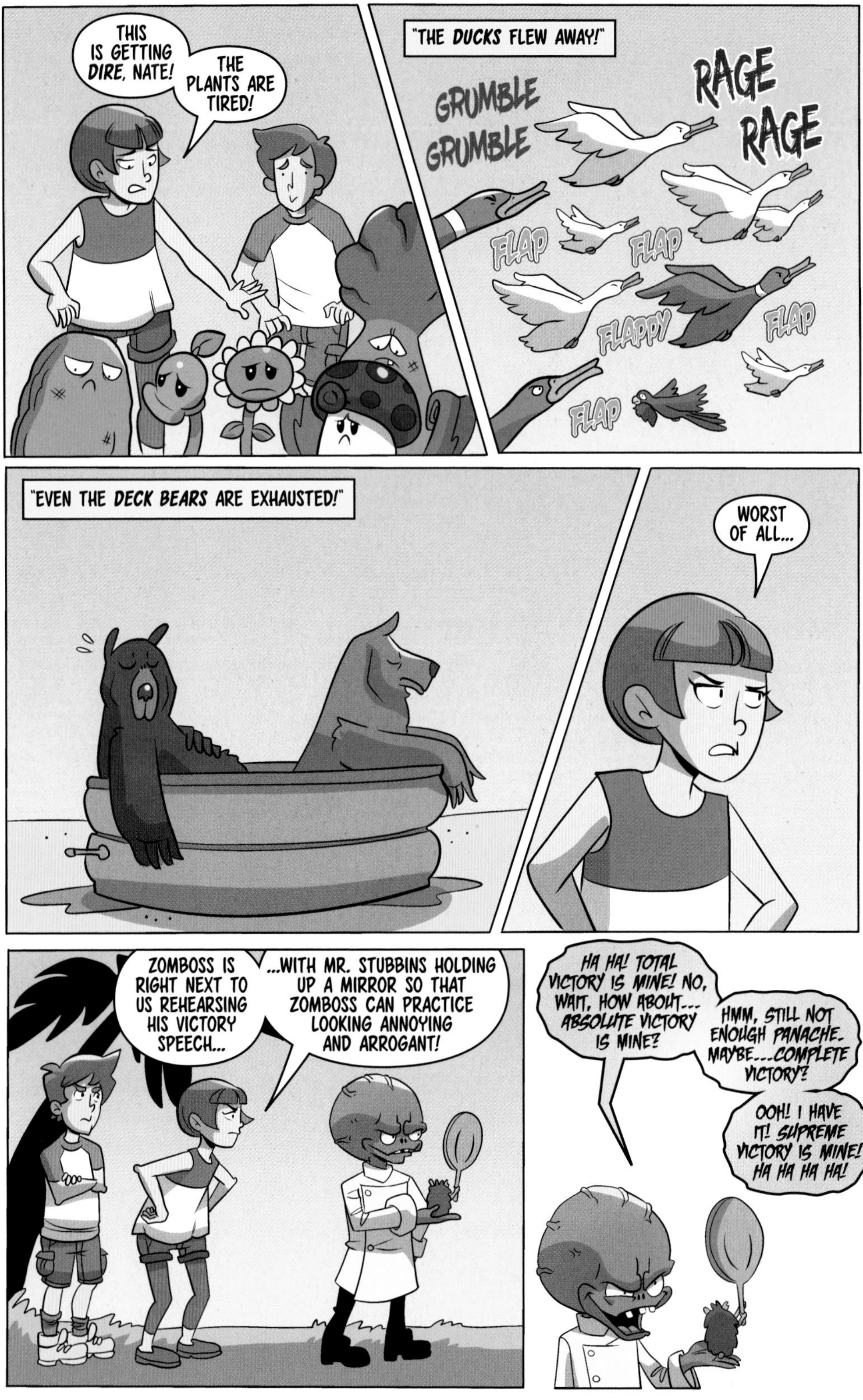
THIS IS GETTING DIRE, NATE!
THE PLANTS ARE TIRED!
"THE DUCKS FLEW AWAY!"
GRUMBLE GRUMBLE
RAGE RAGE
FLAP
FLAP
FLAPPY
FLAP
FLAP
"EVEN THE DECK BEARS ARE EXHAUSTED!"
WORST OF ALL...
ZOMBOSS IS RIGHT NEXT TO US REHEARSING HIS VICTORY SPEECH...
...WITH MR. STUBBINS HOLDING UP A MIRROR SO THAT ZOMBOSS CAN PRACTICE LOOKING ANNOYING AND ARROGANT!
HA HA! TOTAL VICTORY IS MINE! NO, WAIT, HOW ABOUT... ABSOLUTE VICTORY IS MINE?
HMM, STILL NOT ENOUGH PANACHE. MAYBE... COMPLETE VICTORY?
OOH! I HAVE IT! SUPREME VICTORY IS MINE! HA HA HA HA!

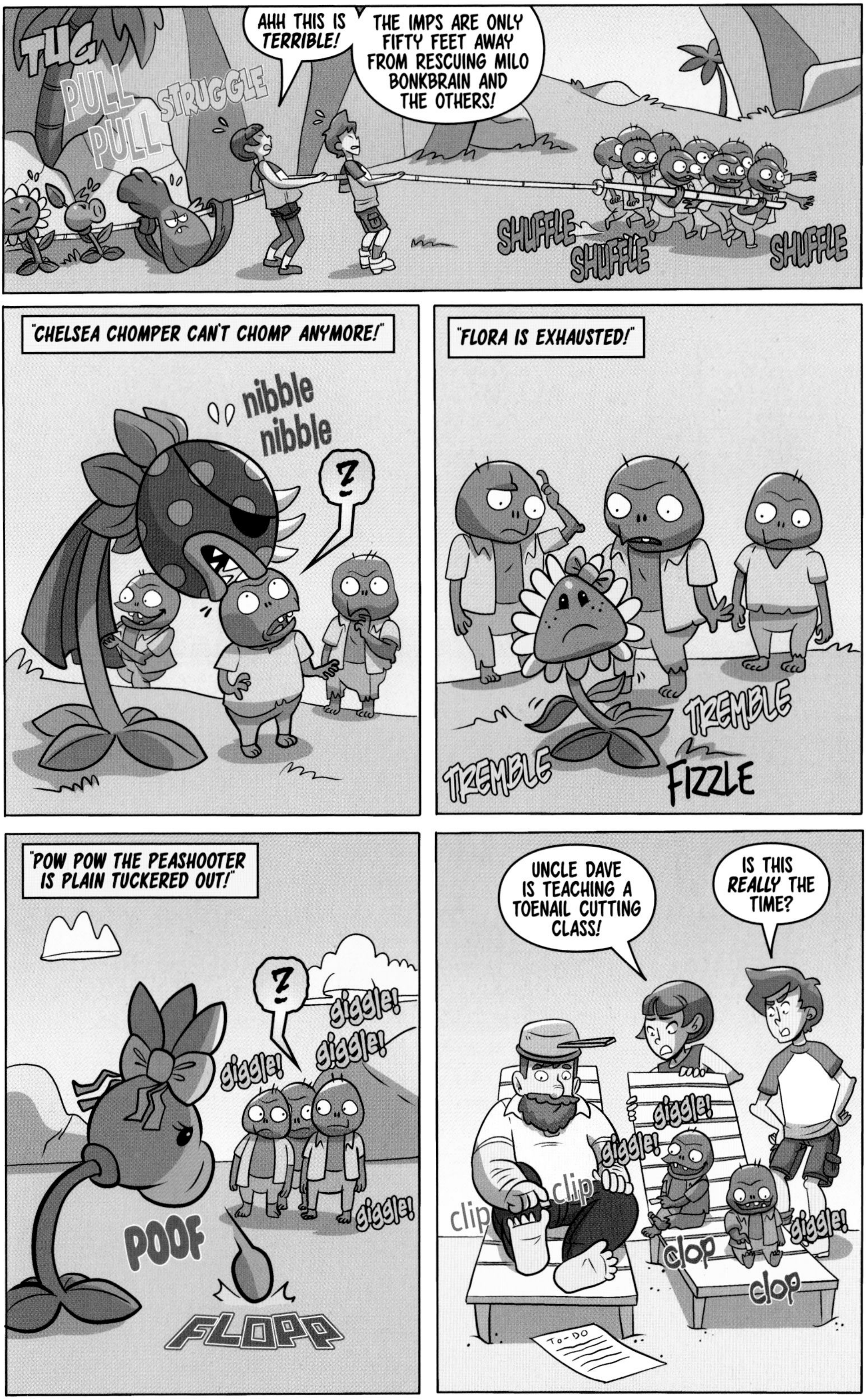
TUG
PULL
PULL
STRUGGLE
AHH THIS IS TERRIBLE!
THE IMPS ARE ONLY FIFTY FEET AWAY FROM RESCUING MILO BONKBRAIN AND THE OTHERS!
SHUFFLE
SHUFFLE
SHUFFLE
"CHELSEA CHOMPER CAN'T CHOMP ANYMORE!"
nibble
nibble
?
"FLORA IS EXHAUSTED!"
TREMBLE
TREMBLE
FIZZLE
"POW POW THE PEASHOOTER IS PLAIN TUCKERED OUT!"
?
giggle!
giggle!
giggle!
giggle!
POOF
FLOPP
UNCLE DAVE IS TEACHING A TOENAIL CUTTING CLASS!
IS THIS REALLY THE TIME?
giggle!
giggle!
clip
clip
clop
clop
giggle!
TO-DO

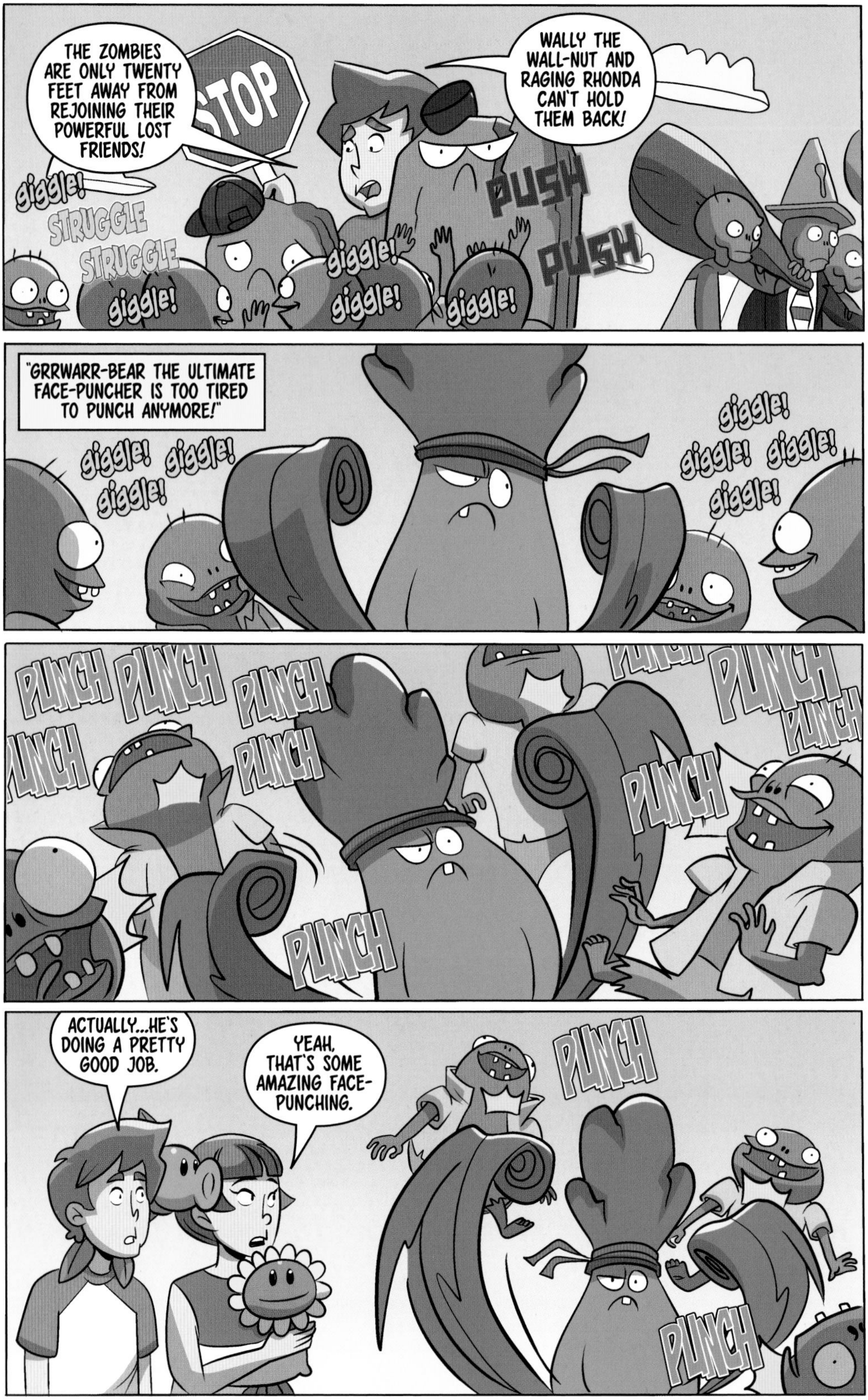
THE ZOMBIES ARE ONLY TWENTY FEET AWAY FROM REJOINING THEIR POWERFUL LOST FRIENDS!
WALLY THE WALL-NUT AND RAGING RHONDA CAN'T HOLD THEM BACK!
STOP
giggle!
STRUGGLE
STRUGGLE
giggle!
giggle!
giggle!
giggle!
PUSH
PUSH
"GRRWARR-BEAR THE ULTIMATE FACE-PUNCHER IS TOO TIRED TO PUNCH ANYMORE!"
giggle! giggle!
giggle!
giggle!
giggle! giggle!
giggle!
PUNCH PUNCH PUNCH PUNCH PUNCH PUNCH PUNCH PUNCH PUNCH
ACTUALLY...HE'S DOING A PRETTY GOOD JOB.
YEAH, THAT'S SOME AMAZING FACE-PUNCHING.
PUNCH
PUNCH

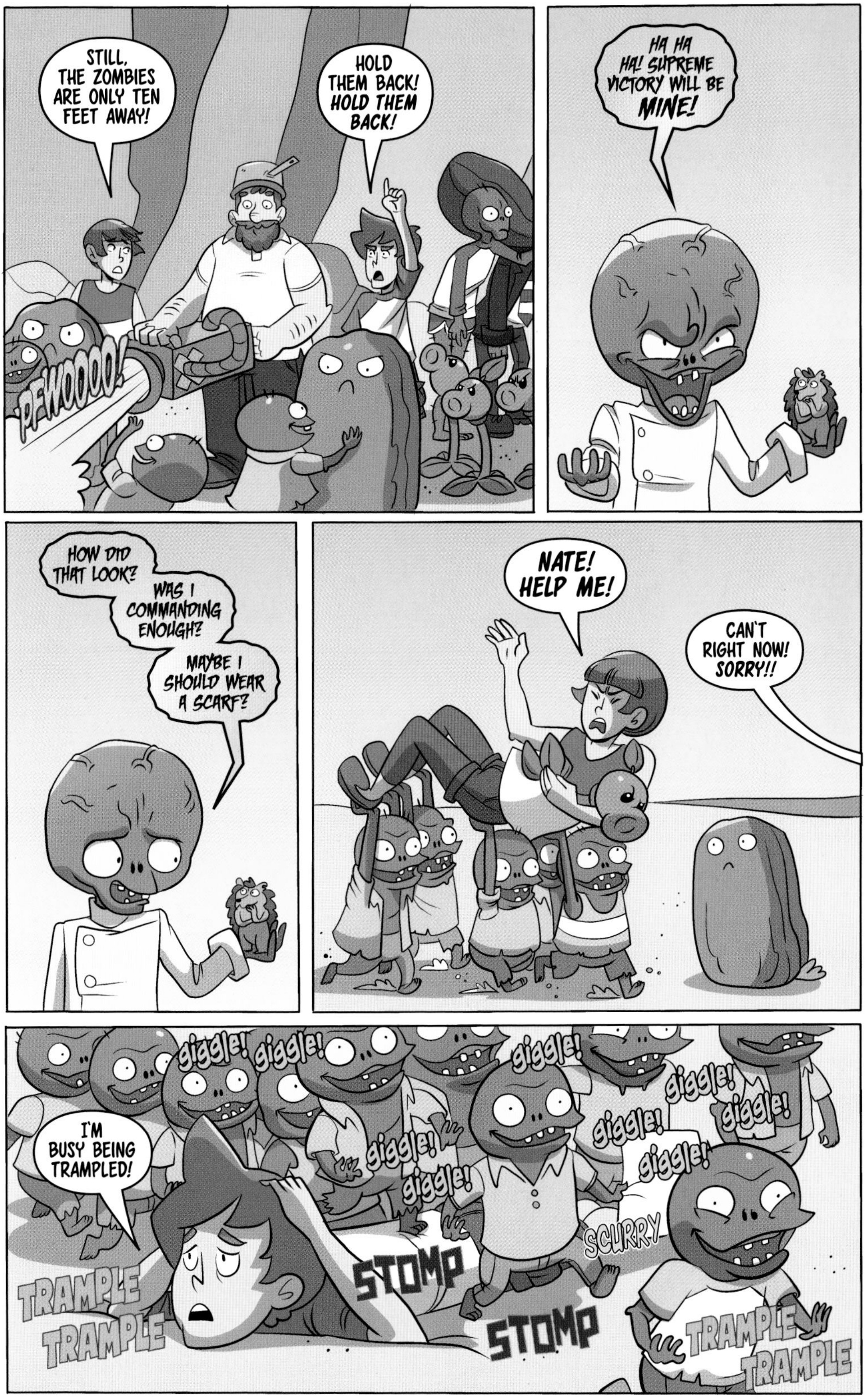
STILL, THE ZOMBIES ARE ONLY TEN FEET AWAY!
HOLD THEM BACK! HOLD THEM BACK!
PFWOOOO!
HA HA HA! SUPREME VICTORY WILL BE MINE!
HOW DID THAT LOOK?
WAS I COMMANDING ENOUGH?
MAYBE I SHOULD WEAR A SCARF?
NATE! HELP ME!
CAN'T RIGHT NOW! SORRY!!
I'M BUSY BEING TRAMPLED!
giggle! giggle! giggle! giggle! giggle! giggle! giggle! giggle! giggle!
SCURRY
STOMP
STOMP
TRAMPLE TRAMPLE
TRAMPLE TRAMPLE

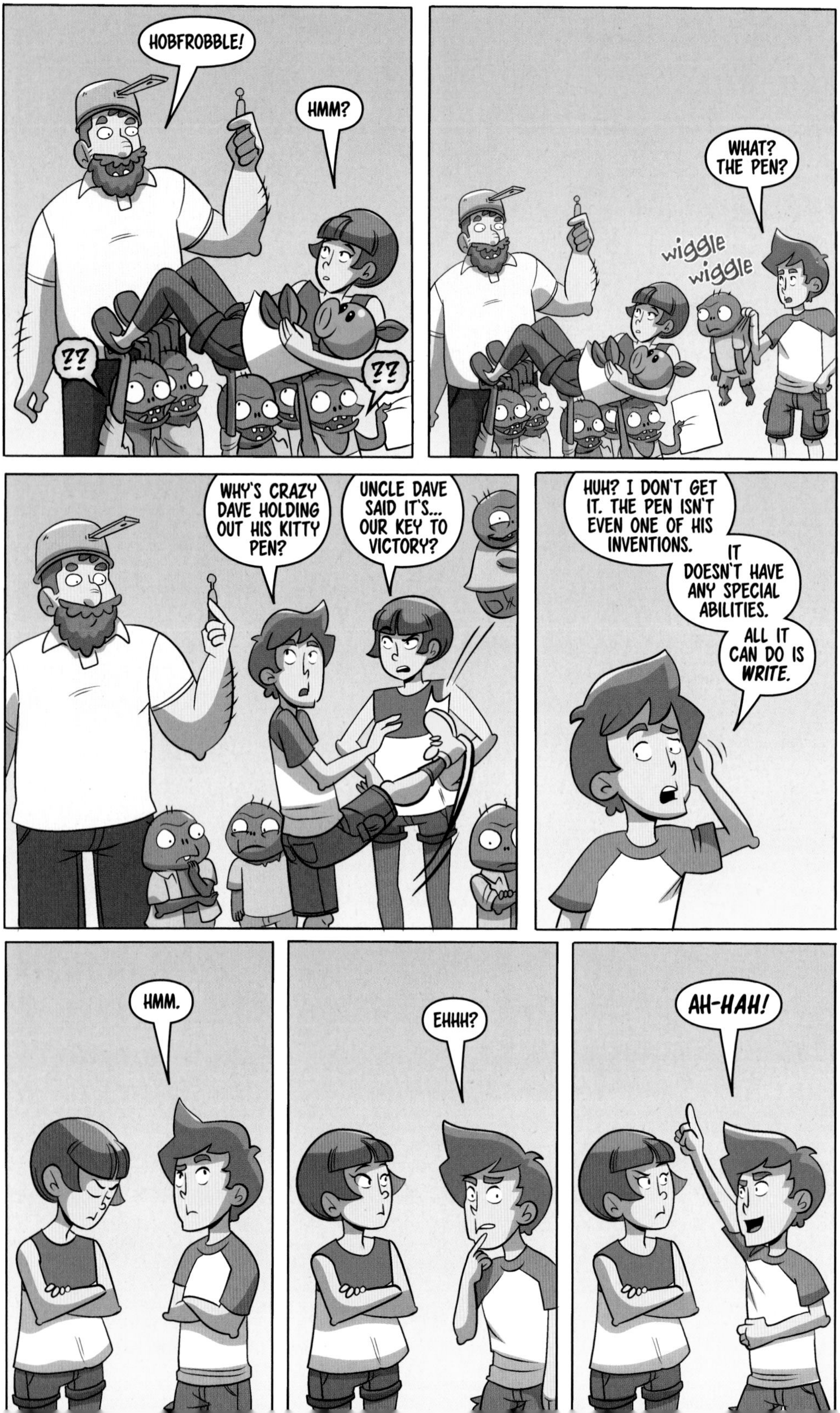
HOBFROBBLE!
HMM?
??
??
WHAT? THE PEN?
wiggle wiggle
WHY'S CRAZY DAVE HOLDING OUT HIS KITTY PEN?
UNCLE DAVE SAID IT'S... OUR KEY TO VICTORY?
HUH? I DON'T GET IT. THE PEN ISN'T EVEN ONE OF HIS INVENTIONS.
IT DOESN'T HAVE ANY SPECIAL ABILITIES.
ALL IT CAN DO IS WRITE.
HMM.
EHHH?
AH-HAH!

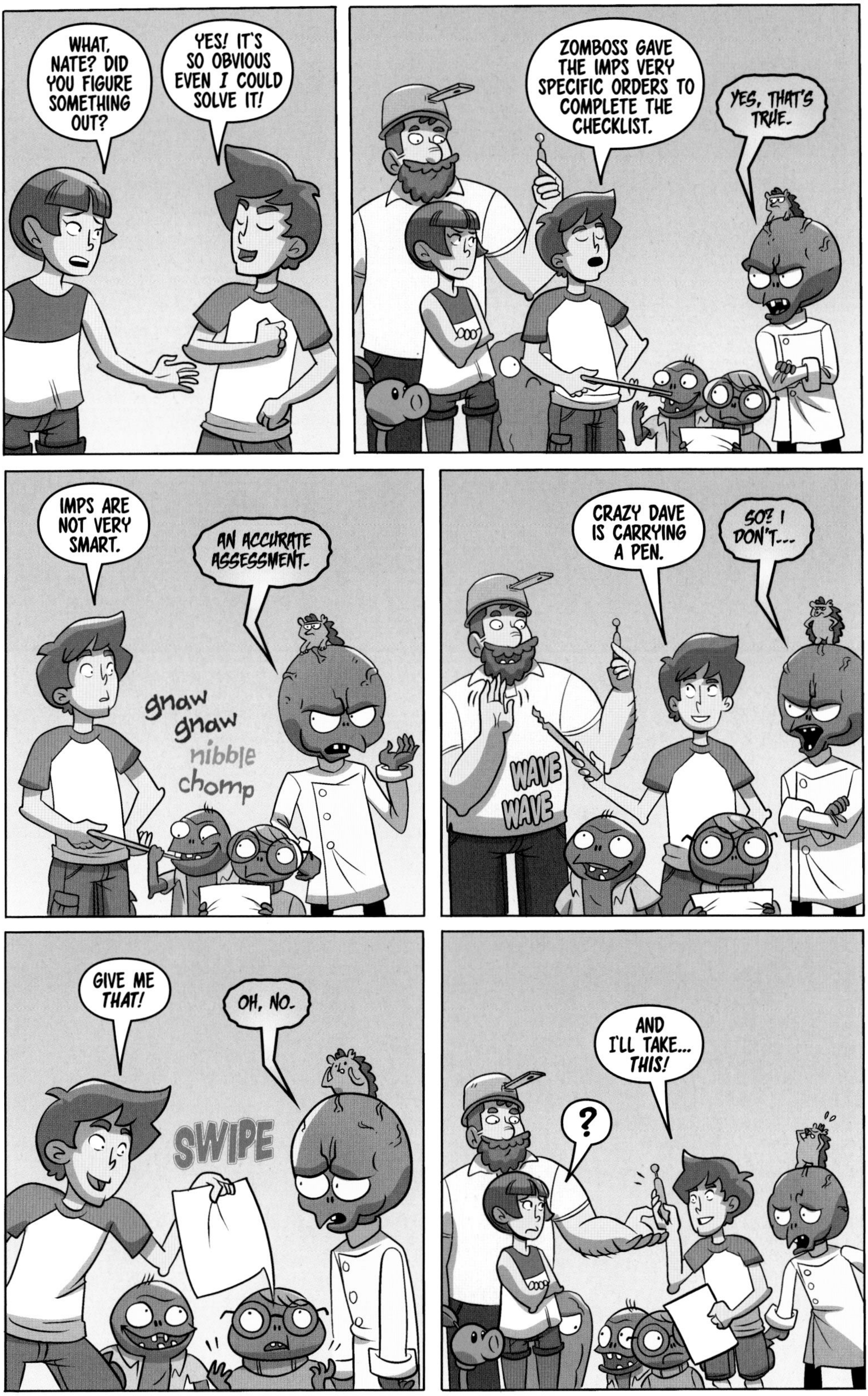
WHAT, NATE? DID YOU FIGURE SOMETHING OUT?
YES! IT'S SO OBVIOUS EVEN I COULD SOLVE IT!
ZOMBOSS GAVE THE IMPS VERY SPECIFIC ORDERS TO COMPLETE THE CHECKLIST.
YES, THAT'S TRUE.
IMPS ARE NOT VERY SMART.
AN ACCURATE ASSESSMENT.
gnaw
gnaw
nibble
chomp
CRAZY DAVE IS CARRYING A PEN.
SO? I DON'T...
WAVE
WAVE
GIVE ME THAT!
OH, NO.
SWIPE
?
AND I'LL TAKE... THIS!

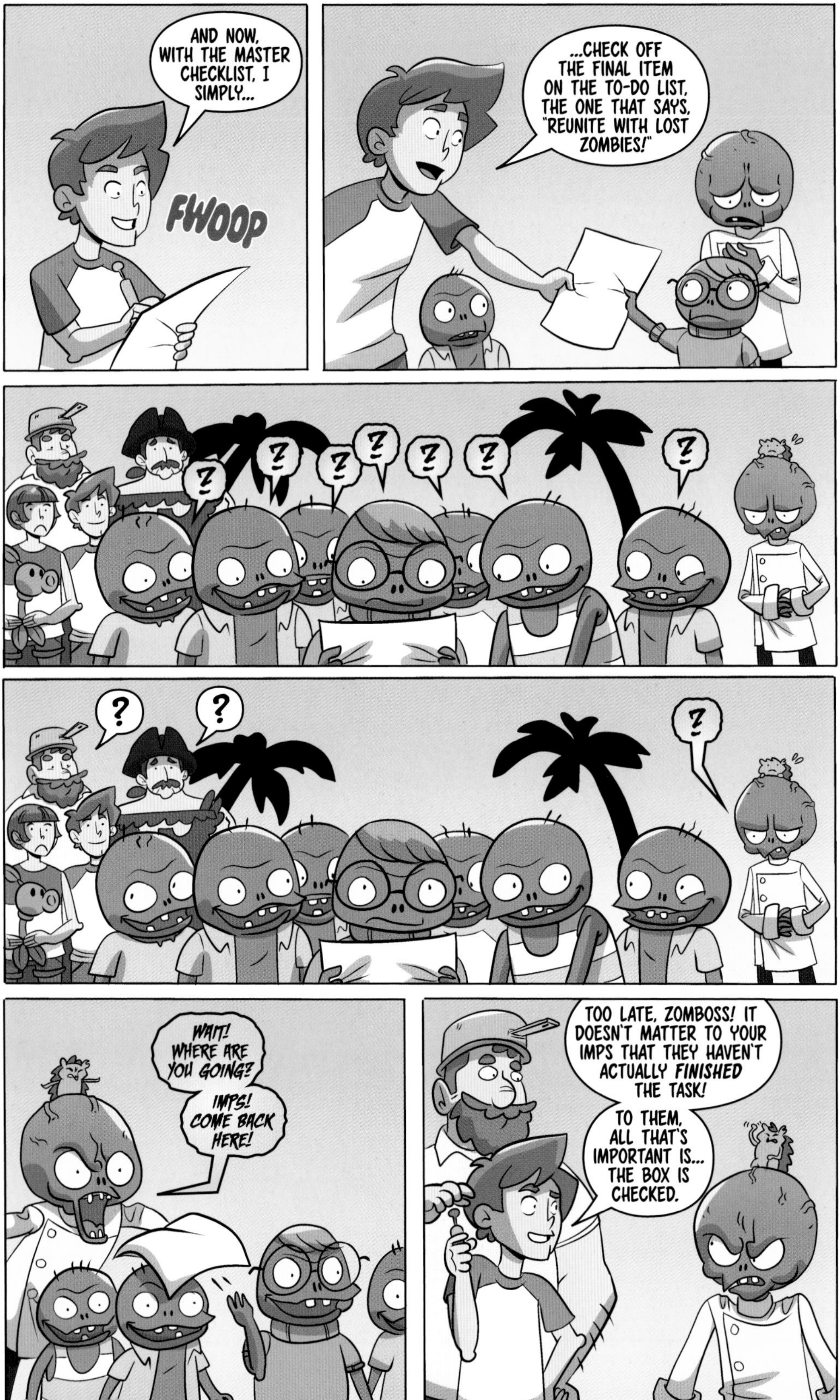
AND NOW, WITH THE MASTER CHECKLIST, I SIMPLY...
FWOOP
...CHECK OFF THE FINAL ITEM ON THE TO-DO LIST, THE ONE THAT SAYS, "REUNITE WITH LOST ZOMBIES!"
?
?
?
?
?
?
?
?
?
?
WAIT! WHERE ARE YOU GOING?
IMPS! COME BACK HERE!
TOO LATE, ZOMBOSS! IT DOESN'T MATTER TO YOUR IMPS THAT THEY HAVEN'T ACTUALLY *FINISHED* THE TASK!
TO THEM, ALL THAT'S IMPORTANT IS... THE BOX IS CHECKED.

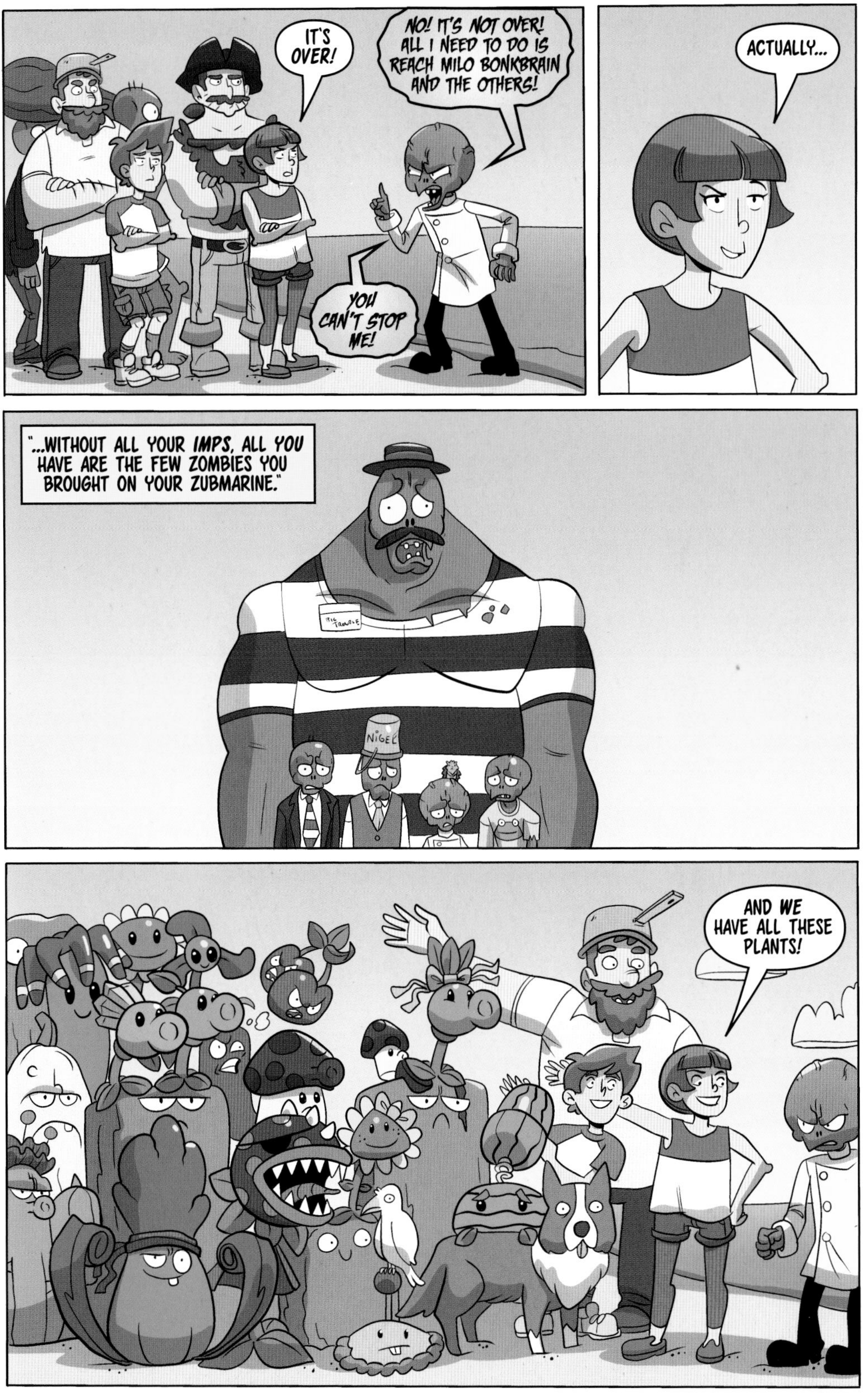
IT'S OVER!
NO! IT'S NOT OVER! ALL I NEED TO DO IS REACH MILO BONKBRAIN AND THE OTHERS!
YOU CAN'T STOP ME!
ACTUALLY...
"...WITHOUT ALL YOUR IMPS, ALL YOU HAVE ARE THE FEW ZOMBIES YOU BROUGHT ON YOUR ZUBMARINE."
NIGEL
AND WE HAVE ALL THESE PLANTS!

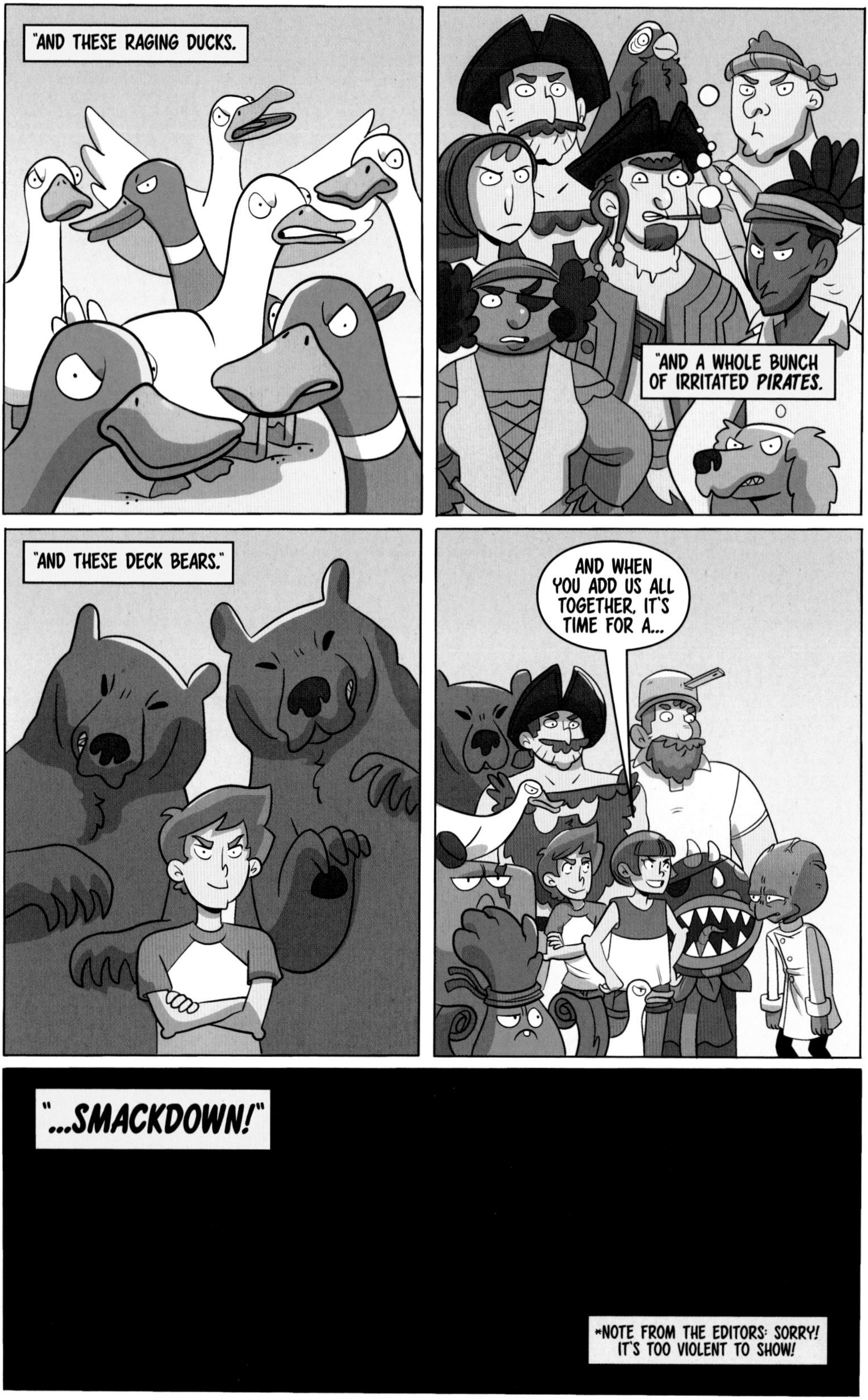
"AND THESE RAGING DUCKS.
"AND A WHOLE BUNCH OF IRRITATED PIRATES.
"AND THESE DECK BEARS."
AND WHEN YOU ADD US ALL TOGETHER, IT'S TIME FOR A...
"...SMACKDOWN!"
*NOTE FROM THE EDITORS: SORRY! IT'S TOO VIOLENT TO SHOW!

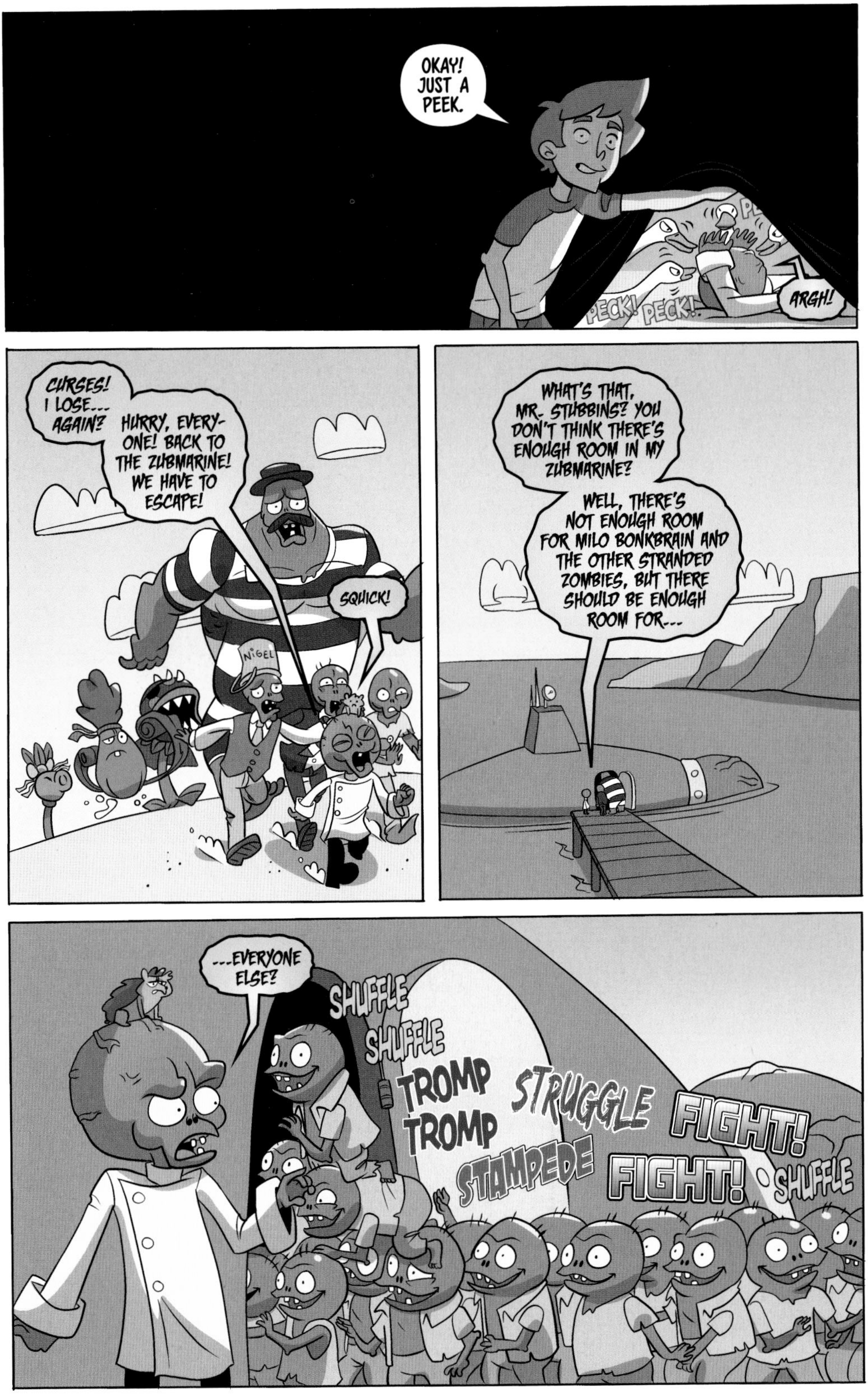
OKAY! JUST A PEEK.
PECK! PECK!
ARGH!
CURSES! I LOSE... AGAIN?
HURRY, EVERY-ONE! BACK TO THE ZUBMARINE! WE HAVE TO ESCAPE!
SQUICK!
NIGEL
WHAT'S THAT, MR. STUBBINS? YOU DON'T THINK THERE'S ENOUGH ROOM IN MY ZUBMARINE?
WELL, THERE'S NOT ENOUGH ROOM FOR MILO BONKBRAIN AND THE OTHER STRANDED ZOMBIES, BUT THERE SHOULD BE ENOUGH ROOM FOR...
...EVERYONE ELSE?
SHUFFLE
SHUFFLE
TROMP
TROMP
STRUGGLE
STAMPEDE
FIGHT!
FIGHT!
SHUFFLE

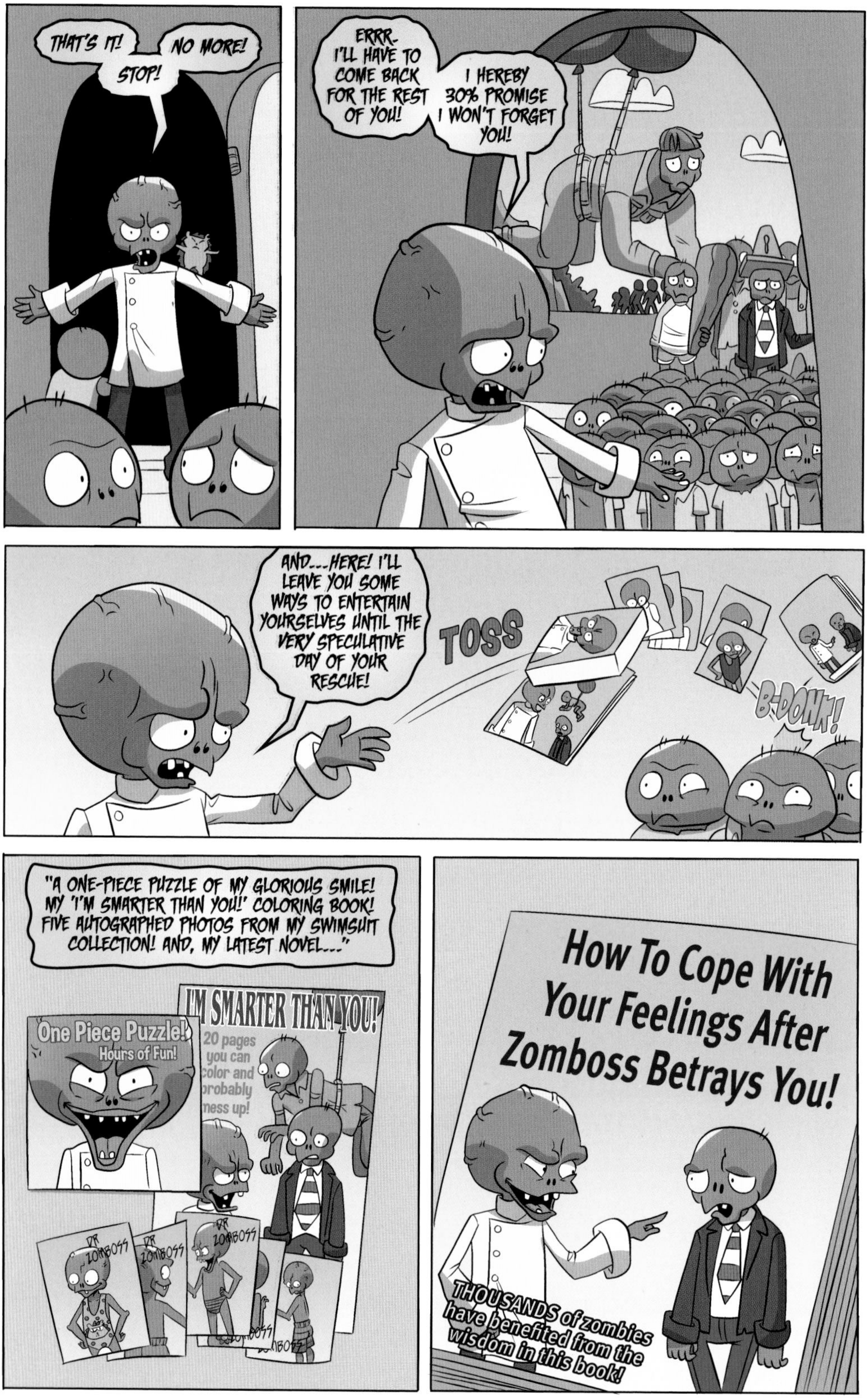

THAT'S IT!
STOP!
NO MORE!
ERRR. I'LL HAVE TO COME BACK FOR THE REST OF YOU!
I HEREBY 30% PROMISE I WON'T FORGET YOU!
AND...HERE! I'LL LEAVE YOU SOME WAYS TO ENTERTAIN YOURSELVES UNTIL THE VERY SPECULATIVE DAY OF YOUR RESCUE!
TOSS
B-DONK!
"A ONE-PIECE PUZZLE OF MY GLORIOUS SMILE! MY 'I'M SMARTER THAN YOU!' COLORING BOOK! FIVE AUTOGRAPHED PHOTOS FROM MY SWIMSUIT COLLECTION! AND, MY LATEST NOVEL..."
One Piece Puzzle!
Hours of Fun!
I'M SMARTER THAN YOU!
20 pages you can color and probably mess up!
DR ZOMBOSS
DR ZOMBOSS
DR ZOMBOSS
How To Cope With Your Feelings After Zomboss Betrays You!
THOUSANDS of zombies have benefited from the wisdom in this book!

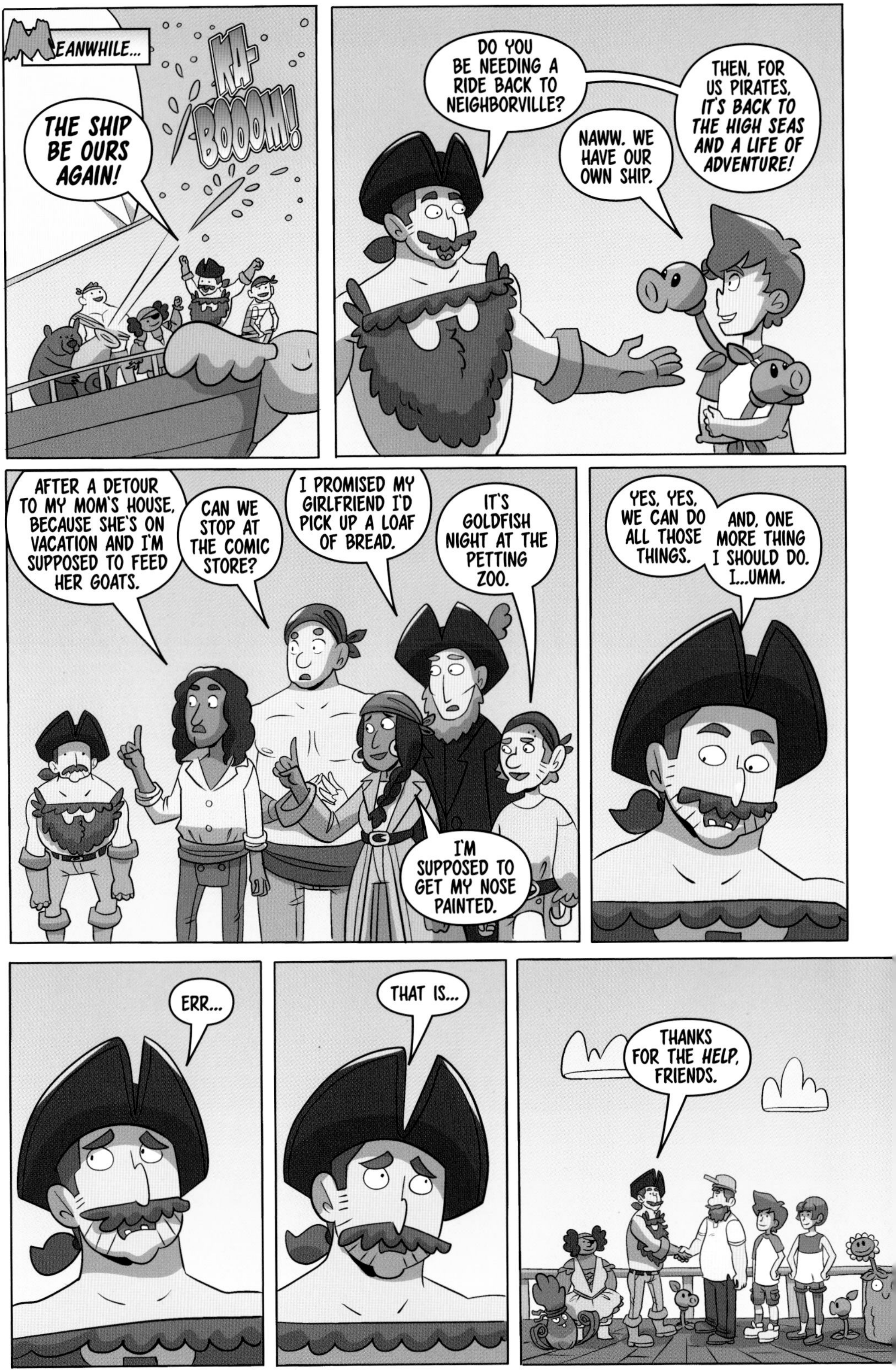
MEANWHILE...
KA-BOOOM!
THE SHIP BE OURS AGAIN!
DO YOU BE NEEDING A RIDE BACK TO NEIGHBORVILLE?
NAWW. WE HAVE OUR OWN SHIP.
THEN, FOR US PIRATES, IT'S BACK TO THE HIGH SEAS AND A LIFE OF ADVENTURE!
AFTER A DETOUR TO MY MOM'S HOUSE, BECAUSE SHE'S ON VACATION AND I'M SUPPOSED TO FEED HER GOATS.
CAN WE STOP AT THE COMIC STORE?
I PROMISED MY GIRLFRIEND I'D PICK UP A LOAF OF BREAD.
IT'S GOLDFISH NIGHT AT THE PETTING ZOO.
I'M SUPPOSED TO GET MY NOSE PAINTED.
YES, YES, WE CAN DO ALL THOSE THINGS.
AND, ONE MORE THING I SHOULD DO. I...UMM.
ERR...
THAT IS...
THANKS FOR THE HELP, FRIENDS.

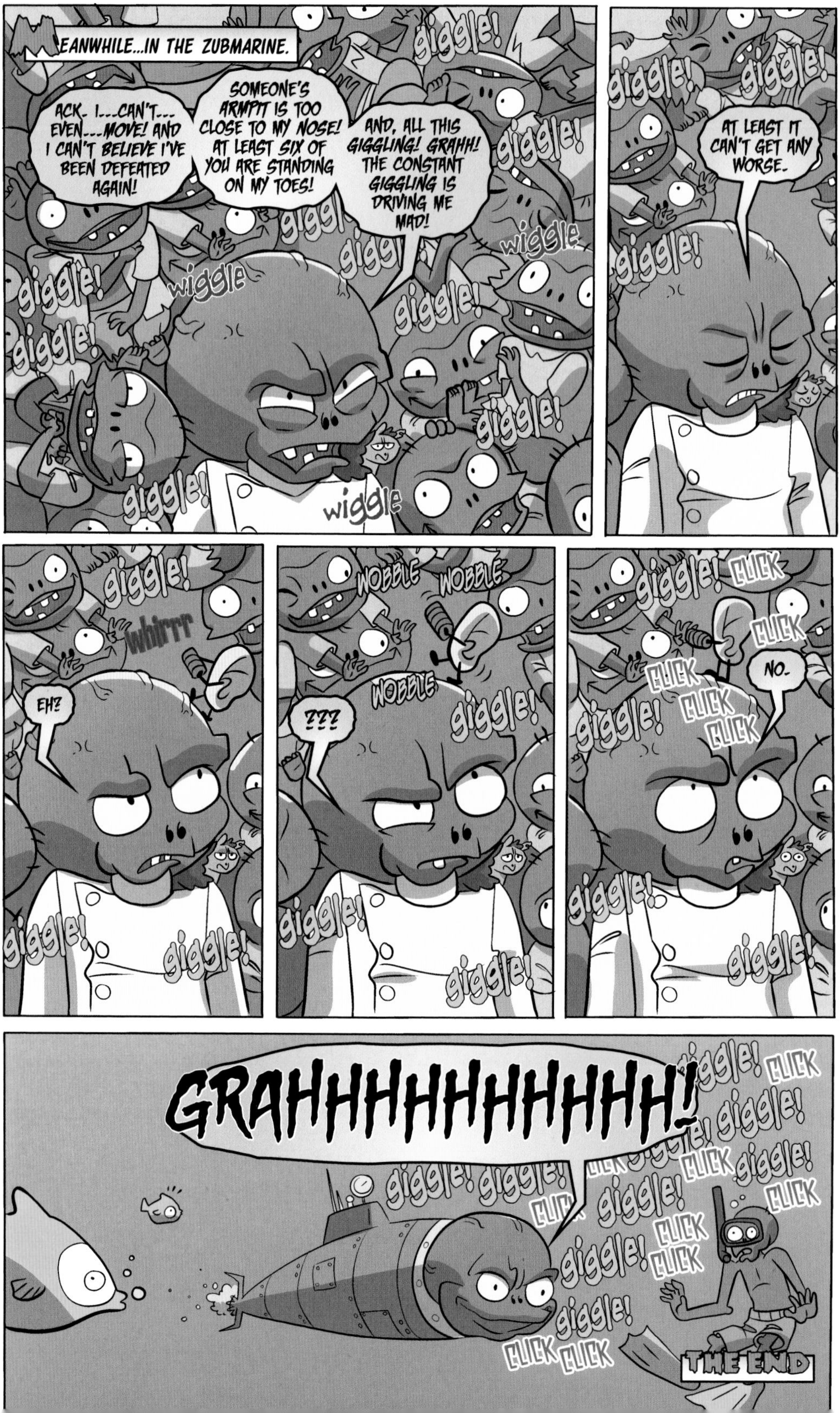
MEANWHILE...IN THE ZUBMARINE.
ACK- I...CAN'T... EVEN...MOVE! AND I CAN'T BELIEVE I'VE BEEN DEFEATED AGAIN!
SOMEONE'S ARMPIT IS TOO CLOSE TO MY NOSE! AT LEAST SIX OF YOU ARE STANDING ON MY TOES!
AND, ALL THIS GIGGLING! GRAHH! THE CONSTANT GIGGLING IS DRIVING ME MAD!
giggle!
wiggle
AT LEAST IT CAN'T GET ANY WORSE.
whirrr
EH?
WOBBLE WOBBLE
WOBBLE
???
CLICK
NO.
GRAHHHHHHHHHH!
giggle!
CLICK
THE END

FROM CAT FARRIS'S *PLANTS VS. ZOMBIES* SKETCHBOOK! INITIAL COVER SKETCHES FOR THE *PLANTS VS. ZOMBIES: IMPFESTATION* COVER.

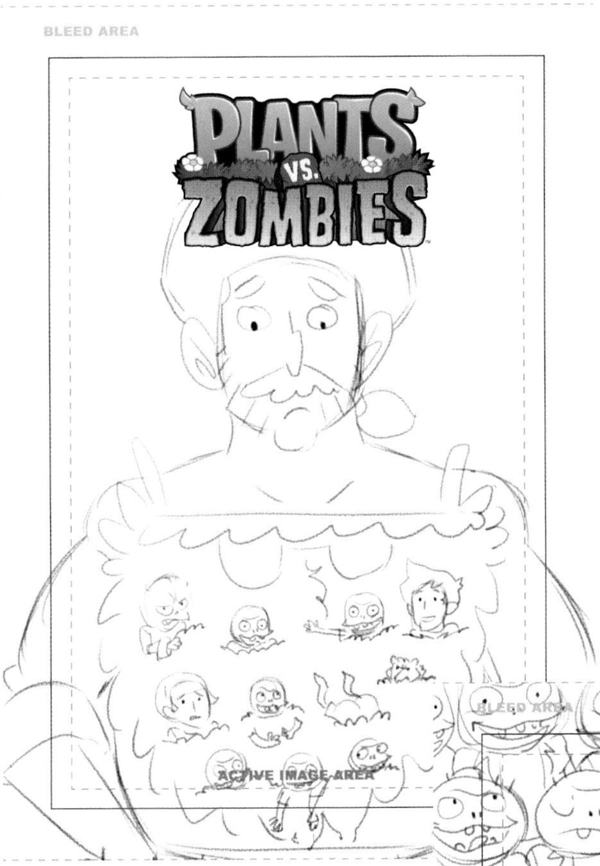
BLEED AREA
PLANTS VS. ZOMBIES
ACTIVE IMAGE AREA

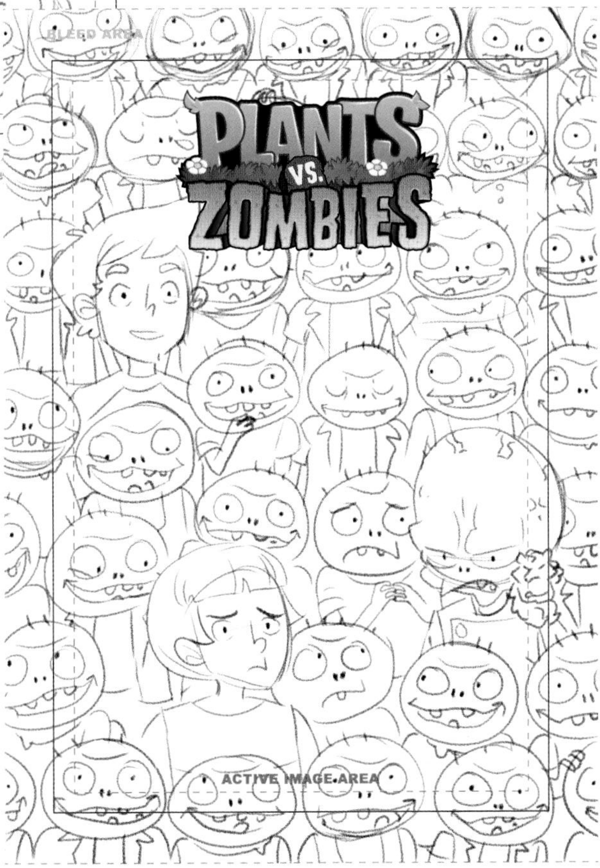
BLEED AREA
PLANTS VS. ZOMBIES
ACTIVE IMAGE AREA

PLANTS VS. ZOMBIES: IMPFESTATION
COVER INKS BY CAT FARRIS

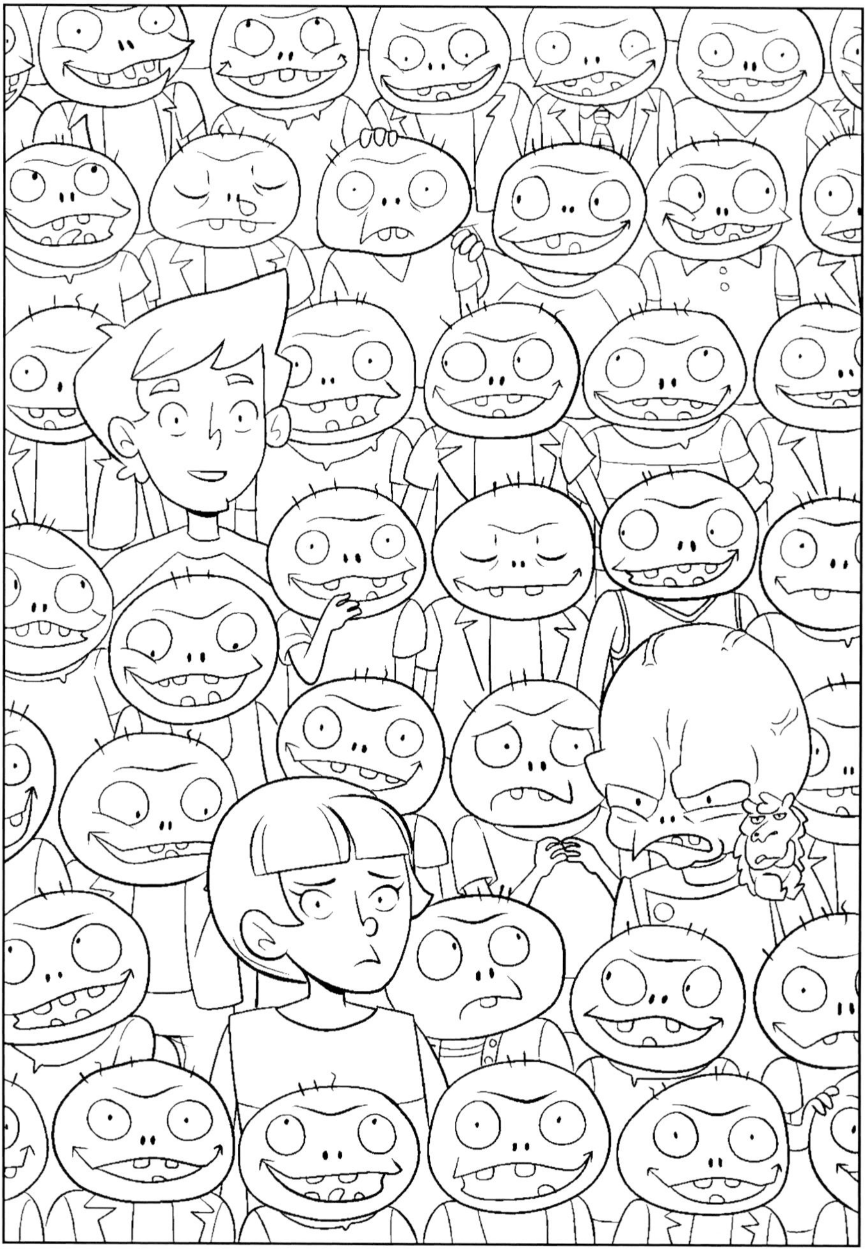

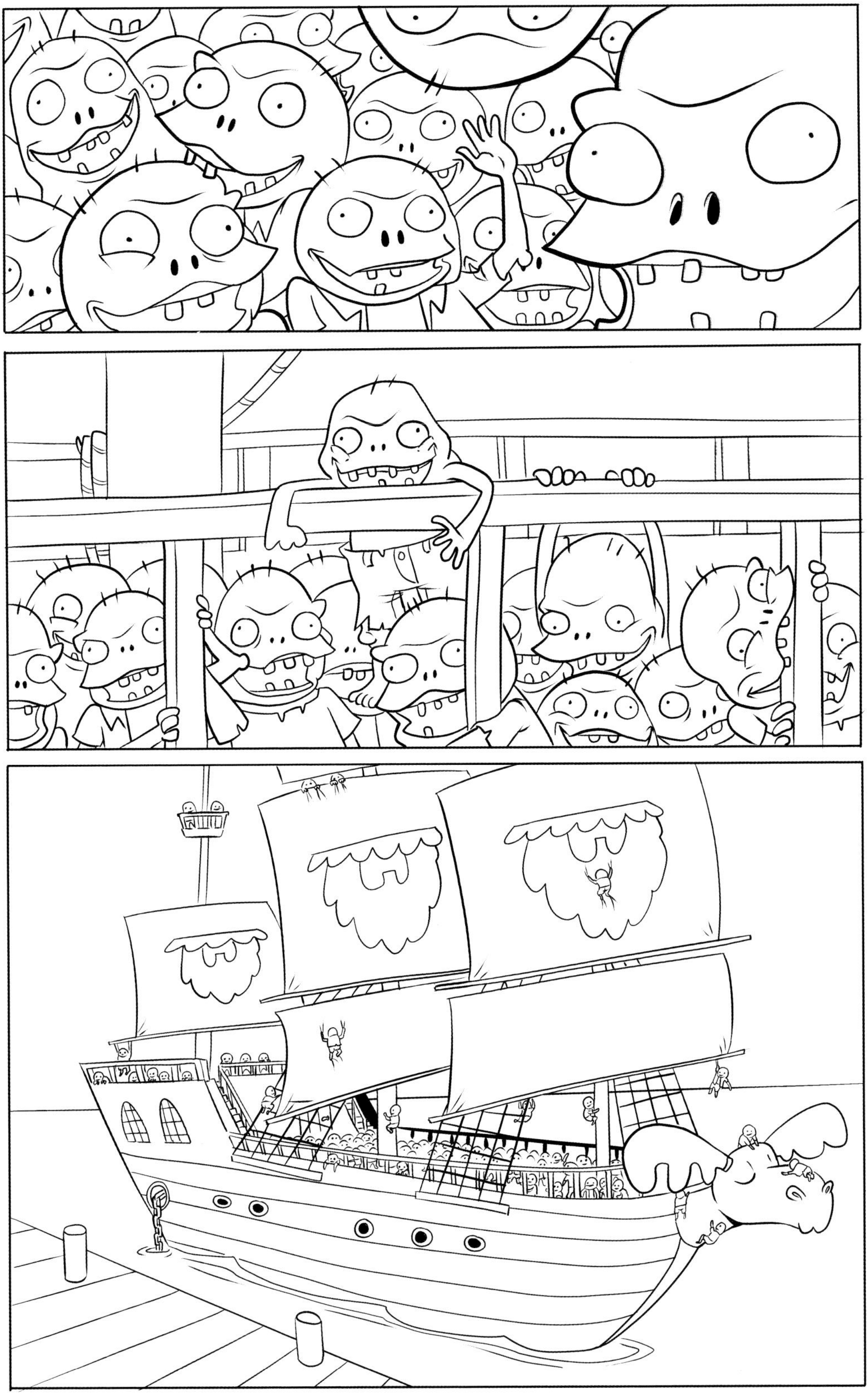

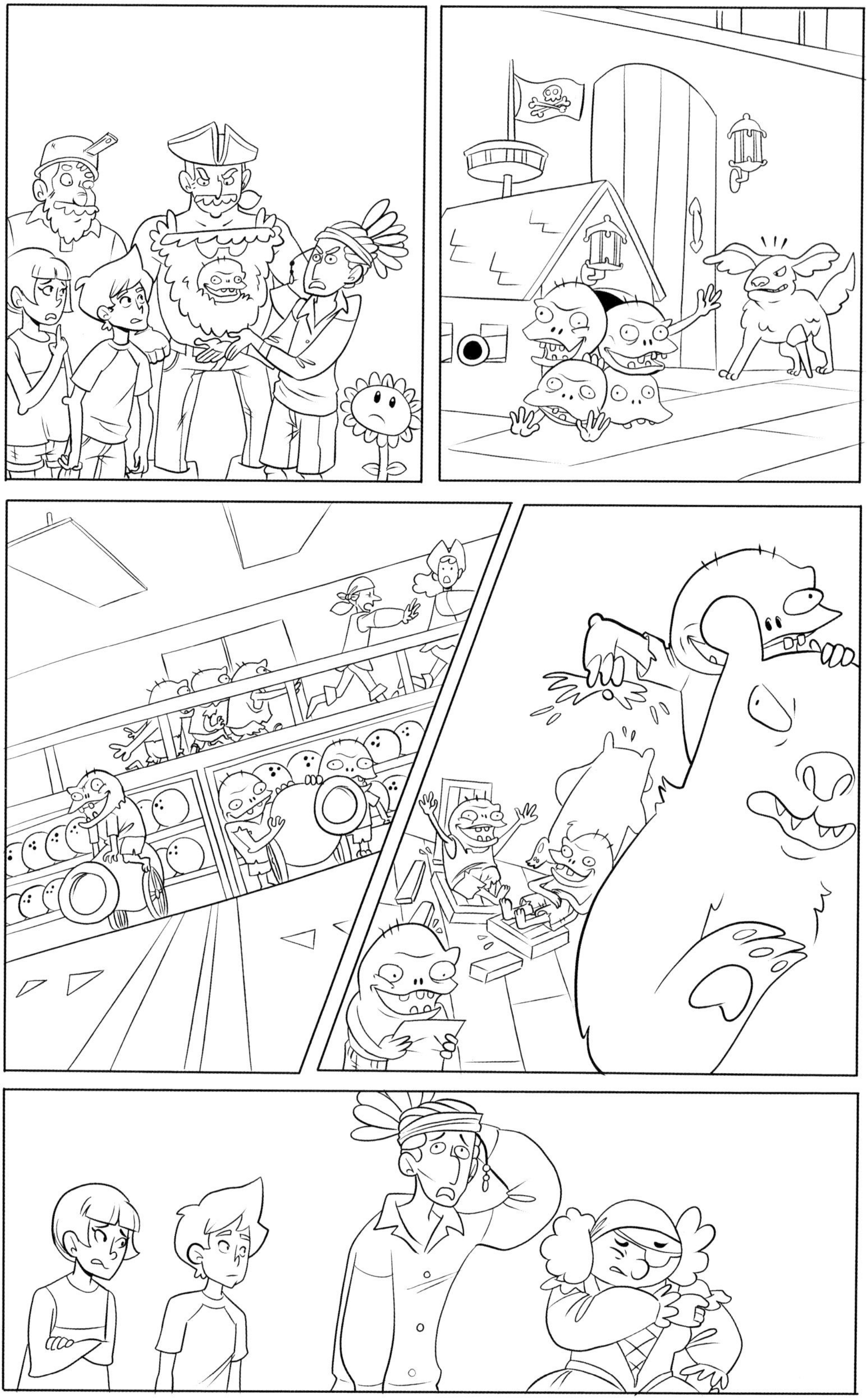

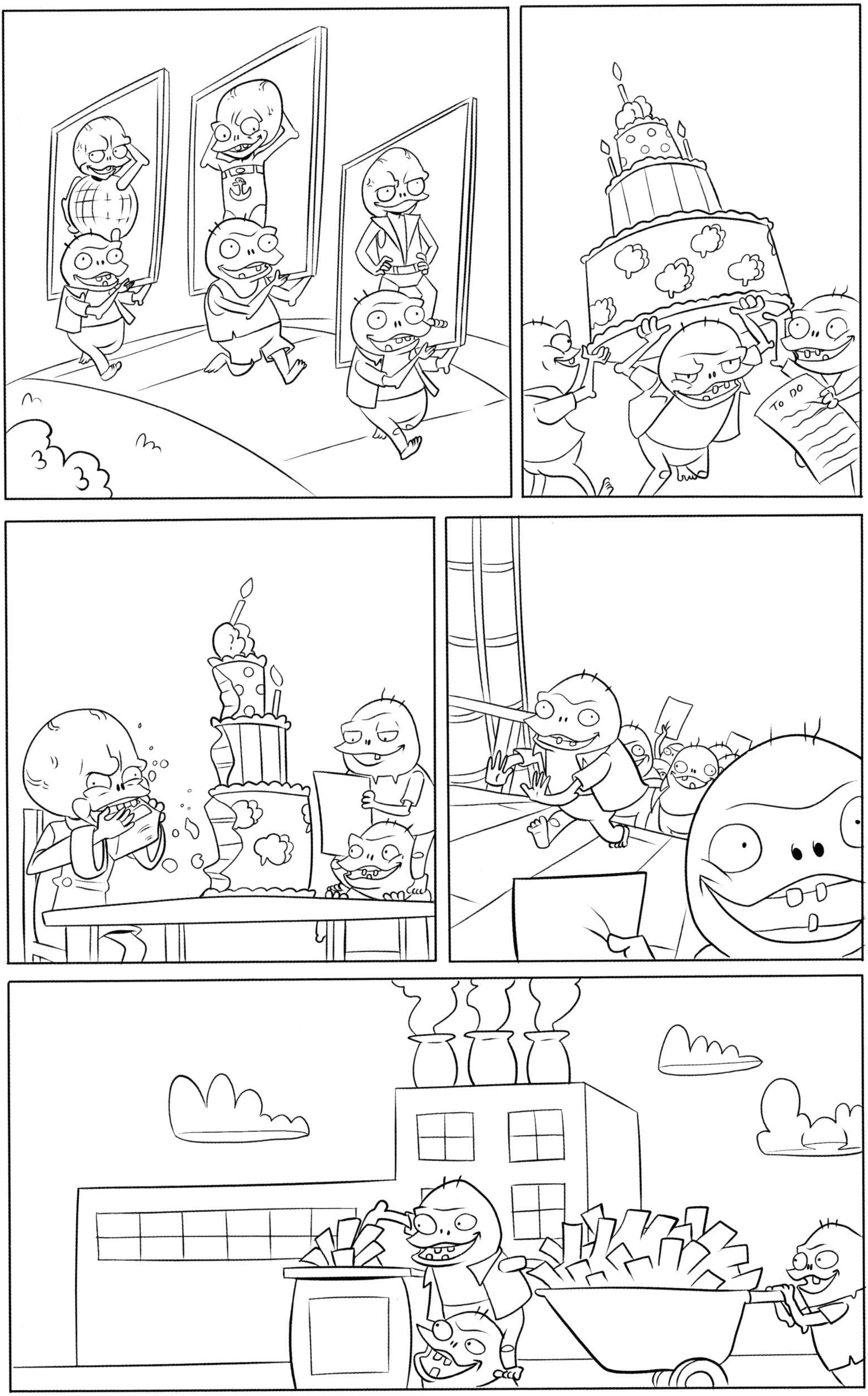
TO DO

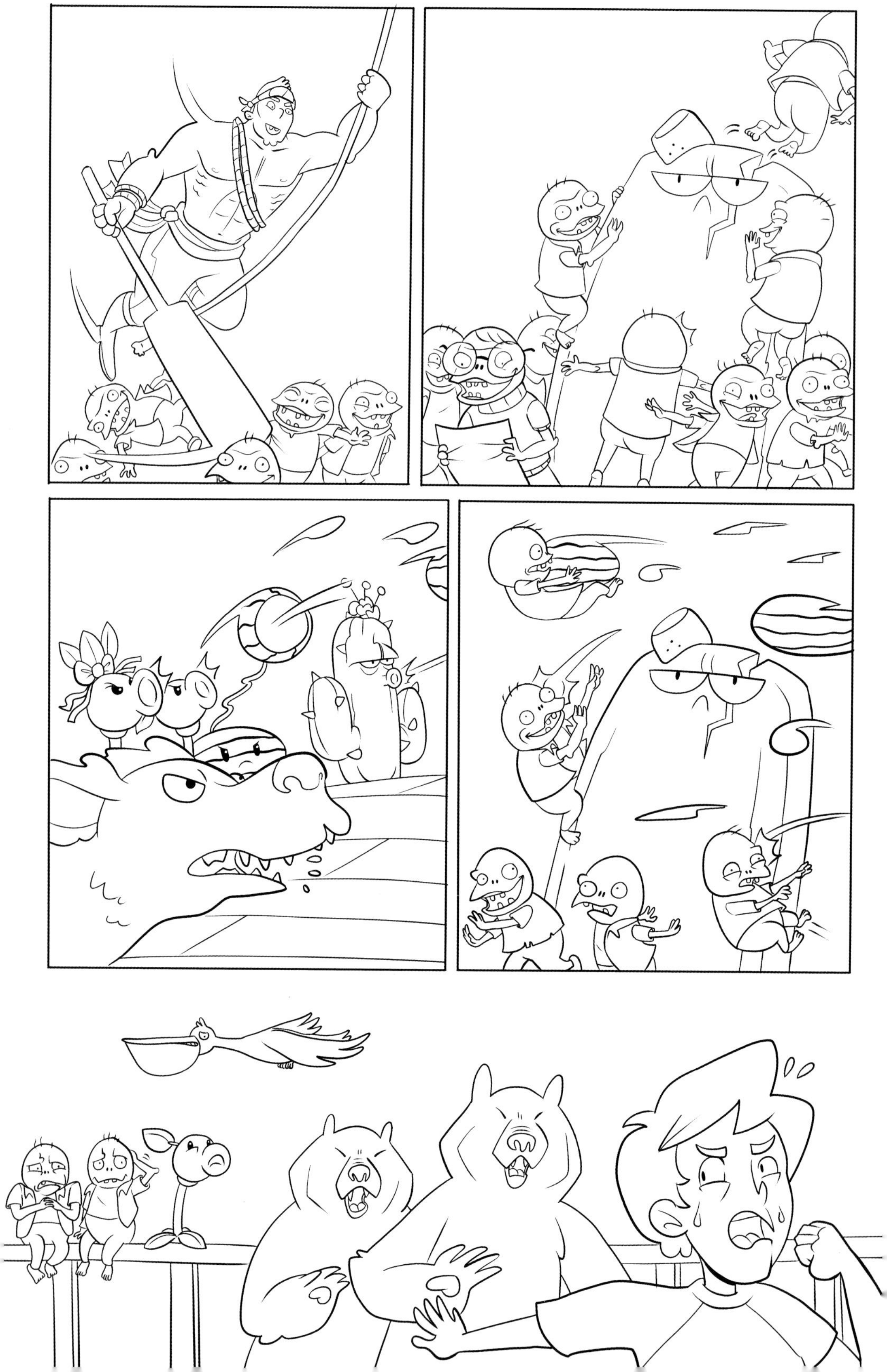

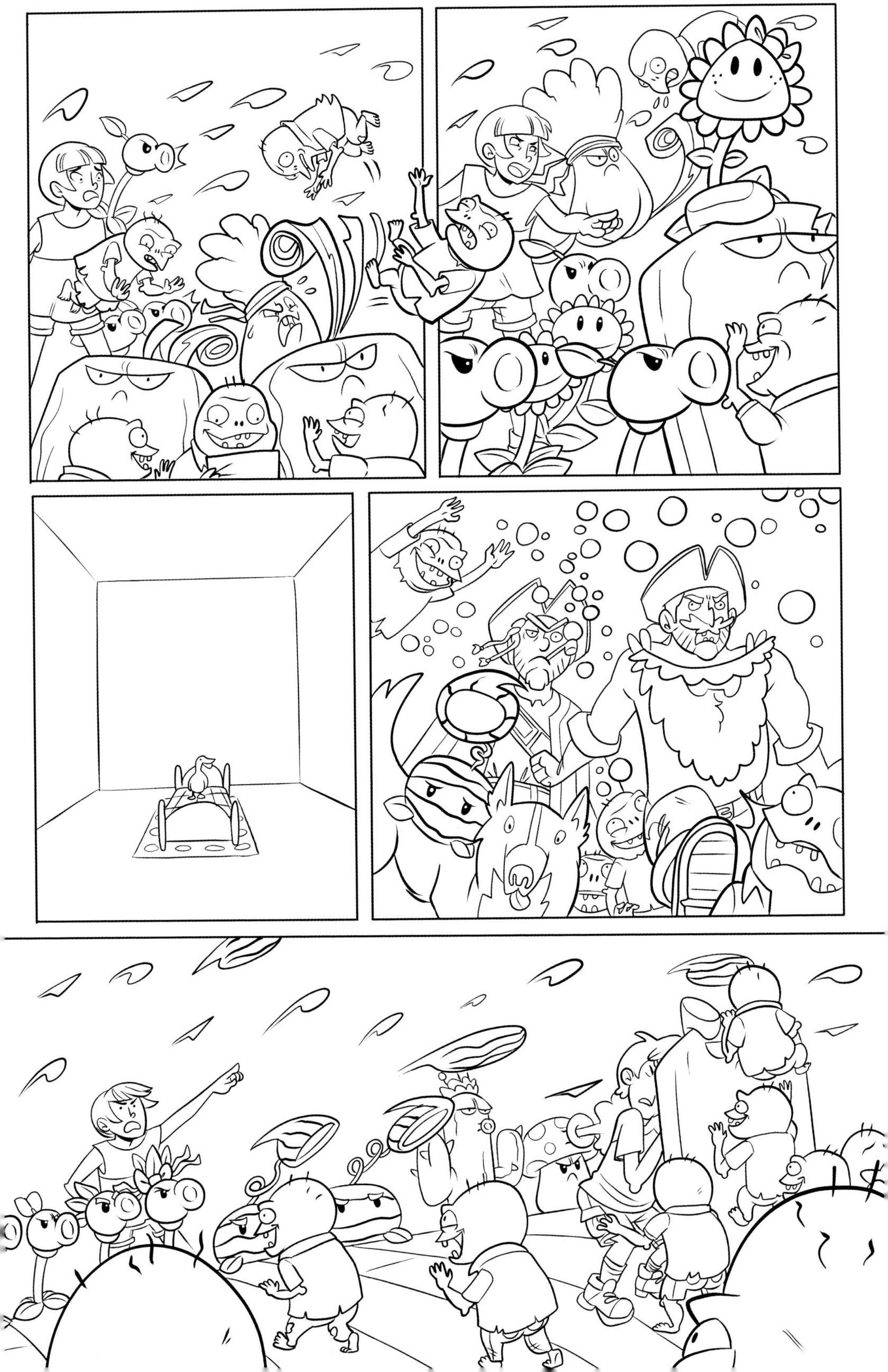

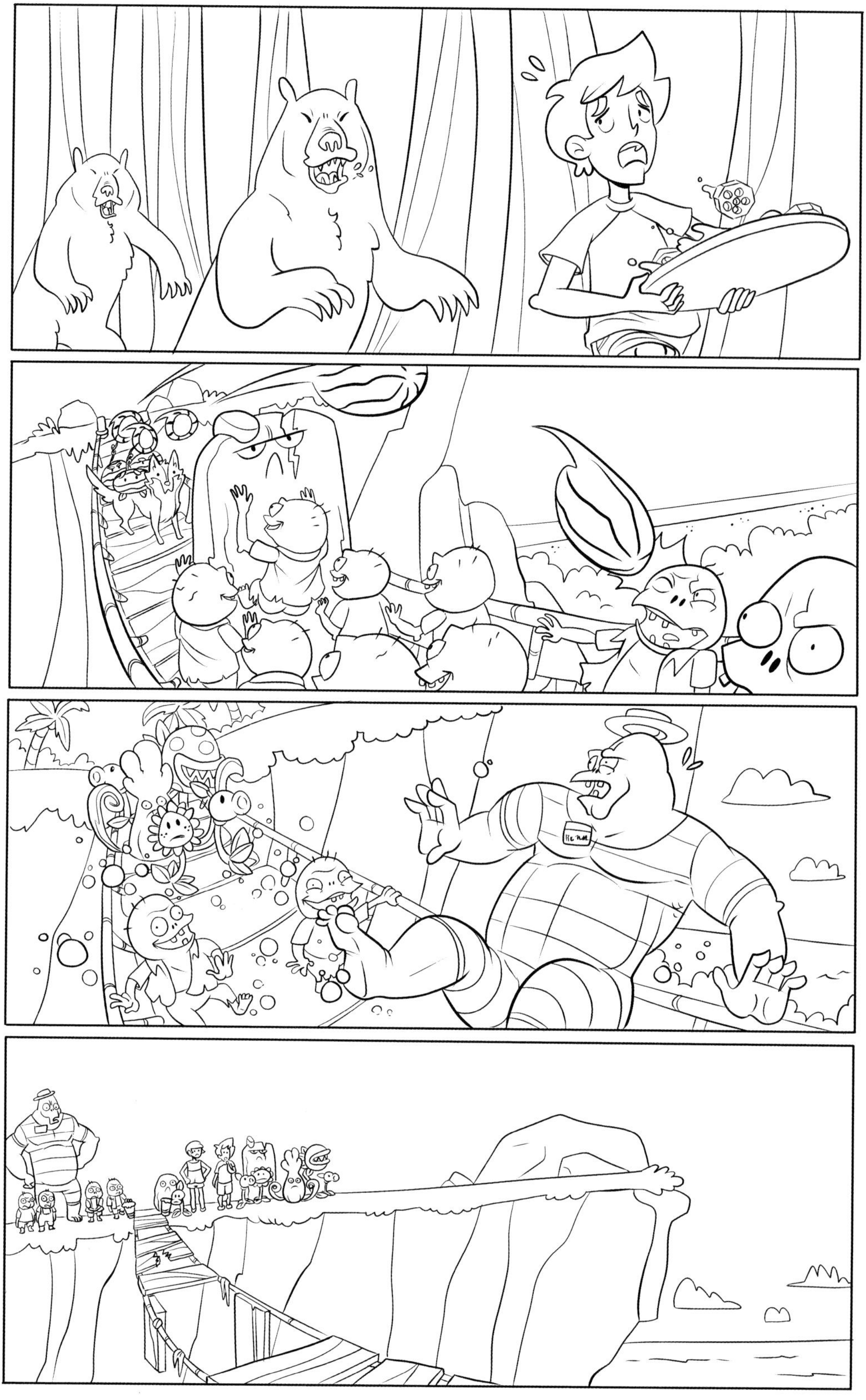

CREATOR BIOS

Paul Tobin

PAUL TOBIN is a 12th level writer and a 15th level cookie eater. He begins each morning in the manner we all do, by battling those zombies that have strayed too close to his pillow fort. Between writing all the *Plants vs. Zombies* comics and taking four naps a day, he's also found time to write the *Genius Factor* series of novels, the ape-filled *Banana Sunday* graphic novel, the award-winning *Bandette* series, the upcoming *Wrassle Castle* and *Earth Boy* graphic novels, and many other works. He has ridden a giant turtle and an elephant on purpose, and a tornado by accident.

Cat Farris

CAT FARRIS is a comic book artist from Portland, Oregon where she lives with her husband and dog. She is a member of the comics collective, Helioscope. Her past works include *Plants vs. Zombies: Snow Thanks* (Dark Horse), *The Ghoul Next Door* (HarperAlley), and *Up to No Ghoul* (HarperAlley). Her favorite plants are Wall-nuts and Tall-nuts!

Heather Breckel

HEATHER BRECKEL went to the Columbus College of Art and Design for animation. She decided animation wasn't for her, so she switched to comics. She's been working as a colorist for nearly ten years and has worked for nearly every major comics publisher out there. When she's not burning the midnight oil in a deadline crunch, she's either dying a bunch in videogames or telling her cats to stop running around at two in the morning.

Steve Dutro

STEVE DUTRO is a pinball fan and an Eisner Award-nominated comic book letterer from Redding, California, who can also drive a tractor. He graduated from the Kubert School and has been lettering comics since the days when foil-embossed covers were cool, working for Dark Horse (*The Fifth Beatle*, *I Am a Hero*, *StarCraft*, *Star Wars*, *Witcher*), Viz, Marvel, and DC Comics. He has submitted a request to the Department of Homeland Security that in the event of a zombie apocalypse he be put in charge of all digital freeway signs so citizens can be alerted to avoid nearby brain-eatings and the like. He finds the Plants vs. Zombies game to be a real stress-fest, but highly recommends the *Plants vs. Zombies* table on *Pinball FX2* for game-room hipsters.

ALSO AVAILABLE FROM DARK HORSE!

THE HIT VIDEO GAME CONTINUES ITS COMIC BOOK INVASION!

THE ART OF PLANTS VS. ZOMBIES

Part zombie memoir, part celebration of zombie triumphs, and part anti-plant screed, *The Art of Plants vs. Zombies* is a treasure trove of never-before-seen concept art, character sketches, and surprises from PopCap's popular *Plants vs. Zombies* games!

ISBN 978-1-61655-331-9 | $10.99

PLANTS VS. ZOMBIES: GARDEN WARFARE TRILOGY

Based on the hit video game series, these graphic novels tie in with the events in *Plants vs. Zombies: Garden Warfare 1* and *2* and *Plants vs. Zombies: Battle for Neighborville*!

VOLUME 1 ISBN 978-1-61655-946-5 | $10.99
VOLUME 2 ISBN 978-1-50670-548-4 | $10.99
VOLUME 3 ISBN 978-1-50670-837-9 | $10.99

PLANTS VS. ZOMBIES: LAWNMAGEDDON

Crazy Dave—the babbling-yet-brilliant inventor and top-notch neighborhood defender—helps young adventurer Nate fend off a zombie invasion that threatens to overrun the peaceful town of Neighborville. Their only hope is a brave army of chomping, squashing, and pea-shooting plants!

ISBN 978-1-61655-192-6 | $10.99

PLANTS VS. ZOMBIES: TIMEPOCALYPSE

Dr. Zomboss attacks throughout different timelines, keeping Crazy Dave, Patrice, Nate, and their powerful plant army busy!

ISBN 978-1-61655-621-1 | $10.99

PLANTS VS. ZOMBIES: BULLY FOR YOU

Patrice and Nate are ready to investigate a strange college campus to keep the streets safe from zombies!

ISBN 978-1-61655-889-5 | $10.99

PLANTS VS. ZOMBIES: GROWN SWEET HOME

With newfound knowledge of humanity, Dr. Zomboss strikes at the heart of Neighborville . . . sparking a series of plant-versus-zombie brawls!

ISBN 978-1-61655-971-7 | $10.99

PLANTS VS. ZOMBIES: PETAL TO THE METAL

Crazy Dave takes on the tough *Don't Blink* video game—and challenges Dr. Zomboss to a race to determine the future of Neighborville!

ISBN 978-1-61655-999-1 | $10.99

PLANTS VS. ZOMBIES: BOOM BOOM MUSHROOM

The gang discover Zomboss' secret plan for swallowing the city of Neighborville whole! A rare mushroom must be found in order to save the humans aboveground!

ISBN 978-1-50670-037-3 | $10.99

PLANTS VS. ZOMBIES: BATTLE EXTRAVAGONZO

Zomboss is back, hoping to buy the same factory that Crazy Dave is eyeing! Will Crazy Dave and his intelligent plants beat Zomboss and his zombie army to the punch?

ISBN 978-1-50670-189-9 | $10.99

PLANTS VS. ZOMBIES: LAWN OF DOOM

With Zomboss filling everyone's yards with traps and special soldiers, will he and his zombie army turn Halloween into their zanier Lawn of Doom celebration?!

ISBN 978-1-50670-204-9 | $10.99

PLANTS VS. ZOMBIES: THE GREATEST SHOW UNEARTHED

Dr. Zomboss believes that all humans hold a secret desire to run away and join the circus, so he aims to use his "Big Z's Adequately Amazing Flytrap Circus" to lure Neighborville's citizens to their doom!

ISBN 978-1-50670-298-8 | $10.99

PLANTS VS. ZOMBIES: RUMBLE AT LAKE GUMBO

The battle for clean water begins! Nate, Patrice, and Crazy Dave spot trouble and grab all the Tangle Kelp and Party Crabs they can to quell another zombie attack!

ISBN 978-1-50670-497-5 | $10.99

PLANTS VS. ZOMBIES: WAR AND PEAS

When Dr. Zomboss and Crazy Dave find themselves members of the same book club, a literary war is inevitable! The position of leader of the book club opens up and Zomboss and Crazy Dave compete for the top spot in a scholarly scuffle for the ages!

ISBN 978-1-50670-677-1 | $10.99

PLANTS VS. ZOMBIES: DINO-MIGHT

Dr. Zomboss sets his sights on destroying the yards in town and rendering the plants homeless—and his plans include dogs, cats, rabbits, hammock sloths, and, somehow, dinosaurs . . . !

ISBN 978-1-50670-838-6 | $10.99

PLANTS VS. ZOMBIES: SNOW THANKS

Dr. Zomboss invents a Cold Crystal capable of freezing Neighborville, burying the town in snow and ice! It's up to the humans and the fieriest plants to save Neighborville—with the help of pirates!

ISBN 978-1-50670-839-3 | $10.99

PLANTS VS. ZOMBIES: A LITTLE PROBLEM

Will an invasion of teeny-tiny miniature zombies mean the party for Crazy Dave's two-hundred-year-old pants gets canceled?

ISBN 978-1-50670-840-9 | $10.99

PLANTS VS. ZOMBIES: BETTER HOMES AND GUARDENS

Nate and Patrice try thwarting zombie attacks by putting defending "Guardens" plants *inside* homes as well as in yards! But as soon as Dr. Zomboss finds out, he's determined to circumvent this plan with an epically evil one of his own . . .

ISBN 978-1-50671-305-2 | $10.99

PLANTS VS. ZOMBIES: THE GARDEN PATH

You get to decide the fate of Neighborville in this new *Plants vs. Zombies* choose-your-own-adventure with multiple endings!

ISBN 978-1-50671-306-9 | $10.99

PLANTS VS. ZOMBIES: MULTI-BALL-ISTIC

Dr. Zomboss turns the entirety of Neighborville into a giant, fully functional pinball machine! Nate, Patrice, and their plant posse must find a way to halt this uniquely horrifying zombie invasion.

ISBN 978-1-50671-307-6 | $10.99

PLANTS VS. ZOMBIES: CONSTRUCTIONARY TALES

A behind-the-scenes look at the secret schemes and craziest contraptions concocted by Zomboss, as he proudly leads around a film crew from the Zombie Broadcasting Network!

ISBN 978-1-50672-091-3 | $10.99

PLANTS VS. ZOMBIES: DREAM A LITTLE SCHEME

Dr. Zomboss invents a machine that allows him to enter the dreams of Neighborville's citizens!

ISBN 978-1-50672-092-0 | $10.99

PLANTS VS. ZOMBIES: FAULTY FABLES

Dr. Zomboss sets out to lull the town to sleep with strange-yet-tedious fables of his own creation!

ISBN 978-1-50672-846-9 | $10.99

PLANTS VS. ZOMBIES: IMPFESTATION

With a seemingly endless infestation of zombie imps aboard his ship, pirate Chestbeard sails to Neighborville Harbor and enlists Patrice, Nate, and Crazy Dave in clearing out the impfestation!

ISBN 978-1-50672-847-6 | $10.99

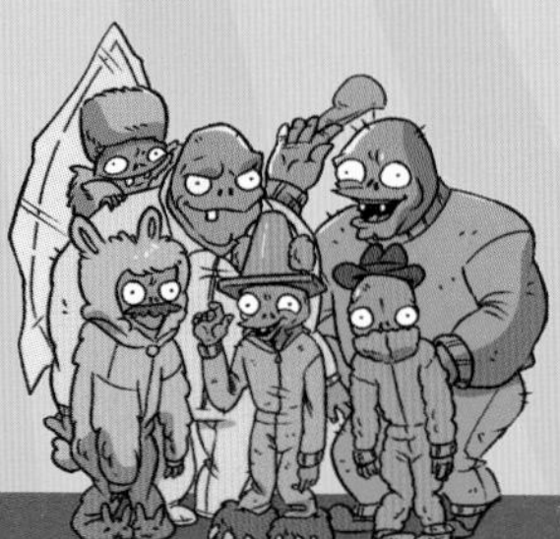

AVAILABLE AT YOUR LOCAL COMICS SHOP OR BOOKSTORE

To find a comics shop in your area, visit comicshoplocator.com. For more information or to order direct, visit **DarkHorse.com**

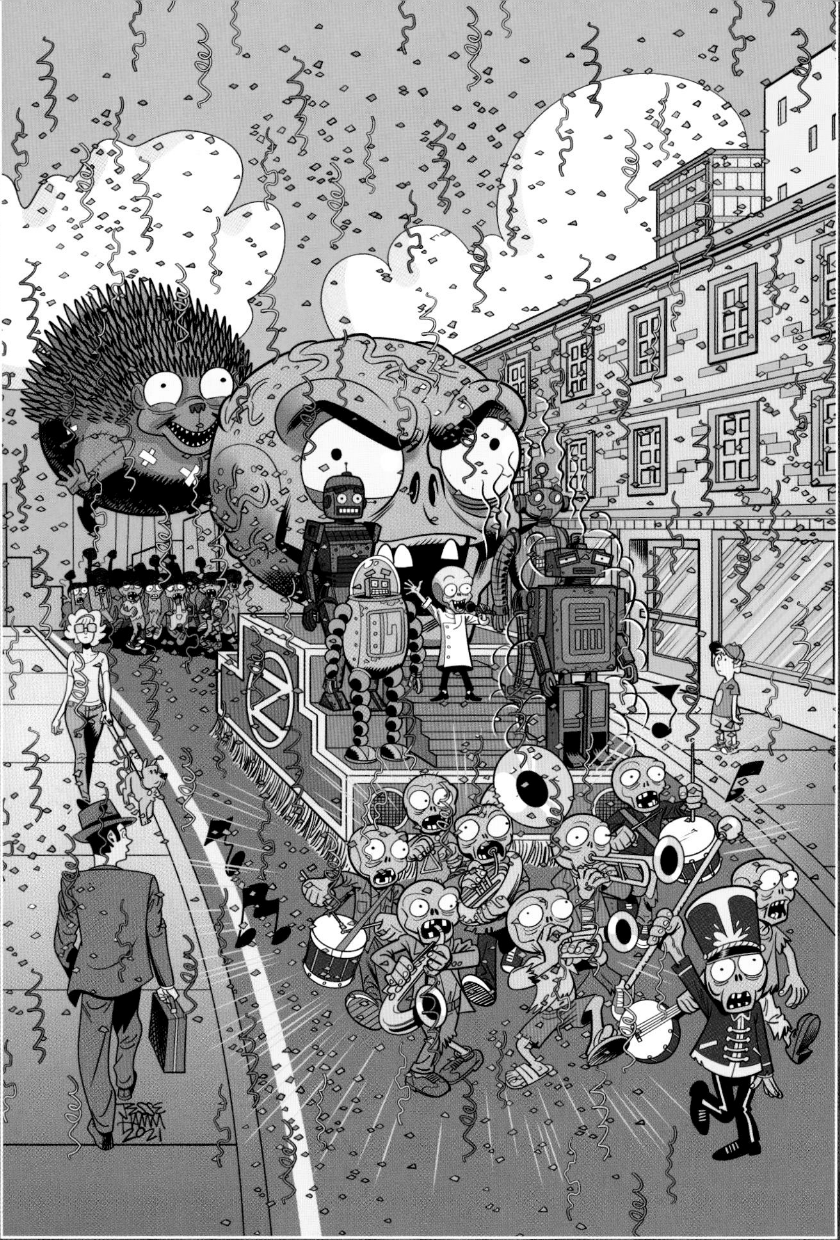

After having countless schemes, capers, and heists easily thwarted by the plant team, Dr. Zomboss needs a win! With Crazy Dave and the gang always one step ahead, Zomboss realizes the only way to achieve victory is by being even one more step ahead than that! So he builds his latest invention: four brain bots called *The Unpredictables*! An all-original graphic novel written by Paul Tobin (*Bandette*, *Genius Factor*) with art by Jesse Hamm (*Plants vs. Zombies: Constructionary Tales*, *Batman '66*), Les McClaine (*Old Souls*, *Maker Comics: Live Sustainably*), Philip Murphy (*Star Trek vs. Transformers*, *Addams Family: The Bodies*), and Luisa Russo (*Grimm Tales from the Cave*)!

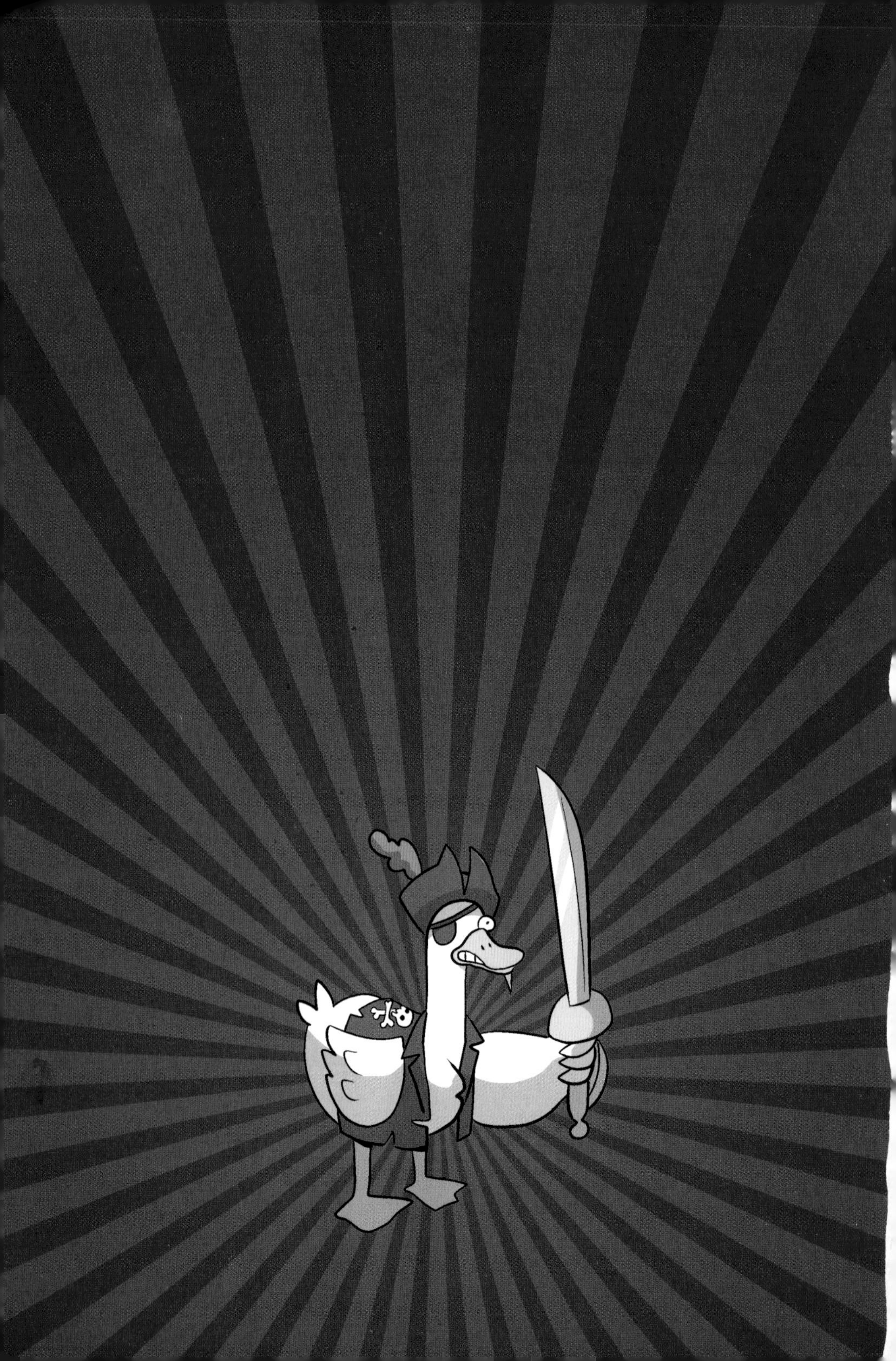

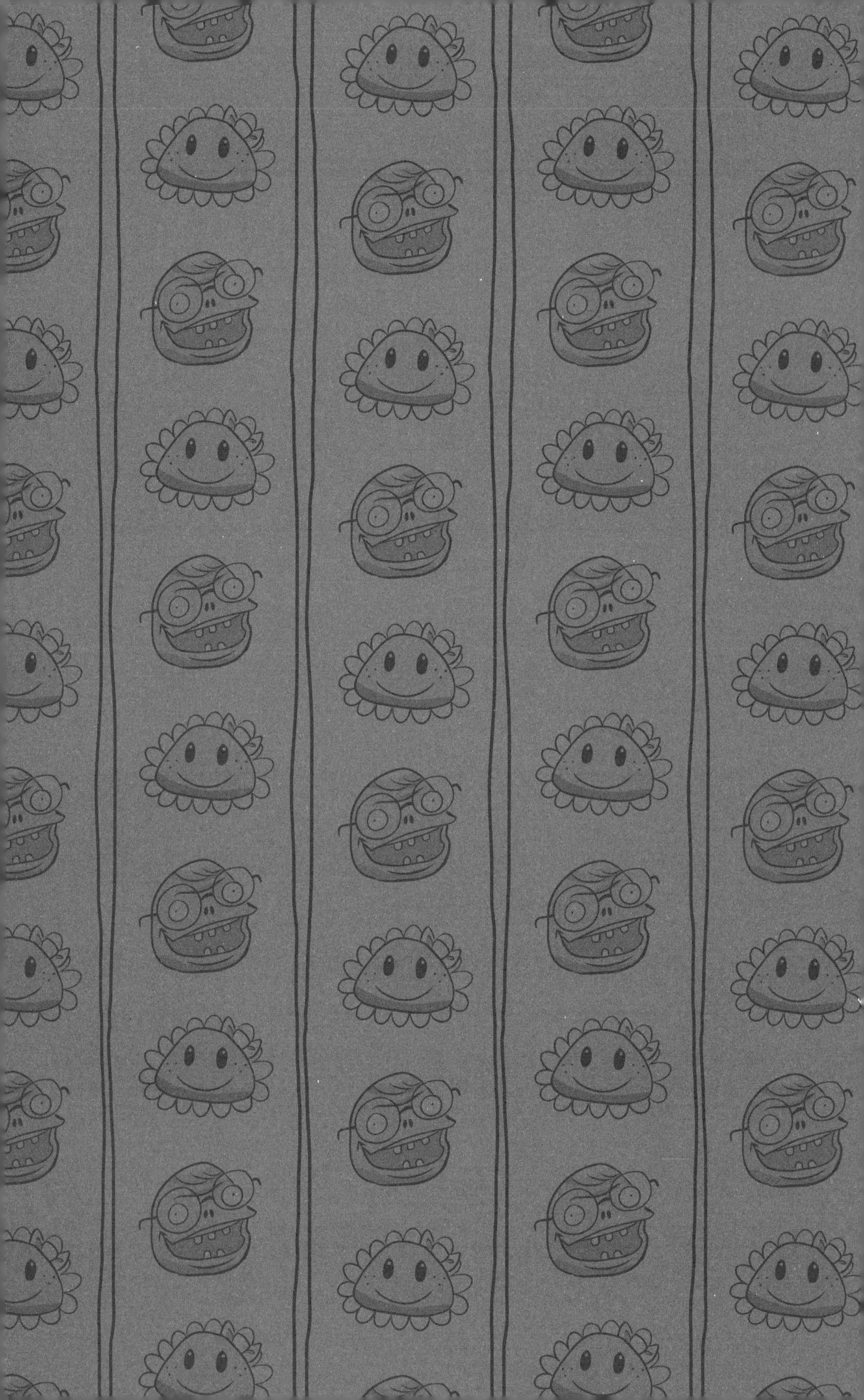